WITHOUT ME

MEN OF INKED BOOK FIVE

Formatting by Brian Morgan
Cover Model Thomas Yarborough
Cover Photo © Eric Battershell of Eric Battershell
Photography

To my father, my hero.

ANTHONY

I'D LED A SELFISH EXISTENCE.

I'd never hidden that fact.

Pussy was the name of the game. I wanted it without attachment or complication. Getting women was never a problem for me, but keeping them away after they'd had their first taste became harder over the years. I was a male slut and fucking proud of it. Every pussy was so spectacular in its uniqueness that I couldn't imagine settling down and fucking the same woman every day.

Watching my siblings fall in love over the last couple of years didn't soften my heart. They changed during that time, growing soft in my opinion. My brothers, whom I'd always thought were tough, became a pile of pussy-whipped humanity in a short time. Their badassness went down a couple of notches in my mind.

It's not women who ultimately change someone, but they affect the actions of the person they love. Why would I want to be different?

I liked who I was.

Fuck, I loved myself.

I wouldn't apologize. I didn't need to be changed.

Perfection's pretty hard to top.

I steered clear of anything that resembled a relationship, including fucking a chick more than a couple of times. Relationships were for pussies or lonely-ass people who needed to feel complete. I wasn't them—the weaker people in the world who craved their second half.

Relationships weren't for me. I loved my time alone, and I wasn't needy enough to require someone to constantly reaffirm how awesome I was. I just needed to look in the mirror, which was a hell of a lot cheaper. Why would I pay for a compliment, whether it was with dates or a fee of the heart, when women openly hurled catcalls in my direction?

Was I cocky? Quite simply, the answer is yes. I had every reason to be. Besides having a plethora of pussy offered to me on a silver platter, I was the complete package. I was handsome and wealthy and could fuck for hours.

My days were spent tattooing clients at my family's tattoo parlor, Inked. During my free time, I sang. I wasn't a rock star by any means. It was a dream I had, one I'd been striving to make real since I was a kid. The years had slipped by. Now that I was older, I thought of it as more of a hobby and enduring passion than a personal goal.

The one thing that singing had given me was an unending stream of pussy. It was like a buffet every night. Women of all colors and sizes offered themselves to me. What man on the planet with a functioning cock would turn that down? Not me—I wasn't stupid.

My upbringing was Italian Catholic. My parents didn't practice their faith weekly, but it always lurked in the background. When I was a kid, my mother would say, "Don't do that or you'll go to hell, Anthony." We all learned to ignore her, and eventually, she dropped the self-righteous bullshit.

I had known I was different since before I could talk; I liked that term more than "special." Being the oldest male had its perks. The worry of many families is the name—would it be carried on? When I was born, the worry vanished. I thanked God every day for three brothers to take that stress off me. Without them, it would have been hopeless. Children weren't in the cards for me. Unless they were the illegitimate type born from a night of passion. Daddy material I was not.

Was I a good person? I thought I was. My family meant everything to me. Family, pussy, and work were my top priorities—and in that order too.

Nothing else mattered.

Women came and went.

Time passed.

Everything and everyone had changed, yet I tried to remain the same.

I sank my teeth into life, holding on to the bitch like everything depended on it.

The one thing I'd learned was that, no matter how hard I tried to fight the inevitable, it would sneak up on me when least expected.

The second I let my guard down and released the hold I had on life... What was my award for such carelessness?

A love so spectacular and heart-wrenching that it threw me for a loop. God had to be playing a wicked trick on me. I'd bet he was laughing his ass off the entire time it played out and sucked me in deeper every day.

When I was in too deep to escape, my greatest fears became reality.

This is my story.

My downfall.

My salvation.

And my love.

THE BEGINNING OF THE END

I propped myself up on the bar, studying the only woman who hadn't bothered to make eye contact with me. Not even a smile or a sideways glance. Nothing.

"What's your name, beautiful?" I asked, trying to get her attention.

Her body inched away as she turned her head to look away from me.

What the fuck was her problem?

I stole a quick glance at the mirror behind the bar. My hair was perfect, just the right amount of stubble was on my face, and my smile was killer. I shrugged and called the bartender over. I needed something cool and smooth after the set.

Singing tonight had set my throat on fire. The change of season wreaked havoc on my system. Even though it had been difficult to sing tonight, it had given me the greatest high. There was nothing like standing on stage and belting out a song that meant so much to me.

"Double Grand Marnier, please," I told the bartender when he came to a stop in front of me.

He nodded and headed to the other end of the bar.

"Can I buy you a drink?" I asked the woman, who was still ignoring me.

"No," she replied without giving me the light of day.

Well, damn. Talk about a cold shoulder.

As the bartender placed the drink in front of me, I motioned to her drink.

"She'll take another too."

She turned toward me and glared. "I said I didn't want a drink."

"Um," the bartender said as he looked between us.

"She'll take another." I lifted my chin to him, giving him the go-ahead for the drink. "Let me buy a beautiful woman a drink. You look like you could use one." I cocked my head, raising an eyebrow as I threw down the challenge.

"I don't take drinks from strangers."

"I'm Anthony." I held my hand out, waiting for her to touch me.

She glanced at my hand before returning her eyes to my face. "Not interested." She wasn't going to make this easy.

"I didn't offer anything but an introduction and a handshake."

"Listen," she said, crossing her arms over her chest.

"Yes?" I repeated her actions, feeling a bit playful. Maybe it was her shitty attitude, but I was ready for whatever she had to throw at me.

We stared each other down. I didn't know what was running through her mind, but I took the opportunity to soak her in. *Exotic* is the word I'd use to describe her. The rich, caramel color of her skin was darker than any member of the Gallo family. It was smooth and blemish-free, and it glistened like silk in the club lighting. My fingers itched to touch it. I wondered if it felt as soft as it looked.

Her eyes were dark, almost black in the dim lighting or the bar. I wanted to stare into them and see them in the light. In the sunlight, did they show hints of gold and specks of brown? Or did they sparkle as the sun hit them? They fit her face perfectly and sat above her high cheekbones and luscious lips.

She reminded me of Keshia Knight Pulliam, the sexy actress who cracked me up in that Madea movie. I remembered watching her as a child when she was Rudy on *The Cosby Show*. She was a dead ringer for her, and if I didn't know better, they could've been twins.

Her lips were large and full. They looked like they had been made for kissing and nothing else. The red lip gloss shimmered in the light, the spots of glitter sparkling. It was like a beacon calling me home and begging for my mouth.

My eyes drifted down, and I noticed the way her arms pushed her tits up in the air. The V-neck T-shirt she wore showed the perfect amount of cleavage. Not enough to be trashy, but enough to entice. I was a tits man. Wait. That's a lie. I was an ass man. Fuck. Who was I kidding? I loved every part of a woman. I could never pick one over another. I wanted the whole package.

"Up here," she demanded.

When I looked up, one shoulder had dropped and her glare had been replaced by a scowl.

"I'm waiting." I grinned.

"For what?" Her lips formed into a firm line and not even a twitch crossed over them.

She was tough. I'd give her that much.

"Your name." I reached for my drink without looking. I needed to maintain eye contact or I'd lose any ground I had won. I knew it wasn't much, but she was no longer ignoring me.

"If I give it to you, will you leave me alone?" Her hands dropped to her sides as her glare disappeared.

"I can't promise anything, but it'll make things go smoother if I know who I'm speaking to." I took a sip, letting the drink coat my throat.

The scratchiness of earlier turned into something entirely different, relieving the strain.

"You're all the same." She rolled her eyes and sighed. "Why can't a girl come to a bar and have a drink in peace without being hounded?"

I took another sip, thinking about my response as I studied her. Before I could reply, she grabbed her martini and placed the glass to her lips. Fuck, I wished I were the glass. I wanted to taste her more than I wanted the tequila that lingered on my tongue.

"First, if you want to have a drink in peace, you need to go to Applebee's. You don't come to the Ritz for a nightcap. Also, you don't have your tits hanging out if you don't want the attention of a man. You can't look like that"—I motioned toward her body—"and expect not to be hit on."

She squared her shoulders as she set her drink back on the bar. If looks could kill, I'd be dead. "Just because I have on a T-shirt doesn't mean I want to fuck. I live nearby and there isn't an Applebee's for miles. This is within walking distance and it's where I want to drink. I don't know if you're clueless or just don't give a shit, but when someone turns their back on you and refuses to answer your questions, it means they don't want to be bothered." She reached for her drink and held my eyes. "You need to get the fuck over yourself."

Oh my God. I think I'm in love.

Well, not really. But fuck, she had my full attention. Rarely did a woman treat me like shit, and for once, I found it refreshing. Her attitude reminded me a little of my sister, Izzy. She wasn't known for being warm and fuzzy, but she was my best friend.

"Meow," I blurted, unable to stop the sound before it left my lips. The one thing I knew was that it would piss her off more.

"You are an asshole," she hissed, glaring at me as she sipped her drink.

I smiled, thinking at least she hadn't thrown her drink on me. "I know I am." I laughed. I knew I was a dick. I'd never claimed to be the nicest guy, but having someone point out what I already knew made me laugh. "So, what's your name?"

"Kitty."

"Now I know you're fucking with me." I couldn't help myself as my laughter grew louder. Not only was she the most beautiful woman in the bar, she was funny and had one hell of an attitude.

"I am, but you can call me Kitty Meow." She grinned and arched an eyebrow.

"I love petting a beautiful pussy," I purred, moving a little closer to her, "cat."

"You're truly a sick fuck, man."

"Anthony," I responded, wanting to hear her say my name.

She moved closer, just as I had. Our bodies were close enough that I caught a whiff of her perfume. The muskiness with a hint of flower made my head a bit dizzy. I wanted to inhale her, fill my senses with her, but I thought that would be pushing the envelope. No one ever said that I was a pansy.

"Thanks for the drink, Anthony."

I didn't waste the opportunity. I moved my face close to her neck and inhaled deeply. Closing my eyes, I let the scent fill my lungs. It was heavenly and made me want to see if she tasted as good as she smelled.

"You're welcome, Kitty Cat."

She drifted away just as my lips were reaching for the flesh of her neck.

"Fuck," I mumbled, missing the opportunity to lick her bronzed skin.

"Not happening, Tony." She shook her head, grabbed her drink, and polished it off. "You have a good night." Then she set her glass down on the bar and picked up her purse.

As she turned to leave, I grabbed her wrist and pulled her toward me. I felt the jolt of electricity that passed between us at the simple touch.

"You can't leave yet."

She looked at my hand and then to me. I couldn't tell, but I bet she felt it too. That lightning that rarely strikes, the thing we all search for. A spark.

"Give me one good reason," she said, her eyes drifting back to where we were connected.

"I'm not done with you." It wasn't the best

line I'd ever given, but I had been thrown by the unexpected zing I'd felt when touching her.

"Well, I'm done with you."

But the funny thing is, she didn't pull away. When a woman was truly not interested, they'd try to get away or slap me in the face. It had happened once. Only one time in my life had a woman turned me down. I chalked it up to the fact that she was probably into pussy more than cock. Why else would she have said no?

"No, you're not." I brought my lips within an inch of hers. "You know you're not. Don't you feel it?"

"You're delusional as well as an asshole." Her eyes sparkled. The hint of possibility wasn't lost on me.

I tightened my grip, but not enough to hurt her. Then I pulled her close enough that I could feel her breath on my face. "Tell me you don't feel it?"

"I don't." She glared at me and lied through her fucking teeth.

"Why aren't you pulling away then, Kitty?" I asked, knowing she felt it every bit as much as I did. I didn't want to be with another human being on this planet, and I'd bet neither did she.

As soon as I asked, she tried to tug her arm away, but I kept my hold on her. She didn't make me believe she meant it.

"I don't know how you'll react if I do."

"Liar," I teased, releasing her wrist but keeping my body close. "Let me buy you one more drink, and if you still think I'm an asshole, I'll leave you alone forever."

She didn't answer right away, looking between the door and me. When her eyes locked on to mine, she finally answered, "Okay. If that's what it takes to get you to leave me alone forever." Then she shrugged, set her purse back on the bar, and sat down on the stool. Raising her hand, she motioned to the bartender, holding up two fingers.

She wasn't going to make it easy on me. I'd have to work for it. My mother always told me that the best things in life needed to be earned and not given.

"So, what do you do, Kitty?" I asked, genuinely interested in more than her body. I wanted to know the woman. What made her tick? More importantly, why was she so damn pissy when it came to me?

"I'm a personal stylist," she replied, keeping her eyes focused on the bartender.

"So, like, you pick out clothes for other people?" I asked, surprised at her answer. It wasn't that she didn't look the part, but jeans and a T-shirt weren't the attire I'd think a stylist would be caught dead in.

"Yes. I help with their entire look."

As the drinks were set in front of us, I slid a twenty across the bar and settled the bill. "You shop for a living?"

"Yes," she answered as she lifted her drink.

I'd hoped for more than curt answers, but felt that nothing would be easy. Maybe the more liquor I got into her system, the easier it would all become.

I must've looked surprised, because she asked, "Shocked?"

I tilted my head and studied her. "Not entirely. You have the look of a fashionista, but I wouldn't expect you to be caught dead in jeans."

"Fashionista? I hate that word." She raised an eyebrow. "Are you sure you're not gay, Tony?"

I closed my eyes, and inhaled before opening them. I wouldn't let her get me worked up. She was baiting me, and if I weren't careful, she'd accomplish her goal.

"Honey, if you give me the chance, I'll prove how wrong that question is."

She chuckled. A full-on laugh bubbled out of her as she tipped her head back. The sound was magical. When she let her guard down and showed happiness, she was even more beautiful.

"In your dreams."

"I think you're the one who's gay, Kitty Cat. Maybe you prefer the purr over a good prick any day."

"You couldn't be more wrong. I love a beautiful cock more than most women, but I don't like the ones that are attached to an asshole."

"You wound me," I said, laying my hand across my chest. "You don't even know me."

"I've known many guys like you. You think you're entitled to everything. You get what you want. Girls fall at your feet. You've spent your life drowning in pussy and throwing women away like trash."

I took a heavy gulp of my Grand Marnier and thought about her response. In all honesty, she wasn't wrong. Would I admit that to her? Fuck no!

"I've never thrown a woman away like a piece of trash."

"Uh huh," she snorted as she crossed her legs.

Out of nowhere, I heard a voice call my name. Fuck. Now wasn't the time for Candy to have found me. Candy wasn't the best example of how I treated women. She had never been my girlfriend, but I had fucked her a couple of times over the last year. I'd say that it was a lack of judgment or maybe too much alcohol, but the girl sucked a mean dick.

"Anthony," she sang as she sauntered up to us.

I closed my eyes, praying that I had imagined her. When I felt her fingers tangle in my hair, I froze.

"Anthony, I've been looking for you. Where ya been?" Her finger traced my ear.

As I opened my eyes, I saw the cocky "I was so fucking right about you" look on Kitty's face.

I pulled Candy's hand away from my face and pushed her backward. "Candy, I'm busy right now."

"But baby," she whined, as she zeroed in on Kitty, "I thought we were going to spend the night together."

I shook my head and let go of my grip on her. "No, Candy. We're not. I told you that last time. You need to move on."

"But," she repeated as her mouth gaped open.

"Move along, Candy. I'm sure one of the other guys would love to spend some time with you," I said, trying to get her to leave me the fuck alone and find a new victim.

"I don't want them, though. They're not as much fun as you." She pouted, clutching her hands in front of her as she stared at the ground.

"Candy, I said no. I'm busy here with Kitty. Can you please excuse us?" Hey, I had tried to be nice, but I thought I'd just gotten a check mark for being a total dick.

When I glanced at Kitty, she was grinning and giving me the "I told ya so" look. For fuck's sake, Candy had ruined any headway I'd made.

"You're a total asshole, Anthony Gallo. Your voice sounded like shit tonight. I'm going to find someone with a dick bigger than a hot dog. You suck," she hissed before she stormed off.

At that point, Kitty broke into hysterics. She covered her face with her hands and laughed and laughed.

"Hardy, har, har, Kitty," I said, joining in on the laughter.

It was my curse in life that shit happened at the most inopportune time. Candy was the perfect case in point.

"She proved my point perfectly. You *are* an asshole." She chuckled harder, enjoying herself and my misery.

"You're wrong about me. I've been a jerk, but if I were a true asshole, I would've gone with Candy and left you here at the bar."

Her laughter faltered at my response. In the

old days, or maybe yesterday, I would've walked off with Candy. I would've taken her backstage, let her suck me off, and walked away a happy man.

"Well, you should've gone with her. She seems like a sure thing. I'm just trying to get through the next ten minutes and then I'm out. Forever." She smiled, wiping the tears that had formed in her eyes.

"You'll change your mind, Kitty Cat." I smiled, moving the stool closer to her and sitting. "So, tell me why you're so cold?"

"I'm not cold," she said as she squared her shoulders in a defensive posture.

"Yes, you are. Why do you hate me so much?"

"I told you already. I've known too many men like you."

"Maybe I'm different. Maybe I want to know you. You may be the one who changes my view on women."

"That's never going to happen. I'm not *the one*." She shook her head and let her body relax.

"Kitty, throw me a bone here, woman. I've

never had to try so hard before. Really, why do you hate me?"

"I don't hate you. I just don't have time for you, Tony."

"What's that supposed to mean? You're too busy with your career to fit me in?"

"I don't have time in my life in general to fit you in. I don't need the complication in my life. I have enough shit to deal with to listen to your bullshit for more than ten minutes. Life is too short to waste on relationships and men."

"Whoa. Wait a minute. I never said anything about a relationship. Maybe we can be friends?"

"Not going to happen."

"Why not?" I asked. I mean, what the fuck? Why couldn't we be friends? In my version of friendship, I'd have her out of her panties, which I was sure were lace, in less than thirty minutes.

"I have enough friends. I don't need more."

"Everybody could use more friends."

"I'm sure Candy could use one right now," she sneered.

"Fuck Candy."

"You have." She burst into laughter again.

"Smartass," I growled.

I brushed my fingertips down the top of her arm. Her skin did feel like silk. My eyes hadn't betrayed me. Now that my hands were satisfied, I wanted to run my tongue along it and see if it tasted as I had imagined. It had to. It fucking had to.

"What are you doing?" she asked as she looked down at my hand, which was still touching hers as goose bumps covered her skin.

"Confirming something."

"And that would be?"

"Seeing if you felt it too."

"I don't know what you mean."

As my hand moved back up her arm, I grazed her breast. She sucked in a breath. I had her. She could deny it all she wanted, but she wanted me. All the sass and bullshit coming out of her mouth was just talk. Her body couldn't hide what she truly felt.

"Kitty," I whispered, moving my face closer to hers. "Tell me you don't feel it."

"I don't," she replied, her eyes growing wider the closer I got.

"You don't?" I asked as I hovered over her lips.

"I don't."

I gave her a quick kiss.

"And this?" I asked as I gave her another peck. "Or that?"

The third time I placed my lips on hers, I kept them there. Her breathing changed as her mouth molded to mine. After sliding my hand up her arm, I held her neck and swiped my thumb along her jaw line.

The taste of the alcohol on her lips mixed with her gloss made my mouth water. Maybe it was all in my head, but I wanted her more than I had ever wanted another thing in my life. I licked at the seam of her lips as she kissed me, begging for entrance. Surprisingly, she accepted, parting her lips and allowing entry.

The tiny victory made me happy. Out of all of my previous conquests, none of them had given me a greater sense of satisfaction than that moment with Kitty.

When she finally touched me, resting her hand on my forearm, I felt the spark ignite something inside me. The kiss had sizzled, but another connection, her reciprocating my touch, caused a detonation of tiny shocks across my entire body.

I had to have her.

I wouldn't accept no for an answer.

Nothing would make me stop until I had her at least once.

As she squeezed my arm, my cock roared to life. The ache grew unbearable with each swipe of my tongue and her grip on my arm. When I finally pulled my mouth away from hers, she whispered, "Fuck."

My work here was done. Even though she thought I was an asshole, she felt it too. She couldn't deny it any longer. Her mouth could move, but she'd be feeding me lines of bullshit.

"You felt it." I smiled, keeping my hand on her neck.

She didn't try to detach herself from me as her eyes fluttered open and she looked at me—really looked at me. For the first time tonight, her eyes were soft.

"I can't," she replied, and averted her eyes.

"Kitty, you can't say that after what you just felt, what I just felt." I shook my head, tightening my grip on her neck. "I've never experienced that before with anyone. You can't shut me out."

Her hand moved away from my arm like I had just burned her. "I just can't." She pushed on my chest with both hands, trying to put distance between us.

"Why not?" I asked, ready to argue the point. I wasn't going to allow her to give up that easily.

"Let me go," she demanded, shoving me away.

"Kitty," I begged, trying to keep our connection. "Please."

"Get your hands off my damn sister!" a deep voice yelled from behind her.

I froze and peered over her shoulder. Fuck. Just what I didn't need. A brother. A big brother. A brother brother. Not like "hey, man, this is my brother," but "hey, this is my big-ass brother and he's going to kick your white-boy ass."

Goddamn it.

"I'm not going to say it again. Get your hands

off Maxine. She asked you nicely to let her go, but I'm not going to be so damn kind."

"Maxine?" I asked, finally learning her name, although it wasn't the way I had wanted to hear it.

"Please let me go," she insisted with tears in her eyes.

I stared at her, not liking that I had caused her distress. "Okay, man, but only because she asked and not you." I released my hand, letting her move away.

She scurried out of my reach.

"Let's get you home, Max," he said to her.

Max. She had a tough name. It fit her perfectly. This couldn't be the end. I didn't want it to be. There was no way in hell I'd let her out of here without at least getting her phone number.

"Max," I said, holding out my hand to her. "See me again?"

Before she could answer, her brother stepped between us. He was at least six inches taller than I was. He was a beast. He'd give any of my brothers a run for their money, but I'd never been a pussy. I never backed down from a fight. Hell, I'd thrown punches over small shit. Max was worth the risk.

"She doesn't want anything to do with you," he stated as he stared down at me.

"I think she can answer for herself," I replied, moving into his personal space.

"Denzel," she said, placing her hand on his arm. "Let's just go."

"Wait!" I yelled, not ready to say goodbye.

"Come on, Max. This fool isn't worth your time and I don't feel like spending the night in jail *again* for assault."

Fuck me.

If I didn't know better, I'd think he was a Gallo. Although I wanted to fight him just to show that I was worthy, I knew it wasn't the way. If some dickhead was fucking with Izzy, getting in a fistfight with any of my brothers wasn't the way to win her heart. I couldn't let my temper and need for her cloud my judgment.

"I'm ready," she said as she reached for her purse.

I clenched my hands at my sides, and it took everything in me not to reach out to her.

Without another word, Max and Denzel turned and headed for the door.

"Turn and look at me," I repeated over and over as I watched her stroll toward the exit. I held my breath, waiting for it.

Before she disappeared through the doorway, she turned and gave me one quick glance before vanishing in the shadow of her brother.

I sucked in a breath, feeling like I'd been hit by a ton of bricks. Never in my life had I experienced something so powerful. To have it ripped away from me so fast and without any warning hurt like hell.

This wasn't the end.

It couldn't be.

I wouldn't give up on finding her again.

I needed to know her.

I craved her.

The feel of her skin, the way her mouth tasted—they'd left me wanting more. And I never gave up on something I wanted. Not without a fight.

3

EVADE AND CAPTURE

I SPENT THE NEXT TWO FRIDAY NIGHTS AT the Ritz hoping to run into Max. Instead, I ran into Candy.

Again, I explained to her that I wasn't interested. If Maxine walked in and saw me with Candy, everything would be shot to hell. Candy was a persistent little thing, but I did my best to rid myself of her.

On the third Friday night, I finished my drink and headed for the door. It was another night wasted, ending in failure. Tucking my hands in my pockets, I walked down the sidewalk toward the parking garage. Ybor City was busier than normal tonight. People lined the streets, filling the tiny café tables outside. The lights over the street twinkled, and there was energy to the area I'd often missed after a night of playing a gig. Usually, by the time I walked out of the Ritz, the only thing I cared about was getting home. I didn't stop to take in my surroundings.

As I walked by the Corona King, something made me stop. When I turned toward the tables, I saw her.

Maxine was sitting toward the back, near the doors, nursing a beer. She didn't see me as she was typing on her phone, oblivious to the world.

Staying out of her line of sight, I walked the outside edge of the tables and headed straight for her. It might have been my only chance to talk to her again. I wasn't going to let it slip past me.

She didn't notice my approach or that I stood behind her, watching her movements. Tonight, she wasn't wearing a T-shirt—she had opted for jeans, heels, and a white off-the-shoulder top with lace sleeves. Her black, pin-straight hair was pulled back into a low ponytail that trailed down her back. She simply looked stunning, more beautiful than I remembered.

"Is this seat taken?"

Her body stilled, the furious typing on her screen ceasing. "It's taken," she replied without even a glance.

"What about the other two chairs at the table?" I wouldn't give up that easily. I knew stubborn women, and eventually, I could wear away their steely veneer.

"Those are too." She started to type on her phone again, pretending I wasn't there.

"When your friends get here, I'll get up," I said as I pulled out the chair and made myself comfortable.

"For the love of God," she muttered, closing her eyes as she set the phone on the table.

"I happened to be walking by and saw you sitting here alone. I had to stop and say hello. It would be rude of me not to." I relaxed back in the chair, resting my elbow on the arm.

It took everything in me not to place a kiss on her luscious lips. Instead, I ran my finger across mine, trying to soothe the ache I felt.

"Did you just get done singing?" she asked, staring straight ahead. She still hadn't looked at me. All progress I'd made the first night had vanished.

Shit.

"You noticed me," I whispered, thrusting out my chest.

"What?" she asked, tearing at the label on her beer.

"You noticed me singing."

"How could I not? You were screeching like a howler monkey." She rolled her eyes.

"You're a horrible liar, Max." I loved the sound of her name. Although "Kitty Cat" would always hold a special place in my heart, Max sounded badass, and she was that and more.

I knew it.

One look at her and I had known she was the most interesting woman in the world. If nothing else, I needed to get to know her. I wouldn't rest until I did.

"What was your name again?" she asked as she balled up the paper she'd torn off her beer bottle with her fingertips.

Normally, I'd have been wounded by a woman forgetting my name, but I wasn't. She knew my name. I knew she did. She was fucking with me, pretending I wasn't important enough to remember. But her body had once again betrayed her. As soon as she'd heard my voice, she'd frozen. Whether she admitted it or not, she remembered me.

"Why do you have to lie, Max? You know exactly who I am." I dropped my hand from my face and drifted forward in the chair. Resting my hand on the table, I moved my fingers within centimeters of hers.

"I remember you're an asshole." She shrugged as she looked down. Even with her face partially hidden, I could see her smirk.

"See? You do remember me." I chuckled, sliding my fingers closer to hers.

"Barely," she lied. Then she lifted her head, giving her drink her full attention.

"Do you want another one?" I asked, noticing that her drink was almost gone.

"I'm good. I was just about to leave."

"But I thought you had friends coming."

"I do, but we're going to go somewhere else."

"Can I come?" I asked, knowing she'd say no, but I wouldn't let her off the hook.

"No."

"Can I get you a drink?" the waitress asked from the other side of the table.

"I'll take whatever she's having, and she'll have another too," I said, keeping my eyes locked on Max.

"I don't want another drink," she replied, finally bringing her eyes to mine.

"She'll take another," I said as I glanced at the waitress and nodded.

"Two drinks coming right up," she said as she rocked on her feet before walking away.

"Anthony, listen—"

"You do remember me," I interrupted her.

"Ugh," she whispered, and blew out a puff of air. "I'm sure you're not a total tool all the time, but I really don't have time for you tonight."

"Tomorrow, then."

"Busy too."

"I can wait."

"I don't have time for you ever." She stared at me without blinking.

"You're an amazing actress. Did you ever think about being in a movie?"

"What?" she asked as her face became distorted.

"You say things you don't mean and make them very convincing. If I didn't know how your mouth tasted and how your breathing changed as I touched you, I may have believed you."

"Stop," she pleaded, holding up her hand. "I can't, Anthony."

"Are you married?" I asked, looking at her hands but seeing nothing that resembled a wedding ring.

"No, but that doesn't mean I'm interested."

"I beg to differ."

"You can beg all you want. The answer is still no."

Before I could respond, the waitress set the beers on the table and asked if we wanted anything else. We both shooed her away, ready to duke it out. I needed to change her mind—or at least show her that she could try to deny what she felt but it was very much real.

"Max, who's this?" a female voice asked behind Max.

Fuck. I guessed that part of her previous statement wasn't a lie. She wasn't going to be alone tonight, but I was all about crashing a party.

"No one important," she sassed.

I jumped up from my seat, holding my hand out to the beautiful female across the table. "I'm Anthony, Max's friend."

She placed her palm in mine and fluttered her eyes as she soaked me in. "Hmmm. I'm Renita, but my friends call me Nita."

I took the opportunity to lean forward and place a kiss on the top of her hand. "Nita, it's great to finally meet a friend of Max's."

"Likewise. Max, where you been hiding this hunk?" Nita asked as she stared at me and licked her lips.

At least one female at the table didn't have a problem showing exactly how they felt.

"Nita, I don't know the man. He's crazy. I told him I'm not interested."

Nita sat down, resting her face in her palm. "This is going to be fun." She batted her eyelashes.

"For the love of God," Max whispered.

"Max likes to pretend we don't know each other. But I know the feel of her pulse underneath my fingertips when I'm kissing her." I smiled, glancing over at Max before turning my attention back to Nita.

Nita's mouth gaped. "Fuck. That's one of the sexiest things I've ever heard."

"You need to get out more, Nita," Max snapped, grabbing her beer and taking a drink.

"What can I get you to drink, Nita?" I had a feeling that, if I won her friends over, maybe— just maybe—I'd find an inroad to Max.

"Yes, I'd love a sangria." She smiled as she stared at me.

"Coming right up. I'll be right back," I said as I pushed the chair back and left them behind.

I kept my eyes glued to the windows, watching them to make sure they didn't vanish as I ordered Nita's drink. When I returned to the table, they both stopped talking and stared at me.

"Miss me?" I asked as I set the drink in front of Nita.

"Yes." Nita smiled and batted her eyelashes again.

Max coughed, and something like "traitor" left her mouth.

"So, what's the plan tonight?" I asked, curious at what my evening would entail. When I'd thought all hope was lost, I'd stumbled upon her and found a new sense of purpose.

"Drinks and dancing," Nita replied as she sipped her sangria.

"I'm tired. I think I want to just go home," Max whined, twirling the beer in her hands.

"Don't be such a pussy, Max," Nita teased, glaring at Max.

"You're both assholes."

"She's just a grouchy fuck. Don't mind her. She's been—"

"I'm just tired," Max blurted out.

I stroked my chin, wondering what I'd missed. There was something Max clearly didn't want me to know.

"She's been what?" I asked.

"Nothing," Nita said with wide eyes. Then she gulped her sangria and glanced away from me. "Is Malia coming?" she asked over the rim of her glass.

Max shrugged. "She's supposed to be here already, but that girl is always late."

"It's fashionable to be late, and you know her, always being trendy," Nita replied, still not making eye contact with me.

"Once she gets here, we'll head to the club," Max said before lifting the beer to her lips.

I wanted to be the bottle, feeling the softness of her lips as she pressed them to me. Reaching under the table, I had to adjust myself to not draw attention to the growing problem in my pants.

"Where are we headed?" I asked, feeling more hopeful with each passing moment.

"We're going to Liquid, but you're not," Max replied, giving me a cold stare.

"Why not?" Whether she liked it or not, I was fucking going. There was no way I'd let her out of my sight now that I'd found her again.

Nita started to giggle, and Max laughed. "What?"

"You don't want to go there," Nita answered, covering her mouth with her hand. "Unless you're man enough to handle it."

"I'm man enough to handle anything, Nita." I smiled, puffing out my chest.

"It's a gay bar." Her entire face lit up as the corners of her mouth reached for her eyes.

Damn, she was beautiful—especially when she smiled.

"So?" I asked. I had always been comfortable in my sexuality. Men, especially gay ones, didn't scare me. I had gay, straight, and bisexual friends —and a few I couldn't classify.

"We wouldn't want to threaten your man-hood," Max answered through her giggling.

"Kitty Cat, other men don't threaten me."

"What if they try to hit on you?" Nita asked, raising her eyebrow as her laughter died.

"I'm not worried about it, Nita. I can handle myself in any situation."

"Somehow, I believe you," she replied.

"Anthony, I really don't think it's a good idea for you to come," Max stated, crossing her arms over her chest.

"Are you worried more men will hit on me than you, Max?" I asked playfully.

"We go to the gay bar so men *won't* hit on us, Anthony. So no, I'm not worried." Max smiled, thinking she had one-upped me.

"I'll never understand women," I mumbled, a little louder than I had intended.

Nita propped her hands on the table. "It's like this, Anth. Can I call you Anth?" she asked, pausing for a second before continuing. "We go there because we don't have to worry about being hit on. It's nice to be able to drink with our friends and dance without having to worry about guys with grabby hands."

"Yeah, you don't need to worry about that at Liquid," Max agreed.

I understood the logic, but that didn't mean I agreed with it. Even in gay bars, there were men who went both ways. They weren't as safe from "grabby" hands as they thought.

"I think Nita and Malia would rather have a girls-only night." Max nodded toward Nita, giving her a death glare.

Nita waved her hand at Max and turned her attention toward me. "Malia and I would love for you to come."

"Would you now?" I asked, raising my eyebrow and loving the playful nature of Nita.

"Uh huh," she murmured as she came closer. "Max would never admit it, but she wants you to come too." Then she lost it, bursting out into laughter as Max hit her in the arm.

"Shut the fuck up, Nita. I most certainly do not want him to come." Max crossed her arms again as she slouched and stared at her legs.

"Looks like I'm getting here at the perfect time," a woman said as she walked up to the empty chair.

"Please save me, Malia," Max said as she stared up at the leggy female to my left.

"I'm Anthony," I said as I hopped up from my seat and offered my hand.

Malia stepped back and looked me up and down. I felt her eyes appraising me with each passing sweep. "I don't know who you are, but I'd sure like to find out more." She slid her hand into mine.

"Any friend of Max's is a friend of mine," I said as I kissed her velvety skin and peered down at her.

"Fuck. I've already made it to 'friends' territory?" she asked as she glanced up at me.

"Max got me first. I'm hers and hers alone, ladies. Unless she wants to share." I grinned, waiting for Max to chime in.

"Max?" Malia asked with a hopeful tone.

"You can have him," Max shot back.

"She's playing hard to get," I responded, letting go of Malia's hand and glancing at Max. "I've always loved a good chase."

"It's not a chase when I'm not running."

"Girl, what is wrong with you? This fine-ass man wants to get to know you and you're being rude," Malia said as she sat down. "I need a drink to get through this night, I think. Ma'am." She waved her hand at the waitress leaving the next table. "Vodka on the rocks, stat."

"There's nothing wrong with me, Malia. I just don't have time to deal with a boy."

"*Man*," I said as I lifted my beer to my lips.

"But he's a fine-looking man, Max. How could you say no to that?" Nita waved her hand in my direction, motioning up and down. "I mean, hell, I'd jump on him in a hot minute."

Max shook her head as she chewed the inside of her lip. "You know why, Nita." She gave her a serious look.

"Yeah," Nita said.

"Does someone want to clue me the fuck in?" It was the second time I'd heard the statement. There was a secret no one would share. My mind started to fill with crazy things. Imagination could be dangerous.

"Nope," Max said, and looked between the two women.

"Be honest, are you married?"

"No!" she screeched, vigorously shaking her head.

I rubbed my chin and thought of all the possible scenarios. "Gay?"

"God, no. She likes cock too much," Malia said, and started to laugh.

"Malia!" Max yelled across the table.

Malia shrugged as she took a drink of her vodka, her lips hidden by the rim of the glass.

"Engaged?"

"No."

"Hmmm," I muttered, trying to think what else would keep her from men. "STD?"

Please say no. Fuck, it would have been such a shame for the beautiful creature in front of me to have something that would stop me from sinking my naked dick inside her wetness.

She laughed, giving me a funny look. "No. Jesus."

"Well, I'm trying to think of all the reasons you wouldn't go on a date with me, Max." I continued to rub my chin and stare at her.

Briefly, I glanced at her friends to gauge their reactions. They weren't giving anything away, though. I was sure they were scared of Max—or at least they made it seem to me as though they were.

"I won't date you because you're an asshole. I think we went over this before, Anthony."

"Is it because I'm white?" I didn't want to throw it out there, but it could be a reason.

Even now, people still seemed to have an issue with race. Not me, but others. Even though segregation had ended more than fifty years ago, people couldn't let go of the past.

She shook her head. "I don't see color, but I clearly know an asshole when they're in front of me."

"I think you have an anal fetish," I said with a smile. Max had brought up the word asshole more than any other person I'd ever met.

"You're impossible."

"No, I'm not. I'm easy, Max. You're the one making this difficult."

Max turned to Malia, who was giggling quietly. "What are you smiling about?"

"I think you two make the cutest couple. Finally, someone who won't listen to your bullshit."

"I'm with Malia," Nita interjected, raising

her sangria in the air. "This could turn out to be a very interesting night."

"I'll drink to that," I said as I raised my glass and clinked it to hers.

"Fuckers," Max mumbled as she chugged the last of her beer and wiped her mouth with the back of her hand.

I'd let her brush me off once, but I wouldn't let it happen again.

Tonight, I'd seal the deal and let her know how wrong she was.

My girls, the two people I shared my deepest, darkest secrets with, had sold me out. They knew me well enough to know that I didn't want him tagging along, but they didn't listen. If I could change things and make falling in love a possibility, I'd be throwing myself at Anthony.

His cocky swagger and killer smile had hooked me from the moment he asked me for my name. I understood why women willingly threw themselves at him, but I didn't have that luxury. I'd sworn off men, even those I wanted to get to know, because it would be easier for everyone in the end.

I know what you're thinking: what does one night matter? How could it hurt? But this was my life, my future, and my heart at risk of being crushed. I wasn't willing to open up to anyone. I couldn't. I didn't have that luxury, and I wouldn't claw my way back from a broken heart.

Nita and Malia had been telling me for months to find someone to be my "friends with benefits," but I couldn't do it. I'd always grown attached to people. I'd never been the type to fuck and run. With my luck I'd fall head over heels and wouldn't be able to climb out of the black hole that would eventually fill my heart.

I'm not cold-hearted. I'm the average African-American girl. I've fought for everything

I have. My life never took an easy path; even today I struggle to be taken seriously. Owning my own business as a female doesn't open as many doors as it would if I had a dick dangling between my legs. I'd made a name for myself in Tampa and done it in a short time. I immersed myself in my work, forsaking love and relationships to keep me sane.

I'd done a good job and succeeded, until he found me at the King Corona. The first time I saw him at the Ritz, I wanted to get to know him. I wanted to chat and look into his sparkling blue eyes. I was a total bitch to him, but I'd become good at the role. Most men would take the hint and get lost, but not Anthony. It drove him forward.

What could a night of dancing hurt? I'd get him out of my system and he'd find out that the last thing he wanted was me—the bitchy black girl that doesn't have time for him in her life. When we said goodbye after dancing at Liquid, I'd never see him again.

I couldn't.

4

FUCK KARMA

I'D LIKE TO SAY THAT WE HAD A SMOOTH start, Max and I. But that was the furthest thing from the truth. Nita and Malia loved me. I spent the entire night buying them drinks and dancing with each of them. Max was my goal, but I knew that friends could be amazing allies.

Max was the best dancer in the place. I took every opportunity to rub against her and touch her exposed skin. She needed to be reminded of the sizzle we had when we touched—the thing I'd never found before and wasn't willing to let go of so easily. She tried to play it cool and act like it had no effect on her, but I knew she felt it too. Even three weeks later, it hadn't waned. The sting from the invisible spark hit me every time.

After a few more glasses of wine and liquor, we stood at the bar, winded.

"So, what do you do, Anthony?" Nita asked, shifting between her feet. Her heels were at least five inches. I didn't know how women danced in them.

"I have two jobs," I replied.

"Oh no. He's a broke motherfucker," Malia blurted out as she swayed.

I laughed and shook my head. "I'm not. I'm part owner in a tattoo shop and I sing in a band during my free time."

"Tattoos, eh?" Nita asked as she swept her fingers across the ink on my arm. "They've always intrigued me."

"I have more than you can see." Just the bottom of my tattoos showed on each arm because my T-shirt hid the rest.

She smiled at me as her fingers inched up my arm and pushed the T-shirt up. "They're so colorful." Running her nails across my skin, she ogled my tattoos. "I want to see them all," she whispered.

"Down girl," Malia said, smacking Nita's hand away from my body. "The man didn't come here to get pawed by you."

"Better me than one of the boys," she said as she tipped her head toward a group of men watching us intently across the bar. "You be quiet, Malia." She pushed her hand away and turned her attention back to me. "Anthony, will you show them to me?" And a smile I could only describe as naughty stretched across her face.

"I'd have to take off my shirt." I didn't care that it was a gay bar, but I wasn't sure how Max would feel about me taking off my clothes.

She rolled her eyes at me and raised her eyebrows. "Go ahead. Give the girls a show," she said with a snarky tone.

"You don't care if I take off my shirt?"

"Why would I? I'm sure the guys would enjoy the view too. It may be the only way you get a date tonight anyway." She smiled and pursed her lips.

"Kitty Cat," I whispered as I reached up and

brushed my fingers on her cheek. "I plan to leave here with you on my arm and spend the night in your bed."

"You better keep dreaming." Her mouth stayed void of emotion.

"I'll show you what dreams are made of, Kitty Cat. Tonight, you'll find out." I stroked her lips with the pad of my thumb.

"It's not happening." She shook her head, breaking the contact.

"Anthony," Nita whined as she tugged on my shirtsleeve. "Let's see the ink, my man. Put up or shut up."

I winked at Max and took a step back as I grabbed the back of my shirt. As I pulled it over my head, I heard a gasp but couldn't tell whose mouth it had come out of. I could've sworn it had slipped out of Max's, though.

After the material cleared my head, I made sure to flex my muscles. Immediately, two hands touched my skin and began to feel my tattoos.

"Ladies," I said, trying to hold in my laughter.

"They're so pretty," Malia said as she slid her fingers up my arm.

"Fuck," Nita groaned as she touched my SOUL tattoo. "The color is so amazing." Her fingers dug into my flesh. "Spectacular, in fact." She groped my pecs, squeezing them repeatedly in her hands.

I didn't know if she was referring to my ink or my muscles. I flexed under her touch, watching her mouth turn up into a beautiful smile.

"Ya like?" I asked, enjoying the attention of them both.

She nodded, glancing over her shoulder at Max. She didn't remove her hands. "Max, get your ass over here and feel this. Damn, this man is stacked."

I wanted to laugh. God, did I want to, but I grinned at Max and arched my eyebrow instead. She rolled her eyes as she took a drink of her beer.

The woman had the emotional availability of a brick wall. She might have been the female version of me. The one time I found someone I wanted to at least get to know, she shut me the hell out. Figured.

"I'm perfectly happy just watching you two fondle him." She faced forward, cutting off all eye contact with me.

"Did these hurt?" Malia asked, raking her nails across my back to my other shoulder.

"Not very much," I said, smiling down at them before returning my attention to Max.

Another night, this would have been the beginning of foreplay. I wouldn't have had to work too hard to get them back to my place. But they weren't my targets. She was ignoring me, acting unimpressed with my physique.

Nita moved her face closer to my chest. I could feel her warm breath as it skidded across my skin.

"Fuck," she moaned as she felt me.

"You said that already, Nita. He's not that impressive," Max shot over her shoulder.

"Max, shut up. You haven't felt him. He fucking is!" Nita yelled into my chest. "Hey," she said, getting my attention. "Don't listen to her.

She hasn't been fucked since Obama became president."

Nita and Malia both started to laugh.

My eyes shot back to Max. It couldn't be. There was no way a creature as beautiful as her hadn't been touched in years. No fucking way. Everybody needs that connection eventually.

Max swiveled on her stool and glared at the girls. Fuck. If looks could kill, they'd both be dead. Yikes, she gave a scary damn look. Scarier than any face I'd ever seen Izzy give me.

"You two bitches need to shut the fuck up. You know that shit isn't true."

I kept my eyes pinned to her, but she didn't look at me. "It can't be true," I whispered.

"It is," Nita whispered. She gave me sad eyes when she spoke. Even if she was yanking Max's chain, I could see she felt bad for her.

Nothing made sense. I couldn't see anything wrong with her. What the hell had I missed? In all honesty, she was the most beautiful woman I'd ever laid eyes on. And hell, my eyes had seen their fair share. Her body was smoking, with curvy hips, a lavish ass, tits that were more than a handful, flawless mocha skin, and straight black hair that grazed her ass when she walked.

I knew I was a superficial fuckwad, but I did have a dick. Looks were the first thing I noticed on a woman.

Maybe she had some nasty habit or was secretly a freak, and not the good kind. Either that or she was a nun in disguise. There was no way she wasn't getting banged or at least being offered to be fucked all the time. I couldn't have been the only one who wanted to taste her. God, did I fucking want to taste her.

"Sir," a male voice said, interrupting my thoughts as I stared at Max.

I shook my head, breaking myself from the trance. A tall and very burly man walked between Max and me and stood behind Nita.

"You're going to have to put your shirt back on. We have a strict nudity policy, and it's becoming a disturbance."

I knew my face was something like "what the fuck" as I started to scan the room. Sets of eyes throughout the club were on me, watching as I gave two out of the three females a skin show. I wasn't nude, but gay or not, I'd end up hurting tomorrow if I fought the guy over a shirt.

"Not a problem. I'm sorry, man," I said as I began to lift the shirt over my head. Then I caught a glimpse of Max laughing behind the bouncer and sighed. It hadn't gone exactly as I had planned when I'd decided to bare my body to her.

The one thing about me, though, was that I never gave up.

"You're such a buzzkill, Donovan. I swear. Finally, a hot straight man is in this place and you want him to put his clothes on," Malia whined as she walked passed me and bumped into Donovan.

He stood stock-still, unaffected by the contact. "Sorry, darling. Rules are rules." He shrugged.

As I slid my T-shirt on, I heard a series of groans and boos in the club. Malia and Nita weren't the only ones upset that I was asked to cover up. I bowed and blew kisses to the crowd. Fuck, I'd take any catcall—even those from other men.

"You're a hit, Anthony," Malia declared as she clapped her hands.

As I stood beside Max, I said, "I wonder what they'd do if I showed them my most impressive asset?"

Instead, she gawked at me. I thrust my crotch in her direction, which caught her attention before her mouth snapped closed.

"You're an asshole and a pig," Max muttered as she ran her hands down her face.

"I caught ya lookin'. You know you want to see it too." I gave her my "I want to fuck you" smirk, knowing my dimple most likely was showing. It was my lady-killer, and it had caused more squeals over the years than a slice of chocolate cake.

"I do. I do," Nita interrupted as she raised her hand and waved it in the air.

"Nita, really. Can't you see the way he looks at Max?" Malia elbowed Nita in the side.

I kept staring at Max. I heard Nita and Malia as they spoke, but paid them no attention. She eyeballed me as I continued to smirk at her while running my tongue along my lips. If I hadn't known better, I'd swear a corner of her mouth twitched.

"Another drink?" I asked, figuring the only way I'd get into her bed, besides with my charm, was with lots of liquor. It needed to be enough to get her to drop her guard—or to at least find a kink in her armor.

Her face remained impartial as she replied, "Sure."

Victory was mine.

I felt it, and I sure as fuck wanted to taste it— taste her—tonight.

"I'll be right back." I headed down to the other end of the bar, unwilling to wait for the bartender. "Hey," I said to him as he reached into the beer cooler and glanced up at me.

"What can I get you, man?" He smiled as his eyes raked over my body.

"Another round for the ladies and me, please." I reached into my back pocket and slid thirty dollars across the bar.

"Coming right up." Giving me a quick nod, he pulled the money toward him.

I stood there for a moment, watching the

girls as they chatted. They kept glancing at me as Nita and Malia stood in front of Max. It looked like they were lecturing her. Hands and arms waved between Max and me as they talked. Ready to rescue Max, I raced to her side.

"Ladies, drinks are on their way," I interrupted, peering down at Max. "Want to dance?" I'd have used any excuse to get close to her, to feel her on me, even if it was only on the dance floor.

"Yes," she sighed as she rose to her feet and snarled at Nita and Malia.

"That looked a little intense." I reached out, grabbing her hand in a tight grip as she tried to lurch away. "I'm just walking you to the dance floor. Don't make a big deal out of everything, Max."

"I don't like it," she replied, trying to jerk her hand from mine.

"What's with you and the bullshit?"

Her mouth dropped open as the words left my lips. "I don't—"

"We're done talking," I said as I gripped her

waist and pulled her toward me. She felt so fucking amazing.

Her mouth formed an O as my hands slid down her back and gripped her ass. Her body tensed in my arms as she stared up at me.

"Anthony."

"No," I said with firmness. I wasn't going to let her ruin this moment.

She needed to stop thinking and just feel. The electricity from earlier had returned. It hadn't been lost entirely, still crackling between us throughout the night. Touching her brought it to the front, reminding me of the reason I had been drawn to her in the first place. Pussy always had my attention, at least for a short time. Max had that unknown quality, the mystery drawing me in and consuming my thoughts.

I thought that, if I had her at least once, the feeling would wane. I just needed a taste to discharge the electric current that passed between us and then I'd be cured. She was a phase, just like the other women in my life.

As my body rubbed against her, the skin of our arms touching, the spark ignited. Our bodies moved together, finding the rhythm of the music, and slowly, her body wilted in my arms. She snaked her arms behind my neck as I drew her closer to my body. Without an inch between us, I brought my lips to hers.

"Tell me you don't want me, Max," I said, knowing she couldn't deny whatever *this* was between us.

Her lips parted as she stared into my eyes.

"Tell me you don't feel that." I brushed my lips across hers before pulling away.

"What?" she asked with an airy voice.

"Your body betrays you," I said on her mouth. "I can feel your heart pounding in your chest."

"You don't," she said as she dug her fingers into the back of my hair.

I drew her bottom lip into my mouth. She tasted better than I remembered. There wasn't an inch of her body I didn't want to sample. As I backed away, I released her lip.

"I do," I growled.

She stopped arguing and let her body move

with mine. I nuzzled my face into her neck; I breathed her in, memorizing the scent.

Nothing else mattered in this moment.

The world melted away as I held her in my arms.

We swayed and stared into each other's eyes. Her face softened, giving me a glimmer of hope. I finally felt like I had a chance with her. All I wanted was for her to give me a shot, and in that moment, I knew it could happen.

"Max," I whispered as I pressed my lips to her ear.

My hands wandered from her ass to her back. With one hand on the small of her back and the other cradling her spine, I dipped her. With her neck fully exposed, I dragged my lips down her skin. The softness of her flesh and the hint of perfume drove me mad as I pressed my mouth to her skin to feel her pulse. It thundered beneath my lips, keeping time with the music. Her heart beat in perfect cadence with the rhythm, matching the flutter of mine.

I'd like to say that my dick ached to be inside her, but it was more than that. As I started to fall down the slippery slope of evaluating what in the fuck was happening to my mind, she grabbed my shoulders and pulled herself up. When her lips connected with mine, the thoughts that had started to creep in vanished.

As I held her to me, I returned her kiss with greater ferocity than I had before. Maybe I'd had too many drinks, and quite possibly, so had she, but the sizzle we'd had weeks ago now felt like a volcano ready to erupt.

"Max," I moaned into her mouth, overcome by the need I felt for her. It wasn't like I'd never felt need before, but not to the extent I did with her.

Our first kiss had consumed me. Never had I chased anyone before. Ybor City wasn't my usual stomping ground except for when I played gigs, yet I'd found myself there numerous times over the last few weeks.

I hadn't dared tell anyone. I spent years making fun of my siblings for being pussy-whipped. The one thing they had achieved that I hadn't was sampling the goods before having their thoughts dominated by another human being.

I'd only had a taste. One simple kiss had sent me into a tizzy.

As I devoured her mouth, tangling my tongue with hers, I had two options. I could excuse myself and fuck the first piece of ass I could find tonight. There was a possibility that it could cure me. It would be the coward's way of dealing with the feelings that lurked in my subconscious. Or I could do what I had come here for—conquer Max and put her out of my system forever.

When the music stopped, our bodies slowly came to a stop. As we stilled, the kiss grew deeper. My mind had been made. I'd dive right in and fuck her brains out. Based on what her friends had said, she needed me as badly as I needed her.

"Let me take you home," I murmured as I lingered over her lips.

Her harsh breathing skidded across my face as she contemplated my words. She blinked twice before she replied. "Okay," she whispered as her body swayed in my arms.

I wouldn't give her the chance to change her mind. I released her from my hold, touching her on the small of her back, and headed toward Nita and Malia. As we approached, I could see the giant grins on their faces. They beamed with excitement as I winked at them.

"Ladies," I said as we reached them, my arm still behind Max. "I'm going to walk Max home."

"Yes!" Malia squealed, bouncing a little bit on her stool. "You do that. She needs to be 'taken' home." She made air quotes.

"Have fun," Nita said, elbowing Malia in the ribs.

The entire time, Max stood silent, giving her friends a sloppy grin.

"I think she's drunk," I said, wondering if I was an asshole. Tomorrow, would she think I had taken advantage of her in her inebriated state? I didn't want to be that guy. I'd never had to be, and I sure as hell wasn't going to start now.

"Anthony," Malia said, beckoning me with her index finger.

I moved in close, placing my ear next to her mouth.

"She's not as drunk as you'd think. Max can out-drink most people on this planet. Let her think you think she's drunk. If she's willing to let you take her home, don't let her change her mind. She needs what you're offering."

I laughed, backing away as I caught Nita and Max whispering back and forth as they glanced at me.

"Got it," I said, nodding at Malia. "Ready?" I asked as I turned toward Max, grabbing her waist. I wasn't going to let her escape.

"Yeah," she answered with glassy eyes and a smirk on her face.

I let Max lead the way, following her movements as we strolled down Seventh Avenue. We walked in silence, nodding at the passersby, focused on our final destination.

When we arrived, I stayed behind her as she unlocked the door. The neighborhood was quiet and only blocks from the center of Ybor. She hadn't lied: the night I met her at the Ritz she said it was the closest bar to her house. I didn't know if it was fate or God's way of fucking with me. He liked to do that from time to time. The fact that she hadn't gone next door to the King Corona that night could've been a cruel joke if I hadn't found her again.

As she entered the house, she held the door open for me to join her. "Can I get you something to drink?" she asked as she turned the light on and sagged into the front door.

I shook my head. The only thing I wanted in my mouth was her. Every inch of her body needed to be sampled, dirtied, and devoured. I couldn't wait another minute to touch her. Fuck, if I waited too long, she could change her mind.

I charged, pushing her body into the door. As I molded to her, I rubbed my denim-covered dick into her abdomen. Smothering her lips, I couldn't resist her any longer. The walk had been torture, but standing in her home made me impatient. I had always been the type to take what I wanted without waiting. Some would think it was a weakness, but it had always worked in my favor.

Her hands drifted underneath my T-shirt. As they glided up my sides, leaving a burning sensation in their wake, I hissed, feeling the sizzle as our flesh connected. She panted as she dug her fingernails into my skin. Her touch branded me. Even when her fingers had moved, the feel of her still lingered, creating a smoldering trail.

I placed my hand on her ribs, feeling the heat emanating from her body, matching my own. The thin fabric of her top did nothing to mask the need that seeped from her body.

"Do you like this shirt?" I asked. I didn't want to take the time to slowly undress her. If I gave her a chance to think too much, she might change her mind.

"Eh," she mumbled into my mouth.

Question answered, I gripped the side of her shirt and pulled. The delicate material ripped, coming apart in my hand, and caused her to shriek.

"Shh," I said as I dropped the cloth to the floor.

I glanced down at her ample breasts, which were peeking out over the top of her bra. They'd been made for me—or at least, I liked to think so. The bra she had on, white to match her top, was a stark contrast to her skin. The lace covered her tits, but I couldn't miss her hardened nipples as they called to my mouth.

She tried to cover her breasts with her hands, but I pulled her arms to her side. Then I dropped to my knees and brought my face level with her bountiful breasts. Leaning forward, I locked my fingers with hers and sucked her nipple into my mouth. She quaked as I sucked the stiff peak into my mouth.

"Anthony," she cried out, gripping my fingers like a vise.

"Mmm," I moaned into her flesh.

"Oh, God." She arched her back, thrusting her chest farther into my face.

When her body rested flat on the door, I released her hands and gripped her waist. Holding her in place, I took my time and gave each breast equal attention. Her fingers knitted into my hair. I could smell her, the need she felt for me rivaling the want I had for her. No longer could she deny what we had. The urgency couldn't be stopped by anything but a complete and thorough fucking.

After using my nose to trace a path down her stomach, I ran my lips along the edge of her pants. Her skin burst into goose bumps as I planted light kisses onto her flesh. I slid my hands across her abdomen to the button hiding my salvation.

"Anthony," slipped from her lips as I started to unfasten her pants. "Wait."

Stilling my hands, I laid my forehead on top of her stomach, trying to catch my breath. "Max, I want you more than anyone in my life." I kissed her. "Please don't stop me now. I have to fuck you."

"Don't stop," she mumbled, pushing my head down with the palms of her hands.

I went back to the task at hand. As the button busted free, I tucked my fingers into the top of her pants and tore them down her legs. The top of her matching white lace panties made my stomach do a backflip. Fuck, my entire body was celebrating.

As I slipped her pants lower, I ran my nose down the front of her panties and inhaled. There was something about the smell of a woman. The hint of musk and sweetness had always brought me to my knees—just like I was in that moment. It gave me a high, making me lightheaded and dizzy. The only thing that could bring my mind back to any sense of normality would have been to taste and fuck the very thing that caused the weakness—Max.

Leaving her pants at her ankles, I shimmied her panties down her legs. Then I roughly gripped her thighs, spreading her open as she slid down the door. My tongue darted out, finally tasting her pussy.

Her arousal filled my taste buds and caused my mouth to water. It drifted across my tongue and drove me forward. One taste wasn't enough. When I went home tonight, I wanted to still taste her and have her scent on my face. There wasn't a part of my body, or hers for that matter, I didn't want to have lingering for hours as a reminder.

I used my tongue to part her as I ran it deeper into her pussy. She moaned and pulled on my hair to the point that it stung, sending a spark down my spine. My cock ached as it grew inside my jeans, which were now too tight to handle the package they contained.

This wasn't the time to think of myself and be a greedy bastard, though. I had to get her to the point of no return. The vehemence with which she'd denied her attraction toward me and the coldness she had displayed could slither into her mind and bring the evening to an end. I couldn't let that happen. I wouldn't.

Even though I could feast on her for hours, I needed to bring her to the brink. As I captured her wetness, I circled her clit. When I sucked it into my mouth, her thighs trembled in my grip. While using my hands to steady her, I assaulted her clit, sucking and flicking with my tongue until she began chanting, "Yes!"

A vocal woman is a pleasure to fuck. There's never a time when you have to second-guess if what you're doing is working for them. Each woman has a different way they like to be handled. Some want soft while others need rough. Experimenting was fun, but finding the perfect rhythm was key. With the way Max moaned, chanted, and screamed, I knew I was on target.

Wanting to add something more to the face-fucking I was giving her, I released one hip, moving my hand between her legs. I ran my fingers through her drenched pussy, massaging her outsides. As her body shook, I tightened my grip on her right thigh and held her upright. Nothing would stop me now. I pushed one finger inside as I continued to play with her clit using my mouth. The heat of her pussy surrounded me as I thrust it in and out.

"More," she grunted, pushing herself down onto my hand.

I lightened the pressure of my mouth on her clit. I'd give her what she wanted, but not without a little begging.

"More," she repeated. Her fingers pulled at my hair as I teased her.

Not wanting to be a total asshole, I complied. Sliding a second digit inside, I slowly felt every inch of her insides. Her pussy molded to my fingers, taking their girth with ease.

"Yes," she began chanting again as I picked up the pace, stroking them inside of her repeatedly.

I sucked harder, pummeled her with my rigid fingers, and held on to her body as I ate her pussy. God, it was spectacular. The only thing I regretted was not being able to see her face from this position. I wanted to watch her come apart from the orgasm I knew would rip through her body and break down her defense.

Just as her pussy started to quiver and draw my fingers deeper inside, I stopped and pulled my fingers out. I had to see her face when she came. I wanted her to see me as badly as I wanted to see her. She needed to remember who was giving her the orgasm, the way I felt inside her as she came apart in my arms.

"Don't stop. What the fuck are you doing?" she said as she pushed my face into her mound.

"I want to see you when you come," I murmured on her clit, feeling the shock waves of need and lust that were so close to breaking free reverberate on my lips.

"You can look at me afterward. You can't leave me like this," she whispered, glaring down at me as I peered up at her.

"I won't leave you like this. I plan to"—I

licked her forcefully and felt her body jolt —"fuck you until you can't breathe anymore and you beg me to stop."

She pulled me up by my hair and I rose to my feet. Her lack of shyness had my dick throbbing for release.

"Let's get to it, then," she said as her hands dropped to my shirt.

"You're so romantic." I laughed, letting her remove my shirt.

"Fuck," she hissed as I stood before her bare chested. "Do you have any body fat?"

I shook my head, happy that my body had finally caused her to have a reaction. At the bar, she'd acted so unimpressed and indifferent. Alone, as I stood shirtless before her, she had an entirely different opinion.

After she tossed my shirt, she settled her hands on my pecs. The warmth of her palms scorched my flesh, causing my heart to beat uncontrollably. What had she done to me? I'd never been like this. So fucking needy that I wasn't acting like myself. Usually, I didn't care if I saw them come, but for some reason, I wanted to see her explode from my touch. This wasn't about getting my rocks off. No, this was something entirely different, and I wasn't sure I liked it one damn bit.

She drifted forward, running her tongue across my SOUL tattoo. I closed my eyes and reveled in the feel of her as she explored my body. It was my turn to sway as the dizziness of the need I felt increased.

As her hands trailed down my stomach, catching on the ridges of my abdominal muscles, my cock jerked. It silently begged to be touched, feeling ignored and angry as fuck.

When her fingers fumbled with the zipper on my jeans, I said, "I have to warn you."

She glanced up with her eyebrows knitted together in confusion. "About what?"

"Well I..." I blew out a breath and suddenly felt unsure of myself. "I..."

"You don't have an STD, do you?" she mumbled on my skin.

I shook my head, wondering how the fuck to say it. I'd never given a woman a warning before, so why in that instant did I feel it was necessary?

"I'm really well hung," I said, feeling a sense of pride. I'd seen plenty of dicks in the locker room, and I'd seen my brothers'. Not one of them held a candle to the package I was carrying. They were mere child's play, while I was all man.

"Well, aren't you cocky," she whispered as she started to giggle.

"Quite literally, I am." I laughed and shrugged one shoulder. "You'll see." I looked down at her and winked. "I have a little something for your pleasure."

"Oh, like Trojan," she teased, and rolled her eyes.

"If you think you're woman enough to handle it, go ahead," I said as I rested my hands on my hips.

I wouldn't give her a heads-up about the hardware I was sporting. I'd let her explore it for herself. It was shocking the amount of women who didn't have any experience with cock piercings, but it always gave them a thrill.

As my pants slid down my thighs, she gasped and her hand flew to her mouth. "What the hell is all that?" she asked from behind her palm.

"I warned you."

"What did you do to your beautiful cock?" Her glance shifted between my dick and my eyes as she gawked.

"You don't like it?" I asked as her fingernails raked across my shaft.

"I do, but you have metal hanging off your junk." She flicked the ampallang with her finger, sending a shot of pleasure down my shaft.

My dick jumped, responding to her touch, as she slid it through her palm.

"Jesus," I moaned, needing the release before my balls exploded.

When she lifted my dick, her hand froze. "Another one?" she asked.

I smiled. "Trust me, Kitty Cat. You're going to fuckin' die when you feel it inside you."

She dropped to her knees, bringing my dick near her face as she inspected the hardware. I stood there with my pants down, fully exposed and loved every fucking minute of it.

"It's just so...much," she whispered, inching

closer.

Her hot breath hit the tip of my cock, and I closed my eyes. I couldn't keep them open. With her face so close to my dick, all I wanted to do was grab her by the hair and jam it down her throat. I needed to push down that urge to face-fuck her. Squeezing my hips, I focused on the bite of her nails sliding across my skin and tried to ignore the warmth of her hands and breath as she explored my body.

She slid my shaft in her palm. "You are impressive, Anthony. You didn't bullshit about your size." She licked her lips as her eyes shot to my groin.

"I don't overestimate my size when I'm about to fuck a chick. It's something you can't hide, no matter how well you move," I said through gritted teeth. My patience and ability to keep my focus off the feel of her was slipping. "If you don't start sucking, I'm not going to be able to control myself, Max. Put it in. Let me feel that hot, wet mouth slide on my dick, baby." My fingers snaked into her hair, coaxing her face closer to my shaft.

She giggled, maybe loving the torture she had to know she was inflicting on me. I pressed the tip to her mouth, shaking my hips as I rubbed it into her soft lips.

"Open up," I commanded, pushing it into her mouth before she could protest.

I blew out a breath, feeling a shock wave of pleasure pass through my system as my dick glided across her tongue. The softness mingled with the wet warmth made me weak at the knees. Even if she couldn't suck a dick worth a damn, I could stay just like this and be satisfied.

As she pulled the tip deeper into her mouth, the piercing touched the arch in the back of her mouth, catching on it. She adjusted and drew it in farther until it touched the back of her throat. My balls grew heavy as the clouds parted, and I swear to Christ I heard angels sing. She could deep-throat. Not even a gag as she took me as deep as she could. I always believed that, if you found a deep-throater, it wasn't a number you wanted to lose.

"Fuck me, Kitty," I groaned as she withdrew my dick until just the tip remained.

sucking me off to perfection. The pressure of her finger amplified everything, causing every muscle in my body to tighten.

"Christ," I whispered, unable to lift my head. All the energy I had was being used to stave off the orgasm that was ready to break free and alter my world forever. There wasn't anything normal or basic about the blow job or Max. She was fucking me, and not just with her mouth.

She bore down and picked up the pace. I became lost, my mind hazy from the feel of her mouth and her finger. Unable to take it any longer, I tensed and rode the wave. Releasing the pent-up frustration, the need I felt for her, and the lust she made me feel, I came in her mouth. As I groaned through the pleasure, my body jerked, raked by aftershock after aftershock of pleasure.

I'd like to say that I held out and came inside her, bringing her to orgasm at the same time, but it would be a lie. I was a selfish prick, after all. Changing who I was at my core wouldn't be an easy process—even when it pertained to Max.

I was a dog, too old to learn new tricks, no matter whose mouth was latched on to my cock.

After I caught my breath and my limbs no longer felt like jelly, I pulled her up by the arms and kissed her. Our arousal swirled together, mixing in our mouths as our tongues tangled. The scent along with the taste surrounded me, making me want more.

I could lie and say that I instantly hardened and began to fuck her, but even though I claimed to be a beast in bed, I knew I wasn't fucking Superman. I spent the next thirty minutes teasing her breasts and eating her pussy like it was the finest meal at a Michelin-starred restaurant. Even though I was sated, I still wanted more of her.

While driving her over the edge time and time again, using nothing but my fingers and my mouth, I felt myself harden. Once I was ready to slide inside her and find out if it felt like home, I grabbed a condom from my back pocket, but I wanted to fuck her in the bedroom.

Without breaking my cunnilingus-athon, I carried her to bed with her knees over my shoulder and my mouth attached to her cunt. I didn't let walking get in the way of me eating her pussy. Although she protested at first, she grabbed my legs and enjoyed the ride.

The rest of the night passed in a blur. I didn't know if the alcohol was causing my memory to be fuzzy or if I was becoming intoxicated and consumed by my lust for her, but the sex was explosive and heavenly.

Those weren't words I used often when describing sex with a girl. But Max wasn't any girl. She was *the* girl. Once I sank my dick inside her, I knew I was doomed.

I knew I'd become one of those pussy-whipped heaps of flesh I'd described my brothers as before Max.

After Max had entered my world and fucked with my head along with my body, nothing else was the same.

If I had known where she'd lead me, maybe I wouldn't have taken the first step on this journey. I might not have chased her and placed myself in her path, giving her no option than to confront her feelings for me.

No matter how hard the journey was and no matter what an asshole I'd been in the past, I wanted her to like me. Trying to find a way for her to accept and reciprocate the feelings I had for her would be the challenge.

Only I, asshole and cocky fucker to the masses, would fall in love with the one woman who wanted nothing to do with me.

Not even after breaking down her walls and catching a glimpse of what could be. She shut me out, tossing me aside like a piece of trash.

The morning after I'd found my way into her house—and, ultimately, into her pussy—she didn't wake with a warm attitude.

"I think you should go," she said as I rolled over and looked at her.

I didn't know what to say as the words soaked in. I'd never been thrown out or excused by a woman. Never.

"What?" I asked.

"I have to get to work. It was fun, but I need you to leave."

"What?" I repeated, still not accepting that her attitude had changed since last night.

I'd thought I'd made headway, that things could be different. I'd really believed that maybe we could date or I could at least take her to dinner. What the hell was I saying? Maybe I'd been drugged the night before, because usually, I'd be elated to have a free pass to leave. In that moment, it just plain sucked.

"Thanks for the good time, Anthony. Last night won't happen again." She slipped her arms through the sleeves of her robe and tied it shut. "So I need you to get dressed and go home."

It was like she had asked me if I wanted coffee. The enormity of the situation was lost on her. If it wasn't, she didn't seem to care.

I sat up and rubbed my eyes. "You're throwing me out?"

"Yes. Get your ass up and leave."

I shook my head. Maybe I was still dreaming. Yeah, that had to be it.

Reaching down, I pinched my skin and instantly felt the burn.

Totally not sleeping. Fuck me.

I was yesterday's news and today's trash.

"Last night meant nothing to you?" I asked

as I crawled out of bed and searched for my clothes.

Goddamn it. All of my clothes were in the living room, sitting in a pile by the front door. I'd have to stand here and have this conversation naked.

"Yes. It was nice, but that's all it could ever be. I don't have time for anything more. I refuse to see you again. We wouldn't work. You're an asshole and I'm emotionally unable to have anything more than a meaningless fuck."

"You're a cold bitch, Max. Last night..." I stopped speaking, swallowing hard, in shock at the words that were about to come from my mouth. "Last night was the first time I actually felt something more than just a cheap thrill for someone. We're different, Max. I want more. For the first time in my goddamn life"—my voice grew louder, to the point that I had started to yell, as I moved toward her—"I want fucking more!"

"I can't!" she yelped as she backed up, staying out of reach.

"You can't or you fuckin' won't?" I said, not

willing to just chalk it all up to a night of fun. I'd had enough of those to know the difference.

"I won't!" she yelled back, finding her footing. The confident woman I'd met in the bar had come back to life.

"Max." I reached out to her as my voice grew softer. "Just see me again. Please." I waited like an idiot.

"No! I can't. I won't. Now, get the fuck out. If you don't go, I'll call the police," she spat. Then she stormed toward the bedroom door.

As she opened it, I caught her by the arm and pulled her backward. When she swung, trying to strike me in the face, I captured it in my grip. "Don't," I said, staring down at her and holding her captive.

"I can't!" she yelled, her nostrils flaring. Then her mouth set in a firm line.

"You can. Please, Max. I can be a better person." I couldn't believe what she was saying.

"Even if you weren't an asshole, Anthony, I can't see you anymore. Get your fucking hands off me. I'll scream bloody murder and my neighbor will call the police." Her fiery gaze bore into me.

I released her and lived to fight another day. "Fine. You have it your way—for now. I'm not giving up on you so easily. I've never chased. *Never!*" I yelled as I walked out of her bedroom to find my clothes. After I dressed, I turned and found her watching me. "You're the first woman I've ever met worth chasing."

She gaped at me, and I swear I could see a tear in her eye, but she hid it well. I was so fucking mad that I didn't have time to ask.

As I opened the front door, taking a step outside, I finished my statement and gave her a warning. "I'm coming for you. I won't stop until I get what I want. You haven't seen how big of an asshole I can be!"

I slammed the door and headed back to the center of Ybor to get my car. Tucking my hands in my pockets, I silently cursed God for being a bigger asshole than I was. Fuck him and fate. Karma was a cunt, and she had come for me, getting the last laugh. The problem with their plan was they hadn't given me enough credit.

I'd have Max again.

Even if I had to cross the line from asshole to prick, I'd do it.

When I started my car, "Thing for You" by Hinder was playing. I slammed my hand down on the radio, silencing it.

I wouldn't let her out of my life.

I'd make a plan and do everything I could to infiltrate her life, giving her no other option than to let me in.

Fuck her.

Next time, I'd be the one to kick her ass out of bed and give her a taste of her own medicine.

When he left, I slid down the door, crumpled to the floor, and sobbed. Seeing the pain in his eyes tore me apart. Anthony was a breath of fresh air. Carefree and fun loving besides being a wild man in the sack, but I had to kick him out like a piece of trash.

I could easily fall in love with the man. I liked them strong, and he was that and more. Not just physically, but he didn't take no for an answer. The way he treated my friends and the way he handled me drove me wild.

In the morning, when I opened my eyes and watched him sleep, I knew I had to be cruel. I had forgotten how much I loved waking up to someone. The smell of him still on my skin had me questioning everything I'd decided long ago. I allowed myself to daydream about the future, being with him and calling him mine. He smelled amazing and looked even more beautiful as he slept.

I let my fingers wander across his body, feeling the hardness of his muscles underneath the softness of his skin. The soft snores that fell from his lips made my heart go pitter-patter and I knew I was doomed. All I wanted to do was curl into his side and feel him against my body. It had been ages since I'd let a man make me feel safe. Anthony could be that for me. He could be my rock if I allowed him to.

The problem with that, though, is that it wasn't fair to him. He couldn't love me.

I wouldn't allow that.

In the end, we'd both be hurt and alone.

As soon as he started to stir, I knew what I had to do.

Through the entire fight my insides clenched, and not in the way he'd made them the night before. Never before had I felt physical pain from telling someone goodbye. It was better to do it now before I got in too deep and couldn't allow myself to save him and myself later.

When his footsteps were no longer audible, I slammed my fists against the floor and let out a cry so visceral and uninhibited that I lost my breath. It took everything in me to stop myself from running after him and begging his forgiveness.

I'd done it.

He was gone.

We were both better off. Right?

5

MISERY

Misery.

It could've been my new nickname.

Over the next two weeks, I tried to put Max out of my mind and rid myself of her entirely. It had sounded easy, but I found out it was impossible.

She invaded my thoughts and filled my dreams. Even when I was flipping through the channels on television after work, I'd find her. Goddamn cable television and their late-night reruns of *The Cosby Show*.

Friday and Saturday night, I found myself wandering through Ybor City, but I couldn't find her. I even went to Liquid and had a drink. If someone I knew had seen me sitting by myself, nursing a beer in a gay bar, it would've spread like wildfire.

Sunday morning, I woke up irritated and crabby as hell. All I wanted to do was stay in bed or drink myself into a coma, but I couldn't. It was the official Gallo Family Dinner, and my mother would kick my ass if I missed it.

When I walked through the door, I put on my best face. I had to pretend that everything was normal. There was no way in hell I'd let on that I was upset. My family would eat me alive if they found out, especially Izzy. She might have been my younger sister, but that didn't mean that she didn't scare the crap out of me.

I sat in my usual chair and ignored everyone, but that wasn't anything new. They barely noticed I was there as I stared at my phone.

How had I not gotten her number? I couldn't just show up at her door. There was no way in hell I wanted to be that guy. I didn't even know Max's last name. Tracking her down would be an issue with only a first name. There was only one way I knew I could possibly find her. Most people had a Facebook profile, and if I were lucky, I'd find her. I started to type Maxine into the search field, but it brought up a bunch of random people. Not one of the photos matched her.

I sighed as I turned the phone over in my hand. There had to be a way. A commercial caught my attention as I stared at the television while deep in thought. Next weekend was Festa Italiana in Ybor. It was a giant street festival celebrating Tampa's Italian culture and heritage. It would be the perfect time to find her. I knew that, if I lived within walking distance, I'd be there every night eating and drinking. Who doesn't love a party?

It was a week away, though. It was too damn long to wait. I had to at least try to find her before then. Every moment without her seemed wasted. I knew she had told me to fuck off and that she didn't want to see me again, but I didn't believe it. I couldn't believe it. There was no way we could have the electricity we did and just throw it away.

I mean, hell, I hated relationships. The last thing I wanted was to be tied down to anyone, but I wanted to see her again. I opened up Facebook again and decided to take a new approach. I visited fan pages for local establishments and scrolled through their followers. Some places had thousands of people. Instead of choosing randomly, I started at one end of the street and looked up each business in order.

"Anthony," Joe barked from his spot on the couch.

I kept scrolling and didn't bother to look at him.

"Hey, douchebag. Are you paying attention?" he asked, and clapped his hands.

"I'm listening, asshat. I'm busy."

"Your face is always buried in that goddamn phone. If you were listening, what do you think?"

"Of what?" I asked, totally busted. I hadn't heard a thing they had been talking about.

Over the years, I'd become very good at shutting them out. You can't have a large family and pay attention all the time. Fuck, I worked with them too. My ability to selectively hear shit was better than most married people's.

"I knew it," Joe grumbled.

A piece of candy hit me in the head. "You're lucky Ma didn't see that," I said, flicking the candy from my phone screen to the floor.

"She wouldn't care. Izzy asked us a question."

I glanced up and looked over at my sister. She glared at me as she snuggled into James's side. James had weaseled his way into her life. I didn't know if that was the right term, but Izzy hadn't always seemed to like him too much. More than likely, it was just her tough-ass exterior. She was like me—she knew any weakness could and would be exploited. We were the lone holdouts in the relationship department, but I feared I'd lost her. More than likely, I was a casualty too.

"What's up, Iz?" I asked, placing the phone on my leg.

She cleared her throat before she took a deep sigh, and her face softened. "I wanted to know about having an open house next weekend. A way to thank our customers for their loyalty."

I shook my head, knowing I wouldn't miss spending next weekend stalking Max in Ybor. "I can't make it."

"What? Why not?" she shot back, and crossed her arms.

"I have shit to do. In fact, I need to clear my entire schedule next weekend." I looked out the corners of my eyes and saw everyone staring in my direction. "I have a gig out of town."

Why in the hell had I said that? Not only had I not been honest about meeting someone, now I had to stay out of sight for a weekend. I'd have to stay far away and pray that my family decided not to attend Festa Italiana. What was the likelihood I'd see them there anyway?

"You do? Where?"

Izzy knew me best. I shared everything with her. But I couldn't tell her about Max. I'd hold on to that information like it was the secret to the universe.

"Vegas." It was the first city that popped in my head.

"Can I come, bro?" Mike asked, causing me to glance at him. "I fuckin' love that city. I could be your roadie or some shit." He smiled, giving me a hopeful look.

"Nope. There's no room. We're booked up and bunking together. Sorry, man."

"I can get my own room. I just want to get away and hang out with you for a while."

He never went anywhere with me. Not since Mia, his lovely, sexy doctor girlfriend, had entered the picture. The one time I'd lied through my teeth, he was willing to hop on a plane and have a brothers' weekend.

"We could have a brothers-only weekend," Joe chimed in, clapping his hands. "The girls can get a break from us and we can blow off some steam."

"No!" I yelled.

The tone of my voice made Pop turn and give me a funny look.

"Sorry, Pop. I can't next weekend, guys. I already have plans. Maybe we can all hit Vegas next time." I grinned, praying that they'd drop the idea of joining me in Vegas. I knew I should've said Branson or some sleepy town no one would want to go to, but my big, fat mouth had dug a hole.

"It's cool, Anth. If you didn't want us to come, you just needed to say so. No need to get your panties in a bunch," Mike said as he squared his shoulders.

I hung my head and exhaled. My patience was very low today. I'd never been described as a patient person, but with all the shit with Max, I was dangling by a thread.

"I thought I did say no...repeatedly," I dead-panned, lifting my head. "My weekend is packed. Otherwise, I'd say yes. I'll be back by Sunday."

"What the fuck? Are you just going for two nights?" Izzy asked as she gave me the "you're full of shit" look I'd grown accustomed to over the years.

"Yes," I replied without blinking.

She still had her arms crossed, one shoulder slumped. Yep, she knew I was lying. I could read her as well as she could read me. Even though we had the biggest age difference, there was something about Izzy and me that just clicked. Since we were best friends, she was going to be pissed off that I hadn't told her about Max.

"I'll be back before Ma has the food on the table next Sunday." I grabbed my phone and went back to my Facebook search, but kept an eye on Izzy.

"How convenient," she said quietly, but loud enough for me to hear.

"Shut it, Iz," I snapped. Not my shining moment. There would be hell to pay for being snippy with her.

She turned as James began to snicker, giving him her full attention. "Jimmy, did I even invite you here?" she hissed.

He slid his arm behind her back and pulled her toward him. "You know you did. Put the claws away, love. Your brother is old enough to do what he wants. Stop being so damn nosy." He grinned at Izzy, stroking her stomach underneath her shirt.

"This is family business." She pouted but didn't say anything more.

"How about the weekend after? I think more

people would come if we made it an all-day event," Joe said.

"Yeah, whatever," I replied, too busy trying to find Max.

"Anyone have plans that weekend?"

"Nope. Sounds good, Joe," Mike replied as he pushed off the couch. "I'm so damn hungry. I'm going to check on Ma."

"Izzy?" Joe asked.

"Yep. It's good." I peeked over my phone to see if she was still giving me the stink eye or if she had already forgotten it.

I caught her glaring at me. Nope. She hadn't forgotten. There was something about Italian women. I swear to God, they had a filing system in their head. There wasn't a thing they forgot. Especially when it was a fuck-up. Izzy didn't forget easily, and I was in her crosshairs.

"Dinner!" Mike yelled from the kitchen just as I got to King Corona, the place where I met Nita and Malia.

"Fuck," I muttered before I turned my phone off.

Ma was known for flipping her shit if we

used any type of electronic device at the table. Sometimes I'd get away with it, but it depended on her mood. As I walked into the dining room, I tucked my phone in my pocket.

Before I could sit, Izzy grabbed my shirtsleeve. "I'm not stupid, Anth. You have some shit to tell me later. Got me?" She glared at me as she fisted my shirt.

Looking down at her hand, I said, "I'll tell you tomorrow before work." I was trying to give myself a sliver of peace for the rest of the day.

"Fine," she snapped, releasing my shirt and sitting in the chair James had pulled out for her.

When he pushed in her chair, he looked at me and shrugged. I shook my head and rolled my eyes as I sat down. I noticed that everyone sat in pairs except for me. I was alone. The way I'd always wanted it to be. But for some reason, it bothered me today.

"Suzy," Ma said as she placed the giant bowl of angel hair pasta on the table. "You get the first serving."

Suzy licked her lips and rubbed her hands together. She'd grown huge over the last so many months. How in the hell a woman as small as she was had expanded so fast was beyond me. Everyone clamored to feel the baby when it moved, but I didn't. That shit was creepy. Straight out of the movie *Alien*. I thought for sure it would break through her skin and try to kill us all. The one thing I knew for sure was that Suzy now ate more than any person at the table.

"I'm starving, Ma," Suzy whined as she rubbed her belly.

"Aren't you always," I mumbled as I laid the napkin across my lap. When I looked up, Joe was staring at me.

"What the hell is your problem today, Anth?" he asked, resting his arms on the table.

"I don't have one. I'm hungry too, but no one's offering me the first serving," I grumbled as I stared back at him, placing my elbows on the edge of the table.

"Get pregnant and then you'll get served first," Suzy teased as she stuck her tongue out at me.

I opened my mouth, about to say something, but when I glanced at Joe, I changed my mind. I had pissed every one of my siblings off at some point since I'd arrived. I needed to eat and get back to my cyber-stalking.

Out of spite, Ma came to me last with the bowl of pasta. "Want some, sweetie?" she asked as she stood beside me, holding the spoon.

"Please." I gave her my best "I'm an angel" smile.

She and Pop were the only two I hadn't pissed off yet. I'd do everything in my power to keep it that way. But I still caught the slightest glare aimed at me as she dug the spoon into the pasta.

She placed two heaping spoonfuls of angel hair on my plate before she set it on the table and took her place next to my father.

"How's Thomas doing?" Pop asked James as he picked up his fork.

Pop never started to eat, even if his food became cold, until my mother had sat down unless she told him otherwise. I'd always thought he was pussy-whipped too, but now that I was older, I thought it was a sign of respect. It was the one thing that stuck out the most when I looked at them.

After I dug into the pasta, bringing it to my mouth, I stopped. I literally froze with my mouth gaping open and my fork hanging in midair. Suddenly, I realized that my thinking process had been altered. Out of nowhere, I'd started to think like my family.

Max.

She had given me more than pussy. She'd changed my thought process. When I'd fucked her, it had to scramble my brains. I never thought like this. Now, my mind was a cluttered mess of pussy bullshit. I almost reached down and grabbed my dick to make sure I hadn't left that behind when she'd kicked my ass to the curb.

"What's wrong?" Joe asked.

I blinked, clearing my eyes of the "what the fuck" haze I'd fallen into. "Nothing. I just re-membered something," I replied, stuffing the pasta in my mouth.

"You looked like you saw a ghost," Izzy added as she gave me a dirty look.

"Just thought I left my house unlocked," I said, my mouth full of food.

"Surrrrre," she heckled me before turning her attention back to her plate.

"What did you say about Thomas, James?" I asked after swallowing. I'd missed his response when I'd zoned out.

My brother had been gone for what had felt like forever. We were all anxious to see him again. James was our only link to him. Without James, we wouldn't have had any information. He wasn't able to tell us much, since the DEA forbade information sharing, especially with family.

"He's doing well," James replied after he choked down a mouthful of food. "We're both hoping for it all to be over soon."

"That would be fantastic," Ma blurted out as she put her hands together in prayer. "God willing."

"He misses you all terribly."

"I can't imagine what he's going through," Pop said as he wiped his mouth.

"It's hell, but he's getting through it," James replied.

I didn't know much about working under-cover. Just the small things Thomas had shared with me before he'd left. He'd promised he would come back home, but even if he were a superhero, he couldn't make that promise be-come reality.

The dinner table and every holiday had felt empty since he'd left. I'd never admit it, but I wanted my brother home. We had always been a fivesome, and being a foursome didn't feel right. We spent out youth trying to pick up women together.

He didn't get as much pussy as I did, but hell, I was a pushy bastard. Being in a band and having my voice alone could make the ladies drop their panties and bend over. It was the one thing Thomas didn't have. He might have been able to flex his giant muscles, but he wasn't as hung as I was and he didn't have my ability to sing.

I ate the rest of my meal in silence. There

wasn't much to say. I had Max on the brain and the rest of the family had happy shit to talk about. Most of the conversation revolved about Suzy and the baby. Ma could only be described as giddy about the upcoming birth. I didn't remember her being as excited as she was now even when Izzy was born.

There hadn't been a baby in the family in well over twenty years. The only thing I could think of was all the crying. They're cute, but they shit themselves continuously, they always cried for food, or they were asleep. Babies didn't have many uses. You couldn't play with them. You just had to hold them and wait until the next time they cried for attention.

As soon as I cleared my plate, I excused myself from the table. I needed to get back to my scavenger hunt to find Max. If I could make contact, maybe I could avoid a crowded weekend in Ybor City, prowling the neighborhood like a creep.

Not that internet stalking wasn't creepy, but it was the only thing I had to go on without showing up at her door. Before I plopped down in my chair, I pulled my phone out and checked my messages. I didn't know what I was hoping for, but the blankness of my screen made me scowl.

I searched Facebook for *King Corona* and started to scroll through their page. There were hundreds of posts, but I checked each one. I looked for Malia, Nita, or Max as I read each post one by one. As my eyes began to burn and I thought about giving up, I saw it. Malia. Even though I'd hoped to see a comment from Max, I'd take any lifeline to finding her.

I viewed Malia's profile page, but it was private. I pressed every button, hoping to find Max, but everything was blocked. The only choice I had was to send her a message and hope she didn't ignore me.

The cursor blinked at me as the screen read *Type a message* while I thought about what I wanted to type. If she ignored me, I didn't know what I'd fucking do. My mind was already fucked up, and every minute had been consumed by thoughts of Max.

Very slowly, I started to type the message. Then I kept erasing the dumb shit I had written.

My words sounded like I was desperate. After another message and a quick erase, I set my phone down and stared out the sliding glass door into my parents' lanai. I needed to stop being a pussy and just send something or I'd kick myself later.

Malia, it's Anthony, Max's friend. Well, she wouldn't call me that, but since I fucked her, I thought it fit.

I erased the message again. Then I shook my head and felt like an idiot. I mean, what the hell do you say when you're trying to track someone down through another person?

Malia, hey. I looked for you ladies last weekend in Ybor but couldn't find you. How are you?

Just when I started to erase the message, Izzy walked in.

"Hey!" she yelled.

I jumped, hitting send by accident. *Oh no. No. No. No.*

That wasn't the message I'd wanted to send. I sounded like an idiot.

"Fuck!" I hissed as I shot a glare at Izzy.

"Why the fuck did you have to scare me to death? Shit!"

"What's your problem today?" She sat down on the floor in front of me. She crossed her legs, sat Indian-style, and stared. "Tell me," she demanded.

I blew out a long breath of air and silently debated if I should tell her. Maybe she'd be able to give me some insight. More than likely, I'd get some shitty comments before she finally had some real advice.

"Are they almost done in there?" I asked, glancing toward the dining room.

She shook her head and rolled her eyes. "Nope. Suzy's still eating and everyone is talking." She exhaled, blowing her bangs in the air.

"James?"

"Him too. He's talking to Joe about some shit."

"Fine. I'll tell you, but you can't tell anyone, Izzy. Not a soul. Understand?"

She rubbed her hands together and said, "Ooooh, okay," as she grinned.

"Seriously, Iz. No one."

She nodded and set her lips in a firm line. "Lips are sealed." She ran her fingers across her lips, pretending to zip them, and tossed the imaginary key over her shoulder.

"I met someone," I said, closing my eyes as I felt my face flush.

"Oh my God," she whispered, scooting across the carpet to sit at my feet.

I hung my head. "It's not what you think."

"I'm not thinking anything," she replied as she touched my leg. "What happened?"

I raised my head enough to look her in the eyes. "I met this amazing girl. We had sex and she kicked me out the next morning."

She burst out laughing. "I'm sorry." She waved her hands in the air and fell backward. "Wait." Her laughter grew loud. "Someone treated you the way you have treated women for years." Her hands slapped the carpet with a dull thud.

"Izzy. Be serious."

"I am. Oh God." She kicked her legs, stomping them on the floor. "Anth, look at it from my perspective. That's some funny shit."

I gritted my teeth, not finding the humor in the situation. "Fuck you. I knew you couldn't listen without being a jackass."

Her body stilled as she tried to catch her breath. Wiping the tears of laughter from her face, she sat up. "I'm sorry," she said, trying to stop the giggle that was at the tip of her tongue from escaping. "I never thought I'd hear you complain about being treated poorly."

"Izzy, don't give me your Nora Roberts bullshit. I know how you treated men. They were a piece of meat to you too. Flash ring a bell?" I asked with a "choke on that" smirk.

"Shhh," she whispered, putting her index finger up to her mouth. Her eyes slid to the dining room. "Don't mention him when James is here. The man goes apeshit."

"See what I mean?" I asked, leaning back in my chair and shaking my leg.

"Fine. I'm really sorry." The smile that had been on her face moments ago vanished. "Tell me what happened?"

"I can't find her."

"You didn't even get her number?" she asked.

"No." It was so unlike me, too. It wasn't that I wanted to see the women again, but it was always good to have a way to contact them. You know, in case they had that deep-throat, never-choke quality I looked for in a woman.

She sat up on her knees and reached toward my head. "Are you sick?" she asked as she pressed her palm to my forehead.

I knocked her hand away. "I'm fine. Stop with your shit."

"So, what did I just interrupt if you don't have her number?" She raised an eyebrow as she pursed her lips.

The last thing I wanted to admit was that I had been cyber-stalking the girl.

"I found one of her friends on Facebook and sent her a message."

"You didn't." Izzy's hands covered her face as she shook her head back and forth. "Say it isn't so. You did not stoop to that level. Not Anthony Gallo."

"He didn't what?" James asked as he walked in the room.

I shot her a look, pleading with her not to tell him.

"Nothing, James." She smiled up at him.

From the look on his face, I'd say he didn't buy it.

"It sounded pretty juicy."

"What sounded juicy?" Joe asked from behind James.

"Nothing," I grumbled before dragging in a breath. If I made it through the rest of the day without blowing a gasket, it would be a freaking miracle.

"What's the score?" Pop asked as he sat down.

"I don't know. I haven't been paying attention," I replied as I grabbed my phone, hoping to see a reply from Malia.

Nothing. She hadn't even seen my message. Most likely, it had landed in her other folder since we weren't friends. She'd probably never see it. It would sit there in message purgatory for eternity while I hopelessly searched for Max.

Everyone fell into the usual routine. They bullshitted about life and cursed at the Cubs. I sat there with my messages open and stared, waiting for it to say *read*. I tried to pay attention to the game, but I couldn't. I wanted to find Max more than I cared if the loser Cubs won a single game during the current losing season.

When I left my parents that night, Malia still hadn't responded. The first song I heard was "I Won't Give Up," and I slammed my palm down on the steering wheel.

I hit number two on the radio, looking for relief from the mushy song shit. Just my fucking luck that "Stolen Dance" filled the car. For the love of God, even Karma couldn't be this cruel. Instead of trying a third radio station, I turned it off and headed home in silence.

If Malia didn't message me by the morning, I'd send her another message. One that was smoother and sounded more like me. The one I'd sent by accident was none of the above. If I needed to, maybe I could track Malia down by her profile. I bet she was the type to list her place of work or at least check in at the places she frequented. Either way, I wouldn't give up until I found one of her friends who would lead me to her.

"What the fuck is wrong with me?" I said to myself as I pulled in the driveway. "She's just another pussy. Nothing more."

I tried like hell to convince myself that I meant those words.

"Yeah, and a bitch at that." I nodded as I turned off the car. "You don't need her," I whispered as I unlocked the door and walked inside.

Maybe I just needed to fuck someone else to get her out of my system. It had been a month and I hadn't screwed anyone besides her. I'd never gone this long without pussy.

Never.

It wasn't my style. I had a large sexual appetite, but over the last couple of weeks, my hand had gotten a lot of use.

"Fuck it!" I yelled, and did the only thing I felt would be right. I picked up my phone and texted Candy.

Me: Want a piece?

I'd never treated her like a lady. Candy liked

being treated like a dirty slut. I liked it that way too. We both got something out of it.

Candy: YES! OMG. When?!?!

Candy was uncomplicated. I smiled as I looked at my watch. It was only seven, so the night was young. Maybe if I banged her for a couple of hours, I could rid my system of Max.

Me: Now. I'll come to you.

I'd never had her to my house. It was my sanctuary. I wasn't saying that I'd never brought a woman home, but Candy was crazy. There was good crazy and bad crazy. She landed somewhere in the middle. Definitely not the type you'd want to give your address to, because there was a high probability she'd show up at your door uninvited late at night.

I grabbed my keys, headed for the door, and went for a piece of ass. Candy would do the trick. She'd feed my sugar fix and wipe Max from my mind.

Right?

6

WHAT THE FUCK DID I DO?

As soon as I opened my eyes, I thought, *I didn't*. Right in front of me was Candy, sprawled out and naked. I wish I could say that alcohol had made me do it and I weren't responsible for my actions.

That would have been the easy way out and a complete and total lie.

I covered my eyes, hoping that, when I looked again, she'd be gone and I'd be in my own bed. Slowly, I peeked through my fingers, but it hadn't worked.

"Fuck," I mumbled, trying to slide out of the bed without waking her.

"Please," she muttered into the pillow.

This was where my luck was headed. First, I met someone I actually wanted to get to know, but she threw me the fuck out. Then I fucked someone I didn't want to know, but she didn't want me to leave.

"I gotta go," I said as I rolled off the bed, barely landing on my feet.

"Why are you in such a hurry? It's early," she said in a sleepy voice as she rubbed her eyes.

"I have a business meeting," I lied as I plucked my pants off the floor next to the bed and slid them on. "Thanks for last night, Candy. It was great."

"That's all I get. No kiss goodbye? When can I see you again, Anthony?" She stretched out, giving me a full view of her pussy.

I turned, trying to avoid seeing her body. Last night, I'd seen it all. Hell, I'd touched and tasted it too.

The one thing I'd wanted out of last night was to forget Max. My plan hadn't worked. She'd found her way into my dreams, haunting me after I'd fucked Candy.

"I'm late," I said as I grabbed my shirt.

"I want to see you again," she begged.

"I'll call you. Don't call me," I replied as I walked out the door.

"You're a fucker, Anthony!" she yelled before something hit the wall with a loud clatter and shattered upon impact.

What the fuck ever. We all had our roles, and she knew what hers was. For a moment, guilt crept in. I knew what it felt like to want more and be denied now.

I showered, brushed my teeth, and collapsed in bed thirty minutes after leaving Candy's place. I tried to rid my system of any memory of her. It was only eight in the morning, not a time of day I normally found myself awake.

I hadn't checked my phone in hours. All I'd cared about was getting home and washing up. As I lay in bed, staring at my ceiling, I wondered if Malia had read my message. I wanted to know. Then again, if she hadn't, I'd make myself crazy.

Temptation got the better of me and I checked my messages. To my total shock, there was a reply from her. My heart started to pound in my chest as excitement coursed through my system. I couldn't see but a few words of her response.

My finger hovered over the message and I froze. If she had told me to fuck off, I'd be livid. Even if she didn't want to tell me about Max, I wouldn't give up. I sucked in air, holding it in my lungs as I pressed the screen and opened her response.

Malia: Hey handsome. We didn't go out last weekend. Max didn't feel like it and we didn't push her.

She had replied an hour ago. If I hadn't spent the night drowning my sorrows in a pussy I didn't want, I would've seen it sooner.

I wasted no time in replying.

Me: Is she sick?

There was something about her message that didn't feel right. Before I closed the app, the message changed to read and she started to reply.

I sighed, feeling relieved. Maybe things were looking up.

Malia: No. She just wasn't in the mood.

I stared at the screen and wondered if I'd

had anything to do with how she'd felt. Could she feel like I did even though she had thrown me out of her house?

Me: Oh.

A moment of joy surged through me. It probably wasn't the right emotion to feel, but thinking of her in as much misery as I felt brought me a bit of relief.

Me: So I was wondering...

I didn't finish the message, but I hit send anyway. I felt like a stalker and wondered how Malia would respond.

Malia: She's talked about you

I blinked a couple of times, staring at the screen. A rush of adrenaline coursed through my veins. She had talked about me. I knew that women talked, but I hadn't thought Max was the type to share the details of what happened.

But maybe the things she'd said weren't good. I closed my eyes and sucked in a breath. I had to ask. I needed to know more.

Me: And? Good or bad?

I waited and waited as she typed. I expected a super-long message with the amount of time that passed before I received the response. Instead, she sent this:

Malia: Mixed.

It doesn't take that long to type five letters. I knew she'd had something else to say and changed her mind. I'd done it myself a time or two, and the fucking Messenger app gave the illusion of typing even when someone was erasing shit.

Me: Did she tell you what happened?

While I waited for her response, I climbed out of bed and began to pace. The stress of not knowing what had been said was making me restless and a bit edgy.

I ran my hand through my hair, yanking on the ends. Candy hadn't rid me of the angst I felt over the entire Max situation. I didn't know what bothered me more: the way she had thrown me out like trash or that I cared how she had gotten rid of me and wanted more.

Malia: Maybe

When I read the message, I looked up at the ceiling and cursed. The woman was being cagey with her answers. Maybe she was chatting with

Max at the same time and telling her that my dumb ass had contacted her.

I couldn't take it anymore. The suspense and not knowing would kill me.

Me: Malia, I like Max. I like her a lot. I want to see her again, but I don't have any way to contact her. Please, please, please tell me she wants to see me again.

The message showed that she'd seen it, but she didn't respond immediately. My nerves were unraveling as I waited. After a few minutes with no response, I needed a drink. I headed to the kitchen and grabbed the tequila and a glass before I started to really beg.

As I climbed the steps, my phone beeped. Although patience was never something I'd been able to deal with, I waited until I sat down on the bed to open her message.

Malia: Sorry, I was in the shower.

I wanted to scream at her response. Curse her out for making me wait and not telling me that she would be missing in action for a short time. I seriously started to panic. Shit like that wasn't cool.

Malia: Max wouldn't want me to give you her number, but… I know she likes you. You know where she lives. Why don't you just go to her house?

My hand began to shake at the possibility that I had a chance with her. Maybe it wasn't really the end like I had thought.

Me: I don't want to seem like a creep. I can't just knock on her door. I need another way. So, how do I see her again if you won't give me her number?

Women could be impossible. I knew that. I'd watched Izzy for years. I'd seen the misery she'd caused in her wake.

Malia: You could show up at her work.

I stared at the screen as my mouth hung open.

Me: How? Do tell.

Malia: Well, she's a stylist. She owns her own business. Make an appointment, dummy.

I laughed at her insult. How had I not thought of that? Why hadn't I Googled her? I was sure that, with enough searching, I would've found her.

Me: Genius. I'll have to use a fake name. Hmmm

Malia: Richard Hung lmfao

I couldn't hide my excitement. From the name Malia had picked, I'd say that Max had shared a lot about me—including the best stuff.

Me: Can I schedule it on a website?

Malia: Yes. She has a store. Make an appointment and then get to it, Anthony. Don't let her get rid of you so easily.

Her words were true. I'd never let anyone treat me the way she had. In all actuality, I'd never given them the chance, always kicking them out of my bed. Maybe she had the same MO as I did. "Hit it and quit it" was a popular phrase when I had been younger, but it had almost become my personal motto. Suddenly, I wasn't as proud of that fact as I used to be.

Me: Does she do that shit often?

Malia: Max? Fuck no. It's been years since she's been with someone. She doesn't want anyone to get hurt.

I read her message repeatedly and was totally confused.

Me: What do you mean?

Malia: I've said too much. Just look her up. Her website is...

With that, we said our goodbyes and I went to her website. I set up an appointment for Wednesday night at seven p.m. I figured I'd be her last of the night.

I'd have her again.

Taste and feel her all over me.

Mark her as mine without letting her escape a second time.

7

HUNG TO THE RIGHT

THE NEXT COUPLE OF DAYS DRAGGED. WORK consumed my evenings, but the days seemed to go on for fucking ever. The shop had been relatively quiet, and I spent more time watching the minutes tick by than tattooing.

By the time Wednesday evening arrived, I was a mess. I had received a confirmation email from Max yesterday. It was one of those that were automatically sent out without a personal touch. We were still on, no matter how it had been sent.

My hand trembled as I pulled on the door handle at five minutes to seven. A loud grumble rolled in my stomach as I looked but didn't see her.

"I'll be right out!" she yelled from the back room.

Hearing her voice again made my heart stutter.

I rubbed my sweaty palms on my jeans and shook out my shoulders.

Calm down and get control.

My emotions were out of control.

The shop was pretty, and looked exactly like it had on her website. A majority of the space was filled with women's clothing and other feminine items, but about a quarter of the store had menswear and shoes. The light hardwood floor and overhead lighting made the space feel warm.

As I looked through the men's shirts, I heard her footsteps behind me. I didn't turn, pretending to care about the clothes in front of me. My heart pounded—no, it thundered—inside the walls of my chest as I listened to her walking toward me.

"Mr. Hung," she said as she came to a stop behind me. "Find anything you like?"

I closed my eyes and turned with a cocky-ass grin. "I have now."

Her mouth dropped open as her eyes grew to the size of saucers. "What the..." she whispered.

"Max," I said, reaching out to touch her.

"Don't." She pulled away and took a step back. "What are you doing here?"

"I'm Mr. Hung." I laughed, enjoying the double meaning as she glared at me.

She rolled her eyes, crossing her arms over her chest. "You're still an asshole."

"That may be true, but I still need your services," I lied. I didn't need her to dress me. I knew how to look good, but it was my only way in.

"I don't have anything to offer you," she said as she turned her back and walked toward the door. After she opened it, she looked at me. "You can leave now."

I shook my head. "I'm not going anywhere. I came here to get your style advice. I'm not leaving until I get what I came for."

"Anthony," she said as she tapped her foot,

still holding the door open. "There's nothing here for you. I don't have time to play games."

"It's not a game, Max," I replied as I stalked toward her. No longer was I willing to take a back seat and let her dictate the terms of how the evening would go. This was my show and I was the frontman.

I reached up, touching her cheek with my fingertips. It felt just as I remembered—soft and silky. Even though her face wasn't flushed, her cheeks were warm to my touch.

"Max," I whispered on her lips. "Everything I want is here, standing in front of me. I won't leave until I get what I want, either. It's not a game, Kitty Cat. I've never chased anyone in my life."

She stared up at me with big eyes as her breath tickled my lips. "Anthony," she whispered as her lip touched mine. "I can't."

"Stop denying that you want me too. Do you feel it?" I whispered.

Her eyes closed as she melted into my touch. "I just can't."

I wanted to argue with her and prove her

wrong. There was no way I'd believe she couldn't. It wasn't an option. Without trying to convince her with words, I pressed my lips to her mouth and tasted the sweet gloss that lined them. The spark from weeks ago felt more like a raging inferno.

She pushed my chest as I held her to me. Her lower half inched away as I gripped her back with one hand. She felt it. I knew she felt it.

"Anthony," she murmured as she stopped trying to escape.

"Max," I moaned as I dug my fingers in her hair. I kept kissing her, not wanting to break contact.

When I felt her lack of resistance, I released her lips. As I rested my forehead on hers, I stared at her mouth. It was slightly parted, swollen, and red, and it glistened in the light.

"Why?" she whispered before she pulled her upper lip into her mouth and licked it.

Our heartbeats thundered wildly in our chests as our bodies touched. I slid my hand down her back and settled it next to my other hand, which was already holding her to me.

"I don't know." I was honest with her. I didn't have a fucking clue what it was about her. Something didn't want me to say goodbye and let go of the single night I'd spent in her bed.

It wasn't fucking her that had my mind in a tizzy, but something about her. I'd never met someone who had so invaded my thoughts after a single kiss. Hell, I'd never had anyone invade my thoughts unless it was while I was jacking off and replaying our sexual escapades. With Max, it was something more, and I couldn't put my finger on it.

"I tried to forget about you, Max. I tried everything to forget about you and rid myself of your memory."

"And?" she asked with a breathy voice as her eyes locked with mine.

I blinked, taking a moment to collect my thoughts. I sucked in a breath and started to speak. "It didn't work. I've been going out of my mind. You've haunted my dreams and filled my thoughts every waking minute." I blew out the breath I hadn't fully released.

"It's not fair," she said, closing her eyes.

I pulled her closer. "What's not fair, Max?" I asked, trying to hide the confusion that undoubtedly was written all over my face.

"I feel it, Anthony. There's something that happens when I touch you." She kept her eyes closed as she continued to talk, her voice dropping to a whisper. "I've never felt that with anyone before. Maybe it's just been so long since I've let a man touch me."

"Are you sure you aren't a lesbian, Max? If you are, I'm okay with sharing you, and it's totally sexy."

The seriousness of the moment was broken as she started to laugh. "Oh my God, seriously?" she asked through her laughter. "You think I'm gay still?"

"You said it's been a long time since a man has touched you," I replied, feeling my face begin to heat. I felt like a complete idiot. Obviously, I'd been wrong when I'd assumed she liked to lick pussy as much as I did.

"You're an idiot."

Yep, I felt like the biggest moron on the planet. Sweat started to collect on top of my brow as I stood there. What the fuck had I done? I'd started out strong and made a complete ass out of myself.

"I'm not gay, Anthony," she said as she stopped laughing and looked up at me. "No one has touched me in years. We've been over this before." She swallowed hard as her eyes dropped to the floor.

"Max." I touched her chin, bringing her eyes to mine. "I'm sorry I just assumed. For whatever reason you've sworn off men, I beg you to give me a chance."

"I can't."

I really started to hate the word *can't*. There was no such thing. Either she didn't want to or something else was holding her back.

"Yes, you can."

"You don't understand, Anthony. I can't deal with a relationship right now. Or ever, for that matter. It's not for me. If it were, I'd give myself to you in a heartbeat."

I held her by the arms, holding her away from me just far enough to look at her entire face. "What's stopping you? I'll do anything to make it happen."

She shook her head and frowned. "There's nothing you can do." She still hadn't looked me in the eyes as I held her at arm's length.

"Max, look at me," I said, gripping her tighter, but not enough to hurt.

When she didn't look up, I repeated myself.

"Max," I commanded. "Look. At. Me."

As her eyes met mine, I could see the tears that had collected in them. When she blinked, a single tear slid down her cheek, leaving a dark, glistening trail on her skin.

"Kitty Cat, you can have me. There's nothing stopping us. I don't get why you're playing hard to get."

"I just can't."

"Have a boyfriend?"

"Anthony, I said no one has touched me."

"Maybe he's a prick who doesn't have sex with you. We've established you aren't gay. Have kids?"

"I don't have any children."

"Want kids?" I asked, cocking an eyebrow at her and trying to hide a smile.

"Never." Her response was swift as another tear drifted down her face and caught on her jaw before falling to the floor.

"It's okay. We can practice a lot." I wanted to make light of the situation. She'd brought the mood down and made the air in the room feel heavy.

"You're impossible."

"I know, but only because I want you so much. Give in to me, Max, and I can make anything possible. I'll move heaven and earth if you give me a chance to get to know you. I don't think I can go through life wondering 'what if?' I'd be a shadow of myself, walking through a world where I knew I'd missed something spectacular."

"How do you know we'd be spectacular, Anthony?" she asked as her shoulder sagged and she relaxed into my hold.

"I've never felt fireworks when I kissed someone. I've never dreamt of anyone night after night as if it were a fucking nightmare. I want to eat, breathe, and live you, Max. I don't care if it's only for a short while. I have to explore what's going on between us."

"Anthony, it's not right." Her eyes dropped back down.

"Is it because I'm white? I know you said it wasn't before, but I can't think of anything else. What's left? It has to be because I'm white." I looked at her. I couldn't think of any other reason. I'd covered all the bases, every obstacle that might keep us apart.

"No!" she shot back as her eyes flew to mine.

"Is it because of your brother?" I asked, because I could understand that. Lord knows we'd tortured Izzy and every man who had tried to get in her pants.

"What about him?" she asked as her eyebrows drew together and her lips pursed.

"Obviously he hates me. He made that very clear. Maybe he doesn't like me because I'm white."

My parents had raised me to not judge a person based off the color of their skin but by the composition of their character. A man was nothing if he wasn't true to his word and honorable. I didn't care if they were white, black, green, or purple. I judged them by their acts and not the amount of pigment in their skin.

Everyone bled the same color and had the same feelings on the inside. We were the human race that had comingled over the years, creating humanity in its perfection that existed today.

Shame on her brother if he judged me because of the color of my skin and not the man I was. There were reasons to hate me, but color wasn't one of them.

"Yes," she squeaked and nodded. "He hates you. He told my mother about you and I'm forbidden to see you."

"What the fuck?" I asked as I released her and stepped back. I raked my fingers through my hair, feeling the anger begin to boil inside me. "You're a grown woman, Max. You're going to let their hatred stop something we both feel? You're going to let them cloud your judgment and possibility of true happiness?"

"Anthony, you have to understand—" she began, reaching out for me.

I shook her off. "There's nothing I need to understand, Max. Either you're the master of your destiny or you let others control you and become a slave to your wants."

"You did not just play the slave card on me," she whispered as her face transformed from sadness to highly pissed off.

"I didn't mean it like that." Fuck. Really, I hadn't. She needed to be an adult and tell her family to fuck off.

"It sounded really shitty."

"I want you to make your own decision. Your family doesn't have the right to deny you your happiness. Or mine, for that matter. I don't care what color you are. We both bleed red, Max." My anger simmered below the surface, ready to break free. "We're not living in the 1950s, for shit's sake. Get a grip, Max. Clearly, you have other thoughts. I didn't hear you saying no to my big white cock as you screamed my name."

She winced. "You just wouldn't understand."

"I don't. I wasn't raised to look at a person's skin color. When I look at you, Max, I see beauty. The inner glow and fierce attitude that emanate from you have drawn me to you."

"My family is my everything, Anthony."

"Mine is too," I hurled back at her. "But I wouldn't let them dictate my future."

"I can't."

"Fucking stop saying that shit!" I yelled, slamming my hand down on a display case next to me.

She jumped from the loud clatter of the jewelry display as it moved with the impact.

"Don't tell them," I begged. "What if you don't tell them about me? I don't need to come over for dinner on the weekends. I don't care if I ever meet your parents. All I want is you. Just you. Only you, Max."

She closed her eyes as tears streamed down her face and fell to the floor. "I don't know."

"Max," I pleaded. "Give me—no, give *us*—a chance. I don't want to look back and wonder what could've been. Maybe we'll fall apart and the flame we have for each other will fizzle out. At least we'll know we tried. To deny ourselves the ability to know if there's something more between us is just plain cruel." I stepped toward her, cradling her face in my hands as I caught her tears with my thumbs.

Small crinkles formed near the corners of her eyes as she strained to keep them closed. Her tears grew until she trembled in my arms.

"I want to say yes, Anthony. I want to more than anything," she sobbed.

"Then do it." I brushed her skin with my lips, basking in her softness. "Be the strong woman I met in the bar weeks ago. I don't care if I have to hide as long as I'm with you."

She kept her eyes shut and didn't respond.

"I'll hide in the shadows for you. I'll be your dirty secret. As long as I get to touch you, kiss your lips, and see where the sparks lead us, I'll do anything. Just don't shut me out."

"Okay," she whispered as her eyes fluttered open. Tears hung in her eyes, ready to fall again as she looked at me. "I haven't been able to stop thinking about you. Your touch stayed with me for days, Anthony. It scorched my skin, burning hotter than the sun. I can't promise a future, but I can give you the now."

Taking a long, slow inhale, I felt relieved that she had given in. All I wanted was the now. We could implode and collapse like the tallest skyscraper during demolition, but I wanted to know we'd tried. That I hadn't let her run away without exploring the first true feelings I'd ever felt for a woman.

That was how we began.

***

Max

I hadn't been expecting him. I thought I'd done enough and been cruel to the point he'd never want to cross paths again. Naturally, I was wrong. He wasn't the type to give up, but the one thing I thought I had going for me was that I was just as bullheaded as he was.

As he turned around, my heart stopped. I felt a void inside my chest from the rhythmic beating that I'd grown to ignore, but when it ceased I took note. I wanted to jump into his arms and kiss his face but I refrained.

I tried everything I could think of to get him

to understand we couldn't be together. The problem with that was he didn't believe a word of it. I felt the spark just as much as he had. Maybe even more since I hadn't let anyone touch me for years.

I'd lied to him. I couldn't believe what popped out of my mouth when I felt backed into a corner. I'd pay someday for that shitty-ass lie. My family wouldn't care that he was white. Denzel was engaged to a white girl, after all. It was the only thing I could think of, though. I figured I could hide behind my family and he'd back off.

But when he kissed me, I couldn't say no to him any longer. Feeling the softness of his lips against mine, tasting him again, and being in his arms made me want to give in and throw my grand plan out the window.

Maybe if I went on one date with him, I'd find out that I didn't really like him. Maybe I only wanted him because I was lonely and horny. An official date with Anthony would be just the ticket. After spending an evening with him and actually talking, I'd be done with him.

His cocky attitude would drive me away and his need to feel he'd captured me would wane. Soon, it would all be over and I'd go back to my simple life and the overuse of my new vibrator whom I affectionately nicknamed Tyrese after watching a *Fast & Furious* movie.

I could go back and be happy again. Couldn't I?

8

I FONDUE YOU

THE FIRST OFFICIAL DATE WE HAD WAS simple. We went to dinner and ended up at her place. I'd like to pretend I was a true gentleman, but it would be a lie. Yes, I opened her door, pulled out her chair, and all that bullshit my father had taught me as a young man, but I didn't waste time before getting her in the sack again.

I couldn't. No matter how badly I wanted to wait, I couldn't. It was hard to be patient and wait when I wasn't sure if the offer would still be there tomorrow. Plus, I was a greedy fuck.

She hadn't promised forever, but she had said that I could have her now. It was more than

I'd ever promised anyone, and since she had my head all messed up, I took what I could. Months ago, before Max, I wouldn't have wanted a second chance. There was no way I'd have accepted taking a back seat and hiding from the people in our lives. Somehow, she made it okay.

I went from not wanting a relationship to being her dirty secret in what seemed like the blink of an eye. Oddly enough, it didn't make me feel inferior or weak. I felt renewed and like anything was possible. Maybe I could be a rock star. Possibly, my destiny wasn't to be alone. Who knew what the future held? I'd always thought I did. I had a set path and I followed it.

Meet 'em. Fuck 'em. Leave 'em.

Roles had reversed, and now, I was the one willing to accept that course of action.

I wanted to show her that I had another side. The non-asshole one that could be sweet. Naturally, I didn't know where a romantic restaurant was, so I Googled it. Listed first was the place that served cheesecake by the tons. I'd been there once and hadn't felt an ounce of romance as I'd listened to Suzy chatter on about school. I went for option two listed in the search—The Melting Pot.

I knew they served fondue, but what I hadn't expected was the amount of time we'd be sitting there. The dinner took hours.

Between the cheese and the meat courses, I thought I'd try and get to know more about the woman who sat next to me. I knew the basics. Name: Maxine. Age: mid-thirties, but she wouldn't be specific. Occupation: stylist. She had at least one brother and a mother who didn't want her to date a white man. Best Friends: Nita and Malia. That was all I knew about her. Not much to go on, and maybe that was why I liked her as much as I did. She was mysterious and magnetic, and I knew that our touch caused sparks.

"Do you only have one brother?" I asked as I poured more wine in our glasses while we waited for our oil pot to arrive.

"Just the one." She played with the edge of the napkin her water glass sat on, rubbing it between her two fingers.

She was dressed in a simple black cocktail

dress. Her hair was pulled up into a ponytail, and the ends cascaded over her shoulders, stopping above her breasts.

I knew that the prick didn't like me, but I was thankful there was only one brother I had to watch out for. "Damian, right?"

She rolled her eyes. "Denzel. Like the actor."

"Sorry. I was paying more attention to you than what you called him."

"Simple mistake. What about you? Any siblings?"

"I have three brothers and a sister."

"Jesus." she shook her head. "I'd go crazy with multiple Denzels. Your poor sister."

"Trust me," I replied as I toyed with the stem of my wineglass. "Izzy handles her own affairs."

"Are you saying I don't?" she shot back as she cocked an eyebrow.

"No. No." I sighed. Fuck. It wasn't what I'd meant, exactly, but maybe I'd said it with a hint of sarcasm. "You certainly can hold your own, Kitty Cat."

"So, you and your brothers never butt into her love life?"

I wanted to lie. Truly, I did. But I didn't think it would be right. "Yeah. We've been known to butt in a time or two."

She laughed, a sweet, soft laugh. "What is it with men always feeling like they need to rescue us?"

Like a dumbass, I replied, "We have to protect what's ours."

"Say that again?" she said with a confused look on her face.

"It's ingrained in us. Part of our DNA. I can't ever stop protecting my sister. She's my family and always will be. Even if she's wrong, I'll protect her with my life."

"Most of us don't need saving, Anthony." She lifted her wineglass and stared at me over the rim.

"I didn't say anything about saving. It's more about protecting, Max."

"That's what guns are for." She grinned on the glass and winked.

"You carry?" I asked, feeling a little afraid of her.

Girls with guns could be a very deadly combination, especially when I had a very good chance of pissing them off.

"Always." Her eyes shifted to her evening bag that was sitting on top of the table, next to the wall.

"Why?" I asked.

"Because a girl could never be too careful."

"Of me?"

"Of anyone, Anthony."

It was laughable, but endearing.

"Max," I said as I set my glass down and inclined forward. "If I wanted to kill you, I would've done it already. I wouldn't have to sit through two hours of fondue to do it."

"Already thinking about offing me?" she asked.

"I don't live in an episode of *The Sopranos*."

Stereotypes crossed all nationalities and racial lines. We all knew what the stereotypes were. Italians weren't usually portrayed in the best light—especially males. Often, we were characterized as mobsters. Seen as dangerous criminals looking for a racket to make our money and "offing" anyone in our way. It was the furthest thing from the truth, but the Hollywood depiction stuck in the minds of all non-Italians across the world. I couldn't blame her for pigeon-holing what she didn't know, but I'd work on changing her attitude.

"I didn't mean to offend you." She tapped her fingernail on the glass.

"You didn't. Tell me about your father," I said, trying to change the subject.

"He's been dead for about three years." A frown covered her face. "He was the best dad ever."

I could've argued that point. Sal Gallo had to be the best dad in the world. My pop was my rock. He was the thing that held the family to-gether. I'd never admit that to my mom, though.

"I'm so sorry to hear that. That has to be hard."

She nodded slowly, looking down at her wine. "It is. He suffered for a long time before he passed. It's horrible watching your father wither away before your eyes." Her fingers swept over the bottom of the glass, making a figure eight. "It was the worst thing I'd ever gone through in my life, Anthony. The day my father died, I didn't know how to feel. I loved him more than anything in the world, but to watch someone suffer is the most excruciating thing you can ever experience. Have you ever lived through something so traumatic it altered your view of the entire world?" Her eyes rose to mine, a thin layer of tears lining the inside.

I thought about it and concentrated on my breathing. I had been blessed with the health of my family. "No. I haven't." I shook my head. A small fissure of guilt went through me at the luck I'd had in life. Unlike a majority of people, I had money, looks, and health.

"Be glad for that. You know how you want to protect your sister—or anyone in your family, for that matter?" she asked, blotting her eyes and capturing the tears on her napkin.

"Yes. Like I said, I'd do anything to keep them safe."

"Imagine if there was nothing you could do. You had to watch as they slowly deteriorated before your eyes. No matter how hard you tried or how many doctors you visited, there was nothing you could do."

"Jesus," I muttered, trying to put myself in her shoes. I couldn't. It would be too painful to watch something like that happen to someone I loved. "Did he have cancer?"

"No." She vigorously shook her head. "He had an incurable disease that's very rare."

"I just can't..." The words got stuck in my throat. "I can't imagine what you went through, Max." I reached across the table and swept my fingers over the top of her hand. "I'm so sorry you had to go through that."

Her eyes dipped to where our bodies touched. "It's over with now," she said as she wiped the tears away. "I don't want to talk about it. It's kind of a mood killer, Anthony." She gave me a small smile that didn't match her eyes.

"Okay," I sighed. I was ready for a new topic. It seemed that whichever way we went, there were landmines waiting to explode.

"Tell me about your family. Give me something happy."

"Well, I'm about to be an uncle for the first time."

"Oh, that's exciting. When?" She smiled.

I'd been waiting for her to move her hand from mine, but she kept it there, letting me stroke it with my thumb.

"This fall sometime. First baby in the family, so it should be interesting."

"Babies always bring joy."

"Yeah, I'd agree if the pregnant woman didn't devour every drop of food at Sunday dinner every week. I swear I've never seen anything like it."

She giggled, and her eyes transformed as her smile kissed the edges of her lips. "I know, right? A few of my friends have had babies, and I wonder the same thing. God, if I look at food, I swear I gain five pounds."

She'd look beautiful with a little more weight. Her body was already lush and soft when I touched her, but I wouldn't complain if she had more to hold.

"Max, you'd look beautiful no matter how much you weighed." I smiled at her, and an image of her with a round belly while she stuffed her face full of pasta made my insides warm. It scared the crap out of me. I knew she didn't want children.

"You're just saying that because you're trying to ply me with cheese, oil, and chocolate tonight."

I shook my head and grinned. "You're beautiful."

"Thanks." She blinked. Then she glanced down at our hands again and had a small grin on her lips. "Tell me more."

I moved closer, making sure no one else could hear. "I love the softness of your thighs when I have my head—"

"No. No. Not that," she whispered. "I meant about your family. Not sex, Anthony." She shifted in her seat before looking at me again.

Knowing that the thought of sex with me turned her on brought me happiness. If nothing else, she couldn't resist me simply because of the number of orgasms I'd brought her.

"Okay. I work with my siblings at the tattoo shop."

"God, I couldn't imagine working with Denzel. I think I'd kill him."

The waitress arrived, placing the pot of oil and a plate of cut-up meats and vegetables besides it. "Do you two need anything else?" she asked.

I looked to Max, and she shook her head. "No. We're fine, ma'am."

She walked away, giving us the privacy I had craved.

"We have a lot of fun. We're all part owners, and sometimes, it gets a little sticky, but for the most part, it's been great."

"You're lucky. Seems like you have a close family, then."

"I do, but one of my brothers is working undercover and I haven't seen him in ages."

"Wow. That's honorable. When will you see him again?"

"Hopefully soon. I think his investigation is just about over. It's like a piece of me is missing when he's gone."

"I know how that feels," she grumbled as she grabbed a long poker and stabbed at a piece of steak. "At least you know he's coming back."

"True," I replied, feeling like a complete tool.

Thomas would come home if everything worked out, but her father? He'd never return to her. I grew silent, cursing myself as I placed a few pieces of food in the pot.

She repeated the process and stared at me over the table. "It's okay, Anthony. You don't need to watch what you say. I like to hear about something other than my family."

The butterflies that had started to flutter inside my stomach began to calm with her words. "If you say so," I mumbled, still feeling like a complete asshole.

"Did you say you have Sunday dinner? Like, every Sunday?" she asked as she twirled the sticks and turned the meat.

"Yeah. My mom cooks dinner every week, and we're required to be there."

"What's she going to do if you don't go? Ground you?" she shot back, and laughed. "You are a grown-ass man."

I chuckled too, knowing that it sounded insane. "You don't understand my ma. She's one woman you don't want to piss off. If you can't make it, you better call."

"You're scared of your mother?" she asked as she pulled her sticks out of the oil, tapping them on top of her dish.

"I wouldn't say scared. I'd say I respect her."

"Uh huh." She placed the first bite of steak in her mouth. "You're scared," she said after she swallowed the food.

"I most certainly am not. My mother is the head of the entire family. I try to never be a no-show out of respect. She spends hours cooking a feast for us and the least I can do is show up. Plus," I added, grabbing another piece of meat from the pot to cool, "it's a free meal." I laughed.

"So, you're a cheap bastard?" she teased.

"What do you think?" I grinned.

"I'd say you are." She nodded and looked down at her tiny plate of meat pieces.

"Fondue isn't a cheap meal. I never skimp, especially when taking a woman on a date."

"Do you do that a lot?" she inquired without looking at me.

"What?" I asked, furrowing my brow as I watched her.

"Take a lot of women on dates."

I couldn't help it. I burst into laughter. "Max, I do not date."

"Well, what's this, then?"

"Let me rephrase that. I've never taken a woman on a date before you."

"Anthony, be honest. God doesn't like liars," she told me as her lip twitched.

"Max, I'm dead serious. I've never found someone I wanted to get to know. Before you, all I cared about was getting them in the sack."

"You've never had a girlfriend?" she asked with a look of shock.

"In high school and in my early twenties, but I wouldn't say I took them to dinner. I wasn't into wining and dining," I admitted, knowing I sounded like a complete pig.

"And you're saying that women are easy?"

"I fucked you, didn't I?" I regretted the words as soon as they left my mouth.

"Not the first night. I believe you had to

work for it." She smiled as she plopped a piece of zucchini in her mouth.

"I did. More than I've ever worked for anything in my life." I returned her smile and didn't feel ashamed that I'd chased her.

"I'm not worth the effort, Anthony." She casually tapped the stick on the side of the pot, letting the oil drip off. She'd said it like it was common knowledge and I shouldn't be offended by her words.

"But you are, Max." I set my sticks down, folded my hands in front of me, and looked directly at her. "The spark when we touch tells me you are worth it. Have you ever felt that with another person? Be honest with me."

Maybe it wasn't the combination of us when we touched that had caused the spark. She might have been the one to generate the electricity. Possibly everyone she had ever touched had felt it. The thought that I wasn't special nagged at me.

"No, I've never felt it before," she admitted as she stared back at me. "I don't know what it is."

"Me either, but I want to know what it means. You may think you're not worth the effort, but I beg to differ."

She gave me a weak smile and returned her attention back to her meal. The rest of the time at the table was spent with small talk, avoiding all discussion of relationships and the electricity we had together. I wouldn't push the issue. Trust me, I wanted to, but for the sake of not pushing her away, I kept my lips sealed.

After she dropped the last piece of angel food cake in her mouth and moaned, she said, "I'm so full." Rubbing her belly, she sighed as her body sagged. "I don't know if I've ever felt this full."

I, on the other hand, felt like I hadn't eaten. The meal had been so drawn out that my body had already consumed the food. "I could eat more."

"I have something you can eat," she replied with a naughty smirk.

"You want my mouth on you?" I asked with a raised eyebrow.

The thought of tasting her pussy made my

cock grow harder. I wished I could lay her out on the table and drizzle the melted chocolate over her body before devouring every morsel.

"Yes." She nodded slowly, staring at me with hooded eyes.

"Check, please!" I called out to the waitress.

9

THIN LINE

I LAY THERE EXHAUSTED, SPENT, AND content. Twirling my finger on top of her stomach, I set my head on her hip and stared at her. Her skin glistened in the light as her chest rose and fell from the exertion of the fuck-fest we'd just had. Thank God I was in shape. If I hadn't been, I would've left her house sore. The woman was a tiger in bed. I'd used everything I had, pulled out all the stops when satisfying her.

"Exhausted," she whined as she threw her arm across her face.

"Me or you?" I splayed my hand out on her stomach, letting it rise with her breath.

"Me. I swear you're trying to kill me."

"Max, I beg to differ. I thought you were trying to suffocate me when you were grinding your pussy on my face." I bit my lip, holding in my laughter.

"Bastard," she hissed. "I was trying to kill you."

"I would've gone out a happy man." I slid my fingers down her stomach before stopping between her legs.

Tiny droplets of cum twinkled in the light. Her taste was like no other woman I'd been with. It wasn't because she was black, but there was something about her that made everything better.

I hadn't seen Max for a week since our first official date. That evening had been much the same way as this night, but minus the face-riding. I'd wanted to see her before, but between our work schedules and her needing space, we'd waited to see each other.

The week had breezed by as I'd tattooed, written music, and practiced with the band. I really had no free time, since I had neglected everything in my pursuit of her. But as I lay there with her, everything seemed worth it.

Peacefulness settled over me as my fingertips grazed her body and felt her softness. The familiar spark hadn't waned with our separation. When I'd seen her after the week apart, fireworks had gone off. We'd torn at each other's clothes like we were animals in heat.

"Do you want to go to my parents' house for dinner tomorrow?" I asked, wondering if she'd take that step.

I'd never brought anyone home with me. Honestly, I'd never had anyone worthy of meeting them. Max was different. I thought she'd get a kick out of them and they'd enjoy meeting someone knew. Plus, I wondered how they'd react to her race. I knew my family would embrace her as just another possible child-bearing female to bring a new Gallo into the world. Maybe if she saw that my family didn't mind the race difference, she'd not worry so much about what her family thought.

When she didn't reply, I added, "It's Sunday and I haven't seen you all week. I thought we could spend the day together, Max." I trailed my fingers between her breasts, watching her skin break out into goose bumps.

"No," she answered. "I can't."

"Have plans?" I asked, not willing to drop the subject.

"No, I just can't."

"Why not?" I asked in an angry tone, propping myself up on one elbow.

"Anthony, we're not a couple. That's what you do when you're a couple." She kept her eyes hidden under her arm.

"We're not a couple?" It wasn't that I was shocked. She had agreed to see me, not be mine. To say that it didn't sting would have been a lie.

"No."

"Friends?"

"I don't know if I'd go that far either," she replied, and drew her bottom lip into her mouth.

"What the fuck, Max?" I shot back, my back growing rigid.

"We fuck, Anthony. That's it. It's nice, but we're nothing more," she said as her voice grew quiet. "We can't be anything more."

I couldn't let my anger get out of control. I wanted to scream, but I knew it wouldn't get me anywhere. I kept my voice low as I spoke. "I'm just a piece of ass to you, aren't I? You can't stand up to your family and tell them you have a right to be with me?"

"Anthony," she said as she sat up, pulling her knees to her chest. "I can't give you anything more than sex. You said you were okay with it."

"I want to see you, Max. I want to be with you. I'm not asking to go to your mother's for dinner. This is my family, and I don't need to hide you." I climbed off the bed and started to pace. "This is all we're ever going to be?" I waved my hands haphazardly, toward the clothing that had been tossed in haste. "Just fuck buddies?"

"I can't give you more." She kept her eyes pinned on me, watching me as I paced.

I stopped and faced her, naked and vulnerable. "What if I want more? Maybe this isn't good enough for me." I had pushed the envelope; I knew it when I spoke.

Max had said that there were limits to our relationship, but I'd assumed the more time she spent with me, the more her feelings would change. Once again, I had it all wrong.

I threw up my arms and put them behind my head, giving her a full view of everything I had to offer. If I was only a fuck buddy, that's what she'd want to see.

"I won't accept it, Max. I know you want more. I can see it in your eyes when I'm inside you. You can pretend that you don't feel what we have, but I can see it." I pulled my hands forward, letting them slide through my hair before resting my palms on top of my head.

"There's nothing you see, Anthony. You don't know how I feel. I don't think we should see each other anymore."

Wait a goddamn minute. It was like déjà vu. I was about to be tossed to the curb again like yesterday's trash.

"That's it? You're ending us?" My anger

rose, causing my heart to beat out of rhythm. "What the fuck, Max?"

"It's best for both of us. You're getting too attached to me. I like fucking you, but I don't want to be with you. I'm not your girlfriend, never will be, and can't give you anything more than this." She waved her arms, motioning across the bed. "If you can't accept just fucking me, then it's best if we end it here."

"You'll change your mind," I said as I grabbed my pants off the floor.

"I won't."

"I don't know who fucked your head up so bad, Max. You really should talk to someone about your issues. We have a good thing going here. No matter what your family thinks of me, we're meant to be together."

I closed my eyes as I spoke the words. In all my life, I'd never thought I'd mutter those words, let alone say them with such conviction. The funny thing was, I'd meant it. Fuck her and her bullshit. I dressed without looking at her and headed home.

Max and I were over, and nothing in the world would make me change my mind.

***

Max

I thought it was hard to say goodbye to him the first time I kicked him out, but that was a cakewalk. I said I'd give us a chance and go on a date with him, but when we did I immediately knew the error of my ways.

The attraction we felt for each other was too great. Not only was the sex amazing, but he was easy to be with. I liked talking with him, surprisingly enough. Telling him about my father had been easy, and he seemed genuinely interested and felt sorry for me. He wasn't the asshole I'd pegged him to be that night at the Ritz. I'm not saying he's a saint, because Lord knows he isn't. He had the perfect mix of cockiness and kindness, which he seemed to hide well.

I had to be brutal with him. When he started talking about meeting his family and possible future plans, I had to put an end to it all. I couldn't let myself fall deeper for the man. I'd never believed in love at first sight. Never did I think you could know someone was right for you after only a few dates.

Anthony said it himself: we were made to be together. The problem with his statement was me. I couldn't change my life and there wasn't a place for him. No matter how badly I wanted to run away with him and forget about everything but us, it wasn't a luxury I could afford.

Not because I couldn't get lost in us. No. I didn't want him to get lost in me.

Saying goodbye to him for a third time was like having my heart ripped out of my chest and watching it beat before my eyes. The sorrow and agony I felt in that moment didn't compare to anything other than losing my father. Having love in front of me then pushing it away was something I didn't want to do again.

Sometimes we can't have what we want. Life has a way of selecting its own course, and there's nothing we can do to hop off the trail.

No matter how badly I wanted to change my future, I couldn't.

My heart would heal and so would his. He'd find his happily ever after while I, on the other hand, would surround myself with friends and family and forsake myself of my one true love.

It was more for his sake than mine.

At least, that was the lie I told myself as I cried myself to sleep.

10

LOVE IS A WICKED GAME

I LIED.

Often, what I said I'd do and what really happened would change along the way without my control. If I were smart, I wouldn't have gone back to her. But since I was a man and often controlled by my dick, I gave in.

Days later, Max shot me a text asking if I'd give her another shot. She missed me, missed my cock, and wanted to see me again. Like an idiot and a man with a cock, I took her back.

It wasn't that we didn't have issues. If we avoided talk of anything that resembled a relationship, everything was smooth sailing. I dropped any thought of taking her to Sunday dinner. We decided that it would be best to keep our visits short, with no wining and dining beforehand. I knew she didn't want to take a chance of someone seeing us.

I knew what it looked like to an outsider. Anthony was pussy-whipped, just like every other Gallo man. There was a bit of truth to the statement, but I would argue my side until the bitter end. I couldn't allow myself to be seen as weak.

I liked to think of myself like a caveman. Max was my prey and I was just waiting to pounce. Eventually, she'd give in. Whether she wanted to admit it or not, I knew she liked me. I'd bet my fortune that her feelings were closer to love than just mere lust.

I'd wait. Be the patient man I'd never been before and wait for Max to admit what she felt for me. The biggest hurdle would be to overcome the fact that her family didn't approve of me. I was sure that, if they got to know me, no matter what color I am, they'd fall in love. If I could just get the chance to show her that we could work and I could get her family's blessing...

But it wouldn't happen overnight. I'd play the part, be her fuck buddy. Be anything she wanted to be until she felt comfortable enough to utter the words I'd always thought I'd be too big of a pussy to say.

Not too long ago, I'd thought relationships were for the weak. Slowly, I evolved. It'd only taken thirty-something years for it to happen. My luck would be that the one woman I finally wanted to chance something more with shut me out. I'd hang on, take what she had to give, and always leave her wanting more.

But eventually, we each have a breaking point.

We usually met up at night when we could find the time in our busy schedules, and I remained in the shadows. It was the lot I'd resigned myself to when I'd begged her to give me a chance that night in her shop, to give us a shot at happiness.

I thought I could handle it, but over time, I wanted to stake my claim and let the world know she was mine. It didn't take me long to fall in love with Max. The only thing that rivaled her beauty was her attitude. I saw myself when I looked at her. Her cockiness and ability to take shit as it was thrown at her and fling it back in the face of adversity were astonishing. She didn't let anything or anybody get in her way.

Except her family. They were in the way of our happiness, her happiness, and a possible happily-ever-after. It had been months since she'd caved in and agreed to see me as we tried to figure out what fate had in store for us.

Not only was our lovemaking epic, our fights could only be classified as nuclear. More times than I'd like to admit, she'd kick me out and put an end to our faux-relationship. She'd cave in, saying that she missed me and had fucked up. Like a dumbass, I'd forgive her and take her back.

I had become the weak one. Roles had reversed, and I'd landed in a position I'd never thought I'd be in. Love can make a person do crazy things. I'd said that I never wanted anything to change me, but without stopping it, I had become someone I barely recognized anymore.

"I'm sorry," she whispered on my lips as she crawled in my lap.

It was about the fifth time she'd called it off and then begged my forgiveness over the last two months. I had come to her house with a plan. I'd fuck her like she'd never been fucked and leave.

Being led by the balls and strung along had been exhausting. It had taken a toll on my music, my work, and my sleep. I was done with feeling like shit. Her moods were too much for me to handle. I wouldn't be a pawn in her life anymore. I was more than a cock and a secret.

"I can't do this anymore, Max." I slumped in the chair and held her hips. "I can't keep taking you back. I won't do it again." I shook my head, unable to comprehend how she had changed me.

"I promise it'll be different. You just don't understand what I'm going through, Anthony." She gripped my shirt, rubbing the material between her thumb and index fingers. "It's so hard having so much love for you and not knowing how to handle it."

"What's to handle? Just feel it and let it happen. Stop running away like a scared child. It's time to grow the fuck up." I played with the loop on her jeans, focusing my attention away from the squeezing pain in my chest.

She had ruined me. Totally destroyed the man I had been not that long ago at the Ritz. I had been a cocky motherfucker who had life by the balls. Now a woman was holding mine in a vise. I'd never understood what my brothers had gone through when they had met "the one." I had ridiculed them and thought they were pussies, but now, I knew. Love wasn't something you could turn off or deny. It became part of you, an ache so deep and full that it had to be filled to feel alive.

I needed to go to an addiction meeting. I needed to admit to someone outside of my family that I was Anthony Gallo and I had lost my way and needed salvation. I needed redemption from a path so cruel that I was a shell of my former self. I hated Max and myself. Her even more for the hell she'd put me through the last couple of months.

Everything in my life was as fake as Kim Kardashian's ass on the cover of *Paper* magazine.

I pretended not to have a girlfriend, she hid me from everyone but Malia and Nita, and we ignored the future. Actually, we swept it under the rug, pretending it wasn't something we'd have to face soon.

She arched forward, pushing her breasts into my chest. "I promise, Anthony. I'll do better."

"I deserve better," I replied. "I've become a better man since I've known you. I'm a shell of my former self, Max. The asshole you met in the bar deserves how you're treating me, but the man sitting before you right now...sure as fuck doesn't."

"You're right," she said as she snaked her arms behind my neck. "I'm sorry. Let me make it up to you, baby." She gave me a devilish grin that made my cock take notice.

"I like the sound of that." I smiled at her, feeling an aching in my balls. I'd spent three days without her and felt the loss in more than my heart.

"I can do that special thing you like so much. It's been a while." She licked my lips as she reached down and palmed my cock.

"Mmm," I murmured as I pressed my lips to her mouth, getting lost in her taste. "Kitty Cat," I whispered into her mouth, "I want you to make me believe that you mean it this time."

She pulled her lips away and gave me a lopsided smirk. "I can do that," she promised before she crawled out of my lap, sliding down my legs.

Her fingers fumbled with the button on my jeans. It took her longer than usual to unfasten them.

"Sorry," she said, glancing up at me. "My fingers don't want to work."

I placed my hands on her fingers. "Take your time. I'm in no rush, and it's not your fingers I care about right now," I said as I lifted my arms and laced my hands behind my head.

"I'm sure you aren't." She smiled as the button popped. "Finally." She breathed a sigh of relief as she dragged the zipper down.

As she opened my jeans, I lifted my ass for her to drag my pants down, giving my aching cock the freedom it had been demanding.

"So you want..." she said before she licked the head of my cock.

My body vibrated, craving more of the warmth that only her mouth could provide.

"...it slow or fast?" she asked before drawing the tip into her mouth.

I shuddered and lost my breath. As my eyes rolled back, I tried to form words but couldn't.

"Like this?" She drew my entire length into her mouth, swallowing the head as it hit the back of her throat.

"God," I moaned as she began to drag my dick back out while pushing her tongue on the underside.

"Mmm," she hummed with the head, dragging my dick back inside.

The vibrations rocked my world. A white-hot streak of pleasure shot straight to my balls, causing the need to amplify. I didn't think I could've handled slow, no matter how badly I wanted to make the moment last.

The warmth of her mouth mixed with the noises she made had me picturing shit that wouldn't drive me over the edge. I wanted to watch. Seeing a woman devouring your cock is one of the sexiest things in the world. It plays over and over again in a man's mind for hours after it happens.

I closed my eyes, shutting out everything but how her mouth felt and her tiny groans as she sucked me off. Her pace was slow as she took her time and paid special attention to the tip. Each time her tongue whirled by my piercings, I lost my breath. The tug of her teeth pulled deep inside my dick. It was the piercing that caused it. I'd picked that type of piercing because it's the most pleasurable for a man. Even though I cared about the orgasm of whichever woman I was with, ultimately, I wanted mine to be better...more explosive.

Her hand slid from my thigh to my balls as she palmed them. One hand worked my cock with her mouth while the other fondled me. It was perfect and heavenly. When I opened my eyes and stared down at her, an internal struggle began.

Should I fuck her and leave? I wanted to make her feel as shitty as I'd felt over the last few weeks. My head had been spinning from the back-and-forth. How could you profess your love one moment and then do a complete one-eighty and turn cold as ice?

I wound my fingers in her hair and yanked roughly, pulling her mouth off my dick. "Not like this," I growled as she peered up at me with saliva hanging from her lips.

I tilted forward, licking her mouth clean before kissing her. As I rose to my feet, I brought her with me, my hands firmly planted on her arms. The tiny silk nighty she was wearing didn't have a chance beneath my hands. I forwent the easier route of letting it fall off her shoulder. It tore from her skin, falling into a heap on the floor.

"Anthony," she mumbled on my lips.

"Shhh," I replied. Honestly, I didn't give a fuck what she thought or how she felt. I wanted to fuck her, and when I walked out the door tomorrow, I wanted her to miss me.

After ripping off my pants, I lifted her and impaled her on my cock. Not working it in gently, making sure she was ready to handle my size. Nope. I slammed her body down over my hardened length, burying myself balls deep inside her.

"Fuck," she hissed as her pussy clenched.

I pushed her down with more force than the first time. "Feel me?" I asked, repeating the motion.

She clawed at my shoulders as she milked me. "Anthony," she pleaded as her feet dug into my ass.

I didn't know if she had been begging me to stop or keep going, but either way, I didn't relent. I didn't make love to her like she was my girlfriend. I fucked her like I'd fucked the countless women before she'd wrecked me.

When I looked at her, watching her mouth gasp for air as I battered her with my cock, I reminded myself that she wasn't the woman I loved. Max had two personalities, and the one fucking me back was the one I hated.

Our bodies crashed into the wall as I tried to get more traction. Resting her body on the wall, I violated her. Pumping into her like a machine, unable to stop myself until I came. Her wet heat surrounded me, milking my dick for more like a greedy bitch.

Her nails tore my skin, causing me to cry out in pain. My grunts melded with hers, sounding like the perfect melody of pleasure. My balls grew heavy, and I felt like the end was near. Without wanting to lose the momentum I had built, I pushed her back harder toward the wall and gripped her under her legs. I pumped, slammed, and fucked her with all the anger that had been pent up inside me for weeks.

She screamed through the pleasure, enjoying every moment of the fucking I was giving her. When I grunted through the last couple of thrusts, my pace became erratic as my dick wept inside of her and I knew it would be the last time I'd feel her from the inside.

"More," she cried out, riding my cock even though I had stopped moving.

I had no breath left, since I'd given everything I had in the pursuit of my pleasure. I released her, letting her use her body to prop herself up and continue on her carnal quest. Resting my hands on the wall and framing her face, I watched as she bucked, chasing her release.

Through my hard breaths I grinned. She had to work for her pleasure. For the first time since I'd met her, I wasn't going to make sure she came multiple times. It was a prick move, but she deserved to be left without the satisfaction only I could bring.

Just as her body stiffened and she began to cry out, the doorbell rang.

"Oh my God!" she yelled as her pussy contracted, milking my softening dick.

Clutching my shoulder, she ignored the door and continued to ride me like a fuck toy. It was how she'd treated me lately, so why would this night have been any different?

When her head fell forward, the doorbell rang again.

"Fuck," she mumbled on top of my shoulder. "I can't," she blew out between breaths.

It double rang. Whoever was standing on the other side of the door was persistent.

"Go get dressed and I'll answer it," I told her as she slid down my body.

"Okay," she said as she tried to stand on wobbly legs, swaying slightly. "Whoever it is, tell them to go away."

"It's probably some asshole selling something," I said, picking my pants up and pulling them on as the doorbell chimed again. "Coming. Christ!" I yelled as I zipped up my pants and stalked toward the door with the button left undone. "What?" I barked as I flung open the door and grabbed for my button.

"Um," a small voice said with a squeak.

My eyes slowly drifted up after seeing a pair of red flats. There were a couple of things I knew in this moment. First off, those were not Nita's or Malia's feet. I'd heard them talk about fashion enough to know they would never wear flats. The flowered dress that hung below her knees screamed *grandma*, or mother at least.

A few weeks before, I might have freaked out, but now I smiled to myself, knowing that Max's charade would come crumbling down.

My gaze meandered up her body, finally settling on her face. I grinned at her. She was definitely Max's mother. I stared at her, waiting to hear her screams, but her reaction totally threw me for a loop.

Her eyes scanned over me, taking time to soak in my chest before they met mine. Instead of yelling, she gave me a sinful stare and held out her hand.

"And you are?" she asked with a smooth, sultry voice.

"I'm Anthony," I said, grasping her hand and placing a small kiss on the delicate flesh lining the top.

"Did you tell them to go away, babe?" Max yelled from the bedroom.

I touched my lips, begging the woman to remain silent. I turned and yelled back, "Yeah. They left, Max."

"Thank shit. They almost ruined my orgasm."

I looked back at her mother, and her mouth had dropped open.

"Take your time, love," I called out.

"Be out in five. I have to put some clothes on."

"And you are?" I asked the woman, who was still holding my hand.

"I'm Max's mother, Ruth." Her smile had transformed into something different. Maybe she was pissed off because I'd just fucked her daughter. No mother, no matter the race, wants to hear that.

"Ruth, I'm surprised you haven't yelled yet," I said as I stroked her hand with my thumb.

Her gaze returned to my face for a beat. "Why?"

"Max told me you had a problem with us seeing each other. I know you don't like that I'm white."

"What?" she asked as her voice grew shrill.

"You don't have to deny it, Ruth. I'm just hoping I can change your mind." I released her hand, letting it drop.

"Baby, I don't know who filled your head with that nonsense. I never said anything about you being white. In fact, I didn't know anything about you. I'm not entirely pleased that you just had sex with my baby, but it has nothing to do with the color of your skin."

My head began to spin. Thoughts swirled in my mind as I tried to piece together what had truly happened. Max had tried to push me away, but when it hadn't worked, she'd pulled the most visible reason from her bag. Racism. It was dirty and underhanded.

"Maybe she was confused. Maybe she just meant her brother."

"No, baby. He doesn't care about color. In fact, his fiancée is a beautiful, redheaded, white woman. I don't know why Max would say that."

My stomach started to knot as my chest tightened. The woman in front of me was looking at me like I was the most beautiful creature in the world. Her words were smooth and kind. No malice or trickery as she spoke to me.

Max had lied.

It wasn't a little lie either. It was the biggest of lies. She'd said it without blinking, making me believe the trash she'd spewed.

"Would you like to come in, Ruth?" I opened the door, stepping out of the way to let her pass. "Sorry. I don't mean to be rude."

She nodded, brushing my chest with her

bare shoulder as she walked into the house. If it were under different circumstances, I would've laughed, but it just made me realize how horrible the lie had been.

As she sat on the couch, adjusting the hem of her dress, I headed to the kitchen. I needed something to deal with the bullshit that would occur when Max saw her mother sitting in the living room.

"Would you like a drink?"

"No. Thank you," she replied as she gripped her knees.

"I'll be right back."

When I opened the cabinet to grab a glass, I heard, "What the..." from the living room and froze. I didn't want to make a sound and possibly miss what was about to be said.

"Max," her mother said. "Sit."

I poured myself a drink and headed back to the living room.

"This fine man," she said as I walked back in the room and glanced at me, "he said I don't like him because he's white. Can you explain this to me?" She glared at her daughter, crossing her arms with her mouth set in a firm line.

"Well, I... I..." she stuttered, glancing between the two of us. "I..."

"Drop the shit, Max. Be truthful with me. Remember, God is listening."

Not only did the woman have the mother guilt, she had thrown religion in Max's face. It wasn't unlike something my mother would do, but when it came from Ruth's mouth, it sounded direr.

Max sat on the opposite couch and bit her lip. "Mama, I didn't know what to say." Max looked down at her hands and knotted them together. "Anthony, can you let me talk to my mother alone, please?"

"No," I replied as I rested on the wall. "I'm not missing this for the world." Lifting the glass to my lips, I sipped the Crown, letting it linger in my mouth.

"Please!" Max yelled, and shot me a glare.

"He's staying," Ruth said, turning to look at me. Before she looked back toward Max, she threw me a wink.

I grinned behind the cup, feeling a bit better about how the night was unfolding. Although her arrival had tossed a wrench in my plans, I couldn't have asked for anything better.

"Mother. There are things I don't want him to know," Max said.

"It sounds like he knows plenty about you, Maxine," Ruth replied. "Stop wasting time and tell me why you said I don't like white people."

"It's complicated, Mama." Her hands unfurled and she reached up, scrubbing her fingers across her face. "I didn't want to see him. I didn't want to like him."

"You used me as an excuse. Why?"

"Because, Mama. I don't deserve him." She peered up at me through her fingers. "It's not fair."

"Child, life isn't fair. You're going to have to get over yourself and figure out what you want in life."

"I know life isn't fair. I'm the one living with this shit!" Max yelled as she jumped to her feet. "I'm the one who will never have happiness. Not you, Mama. Me!"

It felt like I had turned a movie on in the middle, having missed something important that clued me the fuck in on what they were talking about.

"Sit," Ruth commanded. "Do not raise your voice at me. My patience is hanging by a thread right now."

"I'm sorry," Max mumbled as she plopped down.

"What?" I asked, still in the dark. "I'm lost."

Max shook her head, shooting a glare at her mother. "Don't."

"Maxine," her mother said. "You need to stop lying to everyone in your life. Someday, you're going to look back and regret every minute you wasted with your foolishness."

"I'm waiting," I said, taking another drink of Crown. I gripped the glass tighter, feeling my hands begin to shake. The virtual train wreck I'd expected and taken secret joy in watching as it played out was derailing before my eyes.

"I can't." Max shook her head, placing her face in her palms.

The one phrase I had always hated to hear

her say should've been her personal motto. If I never heard the two words again in my life, I'd be a happy man.

"Bullshit," I muttered into the glass.

"Maxine, look at me," Ruth said. When Max's eyes drifted to hers, she began to speak. "Do you love this man?"

Even from across the room, I could see the tears that had collected in her eyes. "I ca—"

"Stop!" Ruth yelled, causing us to jump. "Do. You. Love. Him? It's real simple, Max. Yes or no."

She'd told me many times that she loved me. Never had she admitted it to another person. Even when we were with her friends, she'd gloss over the topic and change course.

I didn't know what I wanted her answer to be. Hearing her tell another soul that she loved me would bring me warmth and joy. The way our relationship had played out—and was in the process of crashing and burning in spectacular fashion—made me want to hear her say no. Could I leave her in the dust if she professed her feelings for me to her own mother?

"Yes," she confessed through gritted teeth as tears began to trickle down her cheeks.

My stomach dropped, filling with butterflies. Renewed hope and the warmth I had sought flooded me. Even though I wanted to stomp on her heart and show her how painful love could be, I felt happy at her confession.

"Does he love you?" Ruth asked Max like I wasn't in the room.

"Yes."

"Then I don't see what the problem is besides you and your lies."

"You know what the problem is," Max bit out as her nostrils flared.

I had had enough. I couldn't stand by and listen to the two of them bicker in code. "Can someone clue me the fuck in on what's going on here?" I growled as I pushed off the wall and headed toward Max. "Excuse my language, Ruth," I added.

"It's okay, baby. Sometimes it's the only way to emphasize what we need to say. Tell him, Max, or I will."

I looked down at Max and saw her trembling. I waited for her to speak.

"I can't," she whispered without looking at me. "I can't be with you anymore, Anthony. I love you, but it's not right."

"I think I should be the judge of what's right for me, Max. Not you. I want to hear that truth."

"No," she said. "I won't." She gave me a steely glare. Even as the tears streamed down her face, she refused to break.

"That's it? Everything I've been through with you. All the abuse I've taken from you and you won't even tell me what the fuck is going on."

She shook her head.

"I'm done, Max. I've had enough of your bullshit. Believe it or not, I do have feelings." I turned to face her mother. "I'm sorry, ma'am, but I can't either." I stalked over, grabbing my shirt from the floor as I slipped my sandals on.

She jumped to her feet and walked toward me. "Son, wait. You need to know—"

"No, I don't need to know anything. It

doesn't matter how much I love your daughter. She still shuts me out. I can't do this anymore."

Without a second thought or a backward glance, I walked out, leaving her and Ruth to talk. I'd done my part, begged enough for her to share the thing that kept her at arm's length, but she'd refused. I couldn't be her pawn in whatever wicked game she was playing.

My time with Max was over.

I stared up at the starry sky as I walked to my car. Everything came crashing down and ended in spectacular fashion.

"Fuck you, Karma!" I yelled as I watched the distant stars twinkle. "You win!"

I headed home, making a vow not to let her have another go at my heart. Max had trampled it to bits, and there was nothing left.

I'd chased her, stalked her as my prey, until she'd caved in and become my trophy.

What happened next would cause my head to spin and have me cursing the gods.

When I found something so pure and real it would be complicated and heartbreaking.

I would be swallowed up, spit out like a

mouthful of cum by a two-bit hooker looking for a fix, and left feeling numb.

It was the ultimate payback for being a cocky asshole my entire life. Karma wasn't done with me yet.

THE DAY MY BROTHER RETURNED HOME should've been a day to celebrate. When he walked in the door, I'd been texting Max and we'd been having a war of words and my mood had turned to shit. Although I wanted to join the rest of the family in welcoming him home, my mind was filled with anger toward Max.

I tried to ignore my phone, pushing her out of my mind while listening to Thomas. Seeing him sitting in my parents' house brought me a bit of solace even as my world had been turned upside down.

On his second Sunday dinner, Thomas brought his girlfriend. Again, I'd been fighting with Max. It was all we seemed to do lately. My family was too wrapped up in him and his girlfriend, Angel, to realize that I was seriously pissed off as well as depressed. I was thankful, because the last thing I wanted to do was have a long conversation about how I'd become a pansy and joined the dark side.

The only person who noticed was Thomas. Even with the overwhelming reception he'd received after being gone for months, he saw right through me. I confessed, telling him as much about the situation as I felt comfortable with.

Although I wanted to spill my secrets and aggravations to Thomas, he didn't need the hassle. He had enough to deal with at the moment to have to worry about my dumb ass.

Walking out the door on Max weeks ago had been the easy part. Living with the pain from the aftermath had become excruciating. There were times I wanted to turn my phone off. Seeing her messages every day reminded me that I couldn't touch her. Even though I wanted to ignore her words and not respond, I couldn't.

My need for any type of communication got the better of me. The one thing I wouldn't do was beg her to give me another shot. I was done with that shit. When she begged me to see her, it took everything in me to say no. She asked if we could meet and just talk, but I knew how it would end up. There would be very little talking, lots of fucking, and I'd leave most likely after she threw me out. I wouldn't do it again. I couldn't relive the last few weeks.

The pain had finally started to dull, the ache in my chest turning into a twinge every once in a while. I wouldn't do it. I couldn't afford the pain. I was too old to deal with the bullshit and life was too fucking short.

When my brother called the family together because Angel had been kidnapped, I didn't have time to think about Max. We worked together, bringing her home safely. When we arrived at Thomas's house afterward, the entire family had gathered. Each person had their loved one waiting for them, but not me. I had no one.

To say that it hurt would be an understatement. What I wouldn't have given to see Max standing there, waiting to see that I was okay. It wasn't in the cards. I'd only thought about her a couple of times in the last forty-eight hours since the insanity of Angel's abduction occurred.

But seeing everyone hugging and kissing with tears in their eyes had made me grouchier. Every feeling that had simmered beneath the surface was ready to bust free. I didn't stay and celebrate with everyone. My heart wasn't in it. I should've been elated, but Max's absence in my life made me feel like shit.

I grabbed a bottle of tequila on the way home and decided to drink myself into oblivion. I was tired and ready to make it all disappear. What better way to do it than at the bottom of a bottle?

***

Max

I was mortified and defeated.

The words I wanted to say to him were stuck on my tongue, but I couldn't say them. Even when my mother threatened me, I still couldn't. I didn't want him to know. It was my secret. It was something that only my family and my closest friends knew.

I didn't want him to look at me differently. I wouldn't be able to survive it. When he walked out the door yet again, I held back the anguish I felt as my insides were shattering.

"What is wrong with you, Max?" My mother shook her head as she climbed to her feet. "That man seems to really like you, and you're being selfish."

"Mother," I snapped as I jumped to my feet. "If I were selfish, I'd let him be mine. I'm saving him from me. He can't fall in love with me. He just can't." I paced the tiny area between the coffee table and couch. He couldn't. I wouldn't allow it.

"He already does, child."

"Ma, what he says and does are two different things."

"I can tell by the way he lit up when you walked in the room. I haven't heard a man fight so hard for the love of a woman. Can't you see how he feels about you?"

I stopped dead in my tracks. "I do! That's why I pushed him away, Mama. It's not fair for him. It's not right of me to love him." I began to pace again.

She gripped my arms, stopping me as she shook me. "Baby, you deserve love as much as everybody else. If you don't get your head out of your ass, you're going to spend the rest of your life alone."

"I have you, my family, and friends. I don't need anyone else."

"Lies. I won't be here forever, Max. Your friends and family have their own loved ones. We all need somebody in life. Don't push away a man that's willing to fight for you."

"Mama—"

She held up her hand. "I don't want to hear it. Go tell that man that you love him and make him understand why you've been acting like a fool."

"I can't," I whispered as my eyes flooded with tears.

"You will. If you don't, Max, I'll find that boy and tell him exactly what's going on."

"You wouldn't!" I yelled as I closed my eyes.

One thing I know about my mother is that she doesn't speak hollow words.

"I will. Try me, child. Get yourself together and go beg for his forgiveness."

There wasn't a point in arguing with her. I knew she'd tell him if I didn't. No matter how hard it would be to tell him my secret, it had to come from my mouth. I needed to look into his eyes when the realization and enormity of it sank in.

11

HOPELESS

LOUD POUNDING ON THE DOOR WOKE ME from my sleep. After half a bottle of tequila, I'd crawled in bed and nodded off watching *Dual Survival.*

I grabbed my pillow, smashing my face into the material. If I ignored the door, maybe they'd go away. As I sighed and didn't hear a second knock, I spread out and started to drift back to sleep.

Another knock had my eyes flying open. This time, the pounding was more forceful, and it made my heart jump. I looked at the clock and wondered who in the fuck would be pounding on my damn door after midnight.

Anything was possible at this point, but most likely, it was one of my brothers popping by with some bullshit. Without looking at my phone, I grabbed a pair of shorts and put them on as I walked down the steps.

The pounding continued, growing louder the closer I moved toward the door.

Finally, I swung it open and yelled, "What?"

Max stood before me with her face covered in tears and her fist in midair. "Anthony," she said.

I crossed my arms over my chest and glared at her. The tequila and the banging on the door had started to give me a headache. Seeing her on my doorstep made my blood whoosh through my veins so fast that my head began to pound harder than her fists had been hitting the door.

"What, Max?" I replied in a scathing voice. "I don't have time for your shit, and I sure as fuck don't need any pussy."

"Oh," she replied, and looked over my shoulder.

"No one is here. I just refuse to let you stomp all over me again. I will not be that man. I'm not weak, Max. I don't need you in my life."

"Anthony, please let me talk." She looked beautiful with her hair shining in the moonlight and taking on a bluish tone in the darkness.

I held my hand out. "There's nothing you can say to me. We want different things in life. I asked for a chance to get to know you so I wouldn't have a regret. I've changed my fucking mind. I regret the day I met you. I'm through. Go home. There's nothing or no one here for you."

Some of it I meant. There was nothing more I wanted to do than hold her and feel her body on mine. I couldn't give in. Standing my ground would be the only way she and I could ever have a future together.

"I don't care how many tears you've cried. Save them for someone who means something to you."

"Stop!" she yelled as tears streamed down her face. "I'm sick, Anthony. Sick! My father died and his condition was genetic." The sob that broke free caused her entire body to tremble.

Every ounce of air inside my lungs had left me in one quick exhale. I stood there not believing what she'd said. Max had lied before, so this had to be another one of her tales.

"What?"

"You heard me," she cried as her shoulders sagged. "I'll never have a future. You need to find someone else to give you a happy life and a big family. I'm not that girl. I can never be her. No matter how badly I want it, I just can't be." She looked at the ground, breaking eye contact.

The knots that had formed in my stomach had changed, turning into a solid punch in the gut. There wasn't a blow I'd taken from my brothers that had caused as much pain as her words had. Sick. She was sick. The strong woman standing before me had something that affected her and made her feel unworthy.

I lifted her chin, needing to look into her dark eyes and understand the depths of her pain. "Max," I whispered. "I don't understand. You don't seem sick."

Her lip trembled as she spoke. "I'm not sick now, but I will be. I know my fate. I never have to wonder what I'll be like in my old age, Anthony. I know that I'll be wheelchair-bound and unable to live on my own, just like my father."

It couldn't be.

Max was vibrant, full of life, and too fierce to let anything stop her. She couldn't resign herself to such a fate. I wouldn't allow her to. All the anger I had been holding inside had vanished and was replaced by a worry so profound that I wanted to move heaven and earth to make her existence different.

"Max, we can go see the best doctors in the world. I have money. I'll help you find a way to change your fate." I wouldn't accept the word of a single doctor.

"It's hopeless, Anthony," she replied as the tears fell onto my fingertips. "I've been to the top doctors in the country. There's no cure. No treatment. I had accepted my future until I met you." She blew out a shaky breath and continued, "Meeting you made me curse the gods and question my faith, Anthony."

"I didn't do anything to you, but love you."

"I tried to push you away," she whispered as her bottom lip quivered. "You wouldn't let me. You chased me, making me give in. God, how I want to change everything, Anthony, but I can't. I don't want the future I've been dealt. I had accepted it, but you fucked everything up."

"Is that why you keep getting rid of me?" It all started to click.

"Yes!" she wailed, and closed her eyes.

I reached out. "Come on, Kitty Cat. Come inside so we can talk."

She didn't speak as she let me guide her inside.

I sat down and pulled her into my lap. "Why would you do that, Max? Push me away."

As she wiped her cheeks, she said, "I decided years ago, when I saw my father wither away, that I wouldn't do that to another person. I avoided relationships, promising to never have to subject someone to that kind of life. I want you, Anthony. I crave you. Being with you brings me so much happiness."

"Then why not let me make the decision for

myself?" I asked. One thing I'd never done well with was people making decisions for me.

"Because you wouldn't make a clear decision. You don't know what you're dealing with." She laid her head on my shoulder as I pulled her closer.

"I always think clearly, Max. It's my decision to make if I want to love you, not yours."

"But—"

I put my finger over her lips. "Max, you've made my head spin since the day I met you. People would think I'm fucking nuts for always going back for more. There was something that drew me to you at the bar that night. That spark between us had me wanting more. Nothing has changed. I need to know if that's the only reason you kept trying to push me away."

"Yes," she replied as she peered up at me. I moved my fingers, giving her a chance to speak. "I was having a battle with myself. I kept telling myself to give us a shot and that maybe you could handle my illness when I was older. That's if we stayed together, of course," she added, and tried to crack a smile, but it was forced. "Then doubt would creep in and I'd try to be as mean as possible to get rid of you."

"You did a good job." I snickered as I brushed the hair away from her face.

"Watching my father disintegrate before my eyes changed me. I look healthy now, but I know what the disease can do to a person."

"Tell me what happens." I played with her hair between my fingertips and listened.

"It affects a person's ability to walk, making them unsteady and weak. It also alters their ability to speak. I'll sound like I'm drunk even when I'm not. My hands will have a hard time grasping objects and I will be robbed of my ability to write. My coordination will be off. I may want to walk to the left but my mind won't get the signal and may go right."

I took in everything she had to say as she continued laying out the severity of the condition and how she'd be changed physically. I knew I had to learn everything I could about it as soon as possible.

"Does it affect your mind?"

"No, I'll still be the same person on the inside."

"You'll still be the same person on the outside too, Max."

"Not really, Anthony. I'll be a shell of my former self."

"Max," I said as I turned her in my lap to face me, "I don't care what your future may be like. I've never loved a woman before I met you. Never. I don't care if we have five years or fifty, I wanted all of them, every second you have on this planet, to be spent with me. I'm a selfish prick, remember? I can't let you push me away again. I won't let you be alone. You've caused enough pain in my life by trying to get rid of me. I won't allow you to do it again."

"Anthony, you don't know what you're saying. You don't want a woman confined to a wheelchair. It's so much more than that. Everything about me will be different. There won't be a thing in my life that won't be a struggle. Someday, I'll need constant care. Do you really want to live like that? With the knowledge that you'll have to take care of me." Her eyes bored into me as they questioned the depths of my love.

I could understand her worry. We both knew I had been an asshole. Love wasn't something I'd wanted or asked for in my life, but it had fallen in my lap.

"I know you think I'm not man enough to love you. I was an asshole. The most selfish prick to grace the planet, but you changed me. Your love has ruined me. I'm not the same man I was when I bought you that drink. Your love seeped into my veins and altered my world forever. If I had to pick between a life without you and one with you, even in a wheelchair, I'd pick you every time, Max. Every time I'd want you in my life."

I paused, feeling my eyes begin to water. This wasn't how I wanted my love to be. I didn't want this to be true.

"No one has made me as happy and pissed off as you have. I've never felt a spark when I touched anyone. It's only you."

"You don't know what you're saying," she said, shaking her head in my hands.

"I fucking do. The last few times you threw me out, I was gutted. Remember what I told you when I asked you to give us a chance?"

She nodded, remaining quiet.

"I said I never wanted to live wondering what could've been. I don't want to have any regrets. I'm in too deep, baby. If I run away from you now, I know I'll be alone for the rest of my life. No one will ever fill my heart the way you have. No one could love me the way you do, both good and bad. When I'm with you, everything in the world seems right. I can't let you push me away. It's not happening."

"Anthony," she pleaded as she touched my hand.

"No, Max. I won't let you ruin our chance at happiness. You've been calling all the shots, and that shit's about to change," I said as I brushed a tear off her cheek.

"But—"

"No. I'm not leaving your side. We're going to figure this out together. Medicine changes every day. They could find a cure before you start experiencing symptoms. Never give up hope. The one thing I now believe is to never give up hope."

"I'm scared to let myself be happy," she whispered.

"Why?"

"Because it'll make it more painful when I start getting sick, Anthony. I'll know everything I'll miss out on once I'm unable to walk." Tears streamed down her face, dropping on my shirt.

"Like what?"

"Like dancing with you."

"Max, I can hold you in my arms and dance. I have the strength for the both of us."

"I won't be able to make love to you the way I do now."

"How many years are we talking about before you start getting sick?"

"I don't know. It could be tomorrow, next week, or in twenty years!"

"If I can still get it up when I'm sixty, we'll figure something out." I laughed.

"Don't be silly." She shook her head, but a tiny smile crawled across her face.

"I'm not. Let's be honest about our future. I

can do it all night now, but in twenty years, who knows. I may not even live that long, Max. Most people don't know their future and wander through life holding on to any happiness they can grasp. You think you know what your future will be, but we could both die tomorrow. Why not hold on to the happiness we've found and face whatever comes next together?" I sounded so grown up that I almost shocked myself. I felt like I was channeling the words of wisdom my mother would say, but for once, I was okay with it.

"Maybe you're right."

"I am. Let's take it day by day. Can we agree on that?" I asked. "If I'm being an asshole, then call me out, but never try to get rid of me because you're scared. When it becomes overwhelming, I'll be there for you."

"I don't deserve you," she whispered.

"I know." I laughed and watched her face break out into the most beautiful, heart-stopping smile.

"You're an asshole."

"I know that too, but that's why you like me."

She rolled her eyes and laughed.

"So, your family doesn't hate me?" I had to bring it up. It was something that needed to be discussed.

"No," she confessed, and grimaced.

"It was wrong of you to use the color of our skin to keep us apart."

"I know. It's the only thing I could think of."

"That was a huge lie, Kitty Cat. A hurtful untruth."

"I know. I'm sorry."

"If your mother hadn't shown up and spilled the truth, would you have ever told me about being sick?"

"I don't know." She glanced down and exhaled. "I'd like to think that I would. I wanted to tell you, but I just couldn't bring myself to."

I raised her face and stared at her, taking in her beauty. "No more lies, Max. We won't survive this if you do."

"Okay, Anthony. I promise."

The one thing I needed was to feel connected to her. Gripping her hair in my hands, I lost myself in her kiss.

"I need to make love to you," I murmured on her lips.

"Yes," she panted.

I lifted her, carrying her to my bedroom without breaking the passionate kiss. Everything we felt but didn't say poured out through our lips as we silently conveyed the emotion of the moment.

Max and I were back, and nothing would tear us apart.

Karma could fuck off.

12

CRYSTAL BALL

"WHAT ARE YOU SO DAMN HAPPY ABOUT?" Mike asked from across the table as I stole a glance at my cell phone.

"I'm not happy. I'm always like this."

I knew that it was bullshit. I usually was a cranky fucker. Typically, I had a headache or not enough sleep and my siblings would make me crazy. At the shop, I could busy myself with something to keep my mind occupied, but sitting at my parents' made it impossible to ignore them.

Max had softened since she'd told me about her illness, and things were smoother. She hadn't thrown me out, either. We talked whenever we had a chance and texted throughout the day. We took turns sleeping at the other's house at least every couple of days. When Sunday had finally arrived, I'd begged her to come to my family's house for dinner, but she'd said that she couldn't make it.

"You're happy. You keep smiling every time you look in your lap. Find something down there finally?"

"Shut up, Mikey." I glared at him, but I didn't feel the anger behind the look. Things were too good right now to be pissed off about anything.

"Get the shit straightened out with the girl?" Thomas asked as he grabbed a piece of garlic bread.

"I think so," I replied, hoping that everyone had been too busy eating to hear what he'd asked.

"A girl?" Ma asked as she stopped eating.

There went the hope that no one had heard. Ma had girlfriend radar, with her overeagerness to be a grandmother many times over. Thanks to

Thomas, I was now on it after having remained free and clear for years.

Even though I wanted to lie to Ma, I couldn't. Plus, she'd see through any fib I told. "Yeah," I answered as I placed a forkful of eggplant parmigiana in my mouth. As I chewed, I saw everyone looking at each other before their eyes fell on me. "What?" I asked with a garbled voice.

My mother corrected her previous question. "As in a girlfriend?"

There was no reason to hold back. Soon, I wanted to bring her to dinner, and it would be better if the shit hit the proverbial fan now instead of in front of her.

I sipped my water, washing down the food in my mouth and making them wait for my answer. They stared at me as they patiently waited for my reply.

"Yes, she's my girlfriend."

"So, you're not gay?" Ma asked as her mouth hung open and the entire table erupted into laughter.

"What?" I replied.

Honestly, I could see her point. I was the only one in the family who'd never had a significant other, and I sure as hell never talked in front of my parents about any of the women I banged.

"I mean, it's okay if you are, sweetie. I'll still love you. Don't be ashamed of who you are," Ma said as she gave me a very serious look. It was the type of look she'd used when we had been kids and tried to lie. She'd lull us into a sense of security to get us to confess.

"Ma, I am not gay." I shook my head, feeling my face turn red.

"If you say so, honey." Ma smiled at me and the laughter grew louder.

"I'm happy everyone is getting a kick out of this," I said as I stabbed at my eggplant.

Ma wiped her lips, laying the napkin back in her lap before she looked at me. "Anthony, you're the only one who hasn't brought someone home. As the oldest, I thought you'd be married with children by now. Hell, I've never, ever heard you talk about a girl."

"Listen, just because I don't kiss and tell doesn't mean I haven't had women."

"Lord has he," Izzy interjected before starting to laugh again.

"Izzy," I said, shooting a "shut the fuck up" glare in her direction. "Ma, I've just never met anyone who was worthy of meeting the family."

"That's silly," Ma replied as she started to play with the food on her plate.

"I'm not gay, I've had women, and I have a girlfriend. Are we clear? I just want to make sure everyone has their details correct."

"Bro, chill out," Joe said.

"I am, Joe. Cool as a cucumber." I placed a forkful of food in my mouth because I knew another question was coming. Nothing in this family was quick or easy.

"Same girl you mentioned before?" Izzy asked as she drew her lips into her mouth, trying to stop her laughter.

I nodded, unable to talk with so much food in my mouth.

"Things change since the last time we talked?" Thomas asked as he stared at me.

Between bites, I said, "Yeah."

"Tell us about her, Anthony. Stop holding out on me," Ma demanded.

"For you, Ma, anything. I met her a while ago, but we were just friends."

"With benefits," Mike mumbled.

I scowled at him before I began to speak again. "It took us a while to get on the same page. She wasn't too keen on the idea of dating. I'm hoping to bring her with me next weekend."

"Thank would be lovely, Anthony. Who is she?" Ma asked as she set her fork down, giving me her full attention.

"I'm sure there are better things to talk about. I can tell you later, Ma."

"No." Izzy shook her head and waved her hand over the table. "We all want to hear this, Mr. I Hate Everything About Relationships. Do tell."

I mouthed the word "traitor" at Izzy before turning my attention to Ma. "Her name is Maxine, but I call her Max. She's a stylist or something like that. Has a little shop down in Tampa."

"I love her already," Izzy said, tilting her head.

"She's black," I blurted out like it mattered, even though I knew it didn't.

"And?" Pop asked nonchalantly as if I'd divulged a secret that weren't so secret or important.

"Just throwing it out there," I replied as I sucked in air. I had known they wouldn't give a shit, but I wanted the information out there from the get-go.

"I don't care if she's blue," Ma said. "Tell me more about her. Why haven't you brought her over sooner?"

"Did you think we'd care about the color of her skin, son?" Pop asked with a raised eyebrow.

Where should I even begin in my explanation? "No, no. I knew you wouldn't care. It's complicated," I replied, because it was the truth.

Ma crossed her arms and tilted her head as her eyes bored into me. "All relationships are. Who at this table had an easy relationship?"

"Joe and Suzy," I offered, because they'd had that insta-love thing.

"Hell no," Joe interrupted.

"Anthony," Suzy said as she stopped eating for a moment. She must've had something important to say, because Suzy hadn't stopped eating since she'd become pregnant. "Your brother and I didn't have an easy love. Mostly because I was an idiot. But it wasn't easy. He was just persistent." She giggled, glancing at Joe and winking.

I slouched back in my chair, trying to remember what happened back then. It felt like ages ago, even though not even a couple of years had passed.

"I guess," I said as I shrugged.

"I'm still waiting to hear why you haven't brought her here for dinner," Ma said.

"We weren't dating a couple of weeks ago. She didn't want a boyfriend and she sure as hell didn't want me."

"Ah, another one like you," Mike mumbled.

"Yes, another one like me, but for different reasons. I just didn't want to be led by the balls like everyone at the table." I laughed, slapping the table. No one else was laughing with me.

"You know what I mean," I added, feeling a little embarrassed.

"So now your balls are in the hands of another," Izzy said with a satisfied look on her face.

"Yes." I sighed, knowing I'd succumbed and become one of the sappy fuckers who'd do anything for the woman they loved.

"Why wouldn't she want to date you? You're such a handsome man with a kind heart," Ma said as she frowned.

"Ma, I'm not. I mean, I am a handsome devil, but kind? Most women would never use that word to describe me." I smiled at her. "Max had reasons to not want to be in a relationship. Plus, she said I was an asshole."

"Oh, I really like her," Izzy muttered with the fork of pasta resting on her lips.

"She called you that?" Ma asked.

I nodded but kept the smile plastered to my face. "I am, though. I mean, I was. I have a reputation that follows me."

I wasn't ashamed of it. It cut down on the bullshit. I didn't have to go into a long spiel about not wanting a relationship. Women knew and I never promised more.

"I thought I raised you better than that," Ma added with a tone of judgment.

"Ma, I didn't treat the women badly. I gave them what they wanted and took what I needed. I never promised more."

"Dirty bird," Pop chimed in, with a small laugh.

Ma glanced at him and shot him a warning glance. "Sal."

"What? There's no reason for the boy to be tied down, Mar."

Ma ignored him and turned her attention back to me. "Why didn't Max want to be in a relationship? Is she like your sister?"

"What the hell is that supposed to mean?" Izzy asked as she dropped her fork onto her plate with a loud clatter.

"You know." Ma grinned as she looked over at Izzy. "Difficult."

"I'm not difficult," Izzy said before her mouth hung open.

James laughed first, followed by everyone else at the table.

"I just didn't want to be tied down and I still don't, but James has made it hard to say no," she grumbled.

"Izzy, we don't want to hear about your sex life," Suzy teased.

Izzy's face turned red as she closed her eyes and dragged in a breath. "Shut it, Suzy. Less talking, more eating."

"She has her own reasons, Ma," I said.

"You're being cagey, son," Pop interjected. My old man never said much, but when he did, it was usually to call one of us out on our bullshit.

"Pop, she has some personal issues that stopped her." I rubbed my face and debated telling the family about her illness.

"Ex-husband?" Mia asked, finally entering the conversation.

"No. Health issues," I blurted out.

I knew it was going to turn into twenty questions and I'd eventually tell them just to shut them up. My family was notorious for their nosiness. I figured I didn't need to hold out.

"Oh no. What's wrong?" Mia asked as her doctor side kicked in.

I glanced down at my mother as she pitched forward, listening intently.

"Her father was sick, but he's now passed. It's a genetic condition called ataxia. So the short story is that she didn't want a relationship because she didn't want to burden someone in the future."

Mia stared at me for a moment with her eyebrows kitted together. "Wow. That's a rare condition, Anthony."

"You know about it?" I asked, hoping she could shine some light on the topic.

"Yeah, a little bit. I know the basic neurology, but it's so rare that not much is learned about it unless you study neurology as your specialty."

"Tell us about it," Ma said to Mia, ignoring her food.

I'd spent some time over the last week researching ataxia online. I spent hours on the

Ataxia.org website reading about the condition and the stories of people affected.

Mia stated the same information I'd found on the website, but explained it in more detail. She said that, often, people appear to be drunk when they aren't, presenting the same symptoms of unbalanced walking and slurred speech.

"Is there a treatment?" Ma asked behind her hand.

Halfway through Mia's explanation, my mother had covered her mouth to hide her emotion. Even though she didn't know Max, her heart was breaking. It was probably out of sadness for me, but she had a tender heart. Once she met Max, she'd be shattered.

Mia shook her head and frowned. "No, Ma. There isn't. No treatment and no cure."

"What the fuck?" Mike asked before he sighed. "With all the advances in medicine, there's still nothing, baby?"

"No. It's so rare that little money is spent on funding the research. There is a research clinic at USF in Tampa that has done some amazing work. But no breakthroughs yet."

"So, it's genetic?" Pop asked. Even though he looked impartial, I knew he fed off my mother's emotion.

My parents were major donors at Mia's clinic. They'd always loved to help the community, especially when it pertained to health.

"It can be. Not all types of ataxia are genetic. Even when it is, the person only has a fifty percent chance of having the defective gene," Mia answered, giving me a weak smile. "Has she been tested?"

I chewed the inside of my mouth. "I honestly don't know, Mia." I tried to recall our conversations about ataxia and if she'd said that she had been or not, but I was drawing a blank.

"If she hasn't, she needs to be. There's a fifty percent chance she doesn't have the gene that causes ataxia."

"Well, shit," I whispered as I grabbed my phone.

"Does it only affect adults?" Joe asked.

Mia continued to answer questions about the condition as I texted Max, needing to find out if she'd been tested.

Me: Hey!
Max: Hey yourself.
Me: Question for you.
Max: Shoot.
Me: Have you been tested to see if you have the gene?

I tapped my foot, feeling nervous as I waited for her answer. I tried to focus on Mia as she spoke, but my attention kept reverting to my phone. She didn't answer immediately, and the waiting was killing me.

Finally, she replied.

Max: No.

At that point, I stared at the phone, totally confused. With the way she'd had her fate figured out and she was all doom and gloom, I would've bet money on the fact that she had been tested.

Me: Why not? Maybe you don't have it.
Max: I know it's in me.

I sat there dumbfounded and confused as hell. Mia had said that a person only had a fifty percent chance of carrying it. At the track or in Vegas, those aren't great odds, but when dealing with sickness, there was a decent chance she didn't have it.

Me: You need to be tested, Max.

Max: I don't need to spend $5000 on a genetic test when I already know the answer.

I stared at my phone and wanted to rip my hair out. I held my head in my hand and rubbed my forehead. Her thinking was off. There was no price tag that could be placed on knowledge. It was a steep price to pay, but I'd gladly fork over the money for peace of mind. If I were in her shoes, I'd sell everything I owned to find out the truth.

Me: You only have a 25% chance of carrying the gene, Max.

Max: How about if I tell you that you have a 25% chance of living. Sound like good odds?

Me: Don't be unreasonable. There's a 75% chance that you're going to have a long, healthy future.

Max: Meh. I have it. There is no doubt in my mind.

I took a laugh and sighed. Women were impossible creatures. They liked to say that men were hardheaded, but I'd never met a reasonable woman. Once they made their mind up about something, it would be easier to become President of the United States than to get them to change their mind.

Me: We aren't done talking about this. I'll be over later.

"What's wrong, baby?" Ma asked across the table.

I looked up at her and blew out a puff of air. "Max has never been tested. She's being a hardheaded woman like the rest of you and claims she doesn't need a test to tell her what she already knows."

Mia's head jerked in my direction. "What? She's never been tested? You need to get her to do it, Anthony."

"I know, Mia," I said. "That's easier said than done."

"I wonder why she's so sure she has it." Mia rubbed her chin as her eyes shifted.

"I don't know. Who knows what a woman is thinking. Ever." I rubbed my forehead as I felt a pressure start to build. I could feel the fight before it happened.

Max would throw a fit, but I wasn't dropping the topic. She'd be tested and we'd know for sure what her future would be. If we were going to be a couple, there was no way in hell I'd let her "feeling" dictate our life.

13

CONFRONTATION

Max had told me not to come.

I'd do everything in my power to get her to agree to take the test. It didn't matter if it showed that she carried the gene. At least we'd know for certain. But if it cleared her of a fate like her father, it opened up a world of possibilities for both of us.

I was nervous as I walked up her sidewalk. I knocked on the door and could feel the sweat that had collected on my palms. My stomach flipped, both from excitement and fear. I was scared as hell of the fight that was about to happen. Max wouldn't make it easy, but I'd spent my entire life dealing with Gallo women. They could teach a course on standing your ground and getting your way.

I knocked again. I could hear music inside, but it didn't sound loud enough to muffle the sound of a knock.

"Max!" I yelled into the door. "I'm not leaving until you open the door!" I pounded on the door this time and then followed it with two rings of the doorbell. "Max! I'll bust the door down if you don't open the damn thing up."

Just as I stopped, the door flew open. Max stood there in a pair of booty shorts and a black tank top. I wanted to reach out and rip her clothes off, but I was here for more important things.

"Don't you get the hint?"

"Listen, woman. We're going to have this talk."

"There's nothing to talk about, Anthony."

"You need to let me say my piece and then you can tell me to fuck off like you used to do."

She sighed before a small smirk spread

across her face and disappeared. "I just have to listen to you?"

"I'd prefer you to do as I say, but listening will work for now." I smiled, knowing I'd find a way to get her to see the light.

Since she'd confessed, she'd become a different woman. The hardass girl I'd met in the bar had melted away. When she'd opened the door, pissed-off Max had returned.

"I'll listen, but I'm not promising anything." She opened the door more and waited for me.

As she closed it, I grabbed her and pulled her to my body. I'd missed her. We'd seen each other yesterday, but the time apart had moved slowly. Plus, I wanted her to feel my touch and remember the spark we'd had before she'd shut me out. That sizzle was what made us different.

I kissed her deeply as I ran my hands over her back. Her smell had intoxicated me from the moment I'd met her, and even now, it had that effect on me. I breathed her in, getting lost in her scent and the softness of her skin.

"Hey," I murmured as I stared at her lips.

"Hi," she mumbled before pulling her lips

into her mouth and running her tongue along them.

I grabbed her hand, bringing her to the couch with me. I wouldn't let her sit across the room. I needed closeness, and more importantly, she needed to feel our connection.

I wanted to drag her onto my lap, but instead, I let her sit and planted myself beside her. I needed to look into her eyes and for her to see my face. Grasping her hands in mine, I started to talk. "I know you said you don't need the test to know you have ataxia, but what if maybe, just maybe, you're wrong?" I asked, keeping my voice calm and level.

"Anthony." She sighed like we'd gone over this a million times. "I don't need a test to know what I have brewing inside my body. I can feel it. Every time I trip or drop something, I know it's just the beginning."

"Max, that's ridiculous." I regretted the words as soon as they'd left my lips. "I didn't mean that."

"Yes, you did," she said as she closed her eyes and inhaled.

"Look at me," I said as I squeezed her hands. As soon as she opened them, I spoke. "Some people are just clumsy. You can't base your entire future on an assumption."

"I can."

"For the love of all that is holy," I muttered through gritted teeth. Time to change tactics. "Do you have feelings for me?"

She blinked a couple of times but maintained eye contact. "Yes," she said on a drawn-out breath.

"If I walked out the door right now and never came back, would you be upset?" I didn't know exactly where I was going with this conversation.

"I don't want to admit it, Anthony, but I'd be devastated." She looked down at our hands and frowned.

"Really?" Dumb thing to say, but *devastated* wasn't the word I'd expected to hear. Yeah, I knew she'd be sad, but devastated, not at all.

"Yes," she replied, bringing her eyes to mine.

"What about the other times you threw me out? You didn't care then?"

"I was upset, but I did everything in my power for you not to want me. I had to push you away. Now, you know everything and I can't deny I have feelings for you."

"Like ya love me?" I asked, jutting my chin out.

"I lo—"

"Don't say it. Not yet," I blurted.

"Why? I've admitted it in front of my mother." she whispered as her forehead crinkled.

"If you're going to say those words again to me, you have to admit you're willing to give something of yourself that I don't think you're ready to do just yet."

"I've told you everything, Anthony. I've given more to you than I have to most people in this world."

"Max, you immediately shut me down when I said I wanted you to be tested."

"But—"

"No buts. You did. If you 'know' you have the gene, what would it hurt to get the test?"

She sighed and blew out a breath, puffing

out her cheeks. "Can't you just believe that I already know?"

"I can't." I threw the line she'd muttered to me more times than I could count in her face, and the corner of her eye twitched. "I won't accept it until you have the test."

"Jesus," she mumbled, and rolled her eyes.

"You've lived your life for too long based on the assumption that you're going to have the same future as your father. What if you don't have it? Imagine how different life could be."

"I don't know. The idea of getting the test is scary."

She confused me. How could a test be scary when she was adamant that she had the gene necessary to cause ataxia?

"Why?"

"Because maybe..." She paused, closing her dark brown eyes for a moment as she bit her top lip. "There's a small part of me that still holds on to the hope that I'm not doomed. Maybe I won't be in a wheelchair. If I have the test and they say I have it, then there's no hope."

My confusion grew deeper. Women. How

could she think knowing would be worse?

"Max, knowing gives you power. If they say you don't have it, then you can live life without the giant ticking time bomb hanging over your head. If you do have it, then we can plan for the future and live every day like it may be our last."

"Why do you have to make so much sense?" she asked with a small smile on her face.

"'Cause I'm a man. We're more logical and less emotional."

She shook her head and her mouth grew slack. "You did not just say that," she whispered.

"I did, and I stand behind that statement." I brought her hand to my mouth and brushed the delicate flesh with my lips.

"Anthony, I still stand behind the statement I made the first night. You are an asshole." She laughed, leaning forward and planting a kiss on my lips.

"As long as I'm your asshole," I murmured into her mouth.

"Mm, you are." Her hands slid up my arms as the kiss deepened.

"Not throwing me out again?" I asked with

our mouths still attached.

"Nope. You owe me big for agreeing to have the test done. I expect payment tonight," she replied, raking her fingernails across my scalp.

I felt a tingle down my back as her fingernails tickled my neck. Tonight, I'd give her a performance worthy of a standing ovation. Something that would make her dream of more, want it so badly that she'd get the test done to keep me.

I'd be lying if I said that what we had was all based on sex. It wasn't. The sex was amazing—some of the best I'd ever had. The thing that brought me to her and kept me coming back for more was her attitude—which was sometimes shitty, but then so was mine—and the tiny sparks of electricity when we touched.

No one in my life had caused my body to come alive from a single caress. The moment I'd kissed her in the bar with my cocky-ass "I know you want me" attitude, I had known I was doomed. When my lips had tingled, feeling her long after I'd left, I had known I'd be lost to her forever.

I moved away and gripped the back of my shirt, pulling it off my body. She did the same and removed her tank top. As the cool air of the room glided over her nipples, they stiffened. Her body was amazing, soft, and begging to be touched.

"Lie back," I said as I stood up, unbuttoned my jeans, and wiggled them down my legs.

"Just jumping right in, are ya?"

"Nope. The jeans were killin' my cock, babe. Shit this big can't be contained when it's hard for you." I smiled. Then I tipped over, grabbed her shorts, and pulled them down her legs. "I plan to eat your pussy until I get lockjaw or you beg me to stop. I just wanted to get comfortable for the feast."

"I want to get lost in you tonight. Make me forget everything in the world except your touch." She relaxed into the couch and closed her eyes as I nestled between her legs.

I placed my hands on her thighs, caressing her skin with my palms as I glided them back and forth. Soft wisps of hairs rose underneath my touch as her skin became dotted with goose bumps. Her lips trembled as she pulled the bottom into her mouth and bit down on the tender flesh.

"Anthony," she whispered.

When my hands drifted down her legs, I clutched them behind her knees. Unable to wait any longer to taste her, I pulled her legs apart and brought her body closer to my face. Leaning forward, I planted my lips on the soft skin above her knee. Skimming across her flesh, I peppered the surface of her body with kisses. I had become consumed by her scent and riveted by the feel of her.

As I followed an invisible path up her legs to her inner thigh, her body shuddered in my hands. She sucked in a breath, causing her breasts to jut out as her back arched. I could smell her arousal—the sweet smell of want I'd missed when we had been apart. It intoxicated me more than any liquor I'd ever absorbed.

Hovering over her pussy, I brushed the soft black tendrils of hair that dotted her flesh with my nose. Nothing else dominated my thoughts more than devouring her and lavishing in the taste of her. Then I captured her wetness on my tongue as I licked her pussy.

I pulled her forward, using my hands behind her knees to gain better access. I wanted to bury my face in her pussy and make the world disappear. She yelped as I got carried away by the moment and drank of her taste.

It wasn't that I only wanted to bring her orgasm after orgasm, she needed to remember me long after I'd been with her, staking my claim. Even if she hadn't said that I owned her, I knew I did, and so did she. The funny thing was she owned me too, but even scarier was that she held my future in her hands.

As I lapped at her flesh, she held on to the cushion, trying to brace herself for the orgasm that was simmering underneath the surface. Using my favorite move, I increased the suction and brought her deeper into my mouth. Feeling her clit swell on my tongue drove me forward. Her breathing grew shallow and ragged as I used the tip of my tongue to play her body like a musical instrument.

"Yes!" she yelled as I tapped her clit with

more vigor.

I hummed my approval, changing the sensation of my lips on her flesh.

"Fuck," she moaned, sliding her hands into my hair and holding my face to her pussy.

She didn't have to do that. I wasn't going anywhere. I'd have lived between her legs if I could. There was no place in the world I'd rather spend my time. No longer was my favorite thing in the world being on stage. It was now worshipping the softness and sweetness of Max's beautiful cunt.

Just as her legs started to quiver, I removed my lips from her body. She gasped, pushing her body into my face.

"Promise me, Max." I gripped her legs roughly. Even though she had said that she would take the test, I didn't trust her to follow through. Promises weren't something either of us had a lot of experience with keeping.

"N-n-now?" she stuttered as her chest heaved.

"Now," I demanded before I swept my tongue across her swollen clit.

She twitched, ready to burst, and needed more friction. I wouldn't give it to her until she said what I wanted to hear. When she didn't answer right away, I nipped her lip to make her focus.

With glazed eyes, she stared at me as if she were trying to focus. "Yes. Yes!" She gripped my hair, pulling my face forward. "Anything you want."

Her answer was good enough for now. I wouldn't let her forget or go back on her word, but I'd use every opportunity to remind her of the promise she'd made me. I sucked her into my mouth, spreading her legs wider, and waited for her body to shake in my hands. She started to writhe on the couch, chasing the orgasm as she mashed her pussy into my face.

Opening my eyes, I watched as she came apart in my arms, a scream sounding from behind her closed mouth. It erupted in her throat and grew to the point that it had to break free. As her mouth fell open, the sound became almost operatic in nature. It was the most beautiful melody I'd ever heard.

When her hands softened on my scalp, her body grew lax into the cushions. I didn't waste a moment as I latched on harder, ready to bring her the next orgasm. I wasn't about waiting. We'd done that enough over the last however many weeks she'd had my dick in a vise.

"I need time," she pleaded as I started to assault her most sensitive area.

I shook my head, not releasing her from my mouth as I drove forward.

"No. Gah," she said as she pushed my head down. "Oh."

Needing to feel her as she came again, I rubbed two fingers on the outside of her before pushing them inside. As I stretched her slightly, she whimpered from the intrusion and I increased the suction of my lips.

Her pussy contracted, sucking my fingers deeper inside. Using a rocking motion, I massaged her G-spot as I grazed her clit with my teeth and flicked it with my tongue. She pushed me away, trying to get out of reach from the onslaught of sensations my touch was causing. Ignoring her, I buried my face deeper and held her in place with my one hand still planted behind her knee. I ate like a starved man until she was writhing on the couch, screaming my name.

As she lay there breathing heavily, her body shook from the aftershocks. Her pussy pulsed as I continued to rock my fingers inside her.

"No more," she begged. "Please. I need to catch my breath." She grabbed her chest. Her skin had grown damp from exhaustion and glowed in the soft light of the tableside lamp.

I didn't have enough. I wasn't done. No matter what she thought, I was in charge now. No longer would I let her lead me by the balls and rule the relationship. I'd use the one weapon I had that I knew worked on Max.

Sex.

Bringing my mouth down on her again, I gave her no rest. I locked my grip behind her knee and pushed my face forward, leaving no space between us.

"I hate you," she whimpered as she tried to use her feet on my thighs to move away. "It feels so good."

I kept to my plan, devouring her pussy like it

was my last meal. I'd forever leave an imprint of my face on her pussy for her to remember. I wanted there to be no doubt who brought her the most pleasure in her life.

Her hands slapped down on the couch before she dug her nails into the white cotton material. "Fuck," she hissed as her back arched.

As the walls of her core pulsated, her body began to shake uncontrollably. Her mouth grew rigid as her lips trembled and hung open slightly. The spasm raked over her body for some time as I kept my lips on her flesh, pulling her through the ecstasy she had fought so hard.

By the time she came down from the last orgasm, I thought my dick was about to break off. I had a hard-on to end all hard-ons. I'd fought every urge I had to stop in the middle of my carnal feast and shove my cock inside her warmth. Who said that I wasn't a patient man?

When I backed away from her, I slid my fingers out and licked every ounce of her arousal off them. She glared, but watched me with her mouth still agape. The look on her face brought me pride. I'd brought her over the edge again and again and I'd accomplished what I set out to do—remind her that she belonged to me.

As I slipped my fingers out of my mouth, I moaned. Even though I'd had my face submerged in her sex for longer than I'd realized, the last drops were still as sweet.

Using my saliva mingled with her wetness, I stroked my cock. My eyes rolled back in my head from the frisson of pleasure that skated over my body. I needed to come. Not for the orgasm, but I needed a release from the pent-up emotion from the day. I needed to fuck her attitude out of her system and mine.

As I stood, she kept her eyes pinned to me. She took in shaky breaths as I rubbed my cock and paid special attention to the tip. I gripped tighter, catching on the piercings, sending a jolt through my body.

"But—" she said as I moved toward her.

"Now," I demanded, unwilling to wait or let her be in charge.

She nodded as her eyes grew wide and I moved closer. Releasing my hardened length, I grabbed her behind the knees and dragged her body forward so her ass no longer touched the couch. I pulled upward as I bent her legs toward her body, moving her ass into the air and folding her a bit as I pushed her knees toward her chest.

I pushed through her opening, feeling a bit of resistance. She was tight normally, but after the numerous orgasms, her pussy had constricted as a means of self-preservation. I tugged her forward and plowed into her.

As her cunt squeezed my length, a shiver went down my spine. I didn't know if anything had ever felt as fantastic as her body impaled by mine.

I wanted to wreck her. Ruin her like she had me. Make her never forget the fact that I owned her body. No one else had sent a spark of passion through her like I had. There was no other woman on the planet that lit my fuse the way she did. It wasn't something I'd give up. Even if she had a future that would be riddled with health issues, I wouldn't turn my back on her.

When you find that something so unlike anything else in the world, it can't be easily tossed aside. I'd fucked enough women in my life to know when there's a magical force at work. The zing I felt when I touched her made it undeniable.

When I'd said that I wanted to wreck her, I didn't mean for life. I wanted her for myself and no one else. The main thing I wanted to wipe from her mind was any thought of running and leaving me behind. I wouldn't let her, even if she tried.

My mind was filled with so many things as I thrust into her repeatedly. I tried to keep my mind occupied, not ready to come inside her yet. The warmth and silkiness of her insides rubbing on my stiff shaft was universe-rocking. The continents collided, changing the landscape of my mind and altering the trajectory of my future path.

Max was mine, and no one else would ever have her.

"Max, say you're mine," I said through gritted teeth as I pulled my dick out before jamming it back inside.

"What?" she whimpered.

I moved my face closer, making sure she'd

hear me. "Say you're mine and no one else's."

"Obviously I am," she replied.

Everything with her seemed to be difficult at times. She liked to yank my chain.

"Max," I said, pushing just the tip inside her and pausing.

She sealed her eyes shut. "I'm yours," she whispered.

Warmth cascaded over me at her admission. "Look at me when you say it, and keep your eyes open this time."

Her eyes opened. "I'm yours," she said in a stronger voice as she stared at me.

"Again," I said as I thrust inside her.

"I'm yours," she said, a little louder, before sucking in a breath.

I pulled out and jammed my dick back inside her heat. "More," I commanded as I picked up the pace. I could feel the orgasm ready to break free, and I wouldn't be able to hold out much longer.

"I'm yours!" she yelled as her body trembled beneath me.

"Max," I moaned, wanting to hear her say it

one more time as I came inside her. "Again!"

"I'm yours, Anthony!" She gripped my legs, digging her nails into my skin.

The bite of her nails coupled with her pussy clamping down on my cock like a vise sent me spiraling over the precipice and to the most body-consuming orgasm of my entire life. Everything inside me awoke. Tiny sparks rocked my body from head to toe as my mind went blank. The only thing I could focus on was the rush of bliss that had ravaged me.

Although I'd wanted to ruin her and remind her that she was mine, her words and body had made it quite clear that I was hers and hers alone. Never again could I look at another woman in the same way. My heart, mind, body, and soul were Max's.

"Mine," I whispered as the last aftershock shot through my body.

"Yours," she replied, reaching forward and pulling my lips into a kiss.

We were irrevocably locked together forever with no other course than to roam this path together.

14

GALLO TIME

I RANG MAX'S DOORBELL AND COULD HEAR her heels on the hardwood floor as I waited. Yesterday, after much prodding both verbally and with my pecker, Max had finally given in and said that she'd come to a Gallo Sunday dinner. I had to agree to going to her mother's next week out of respect.

Since I'd met her mother already, although not how I would've liked it to happen, I'd said yes. I knew that her mother was okay with everything, but her brother, Denzel, would be there. I remembered him from the first night at the bar, when I had become a little overeager about getting to know Max. Hopefully he'd let it slide, understanding that I cared for Max.

Actually, when I really thought about her, I knew I loved her. Maybe I loved her from the moment I saw her. I never believed in that shit, but she'd crept inside me and made it impossible to forget her. I swear to shit, they should have taken my man card away from me. Next stop, I'd grow a pair of tits for the way I'd become all sappy and shit.

"Fuck," I muttered to myself as I rolled my eyes.

I'd never admit it to anyone, but I was pussy-whipped. More accurately I was Max-whipped. She could have anything she wanted. I'd give in to everything. Everything unless it came to her health. Then I'd give nothing.

After much resistance, she had taken the DNA test for ataxia. I went with her to the clinic in Tampa, and we were told the results wouldn't be available for several weeks, but we weren't given a specific time frame. I held her hand, reassuring her that, no matter what, I'd stay by her side.

Outsiders would think I was fucking nuts. The woman had treated me like a piece of trash. More accurately, like a piece of cock she could use and get rid of like a cheap whore. Before Max, I would've been okay with it and happily moved along. She had driven me mad for longer than I'd like to admit with her "please fuck me" and then "get the fuck out of my life" statements. My head had spun from the back-and-forth.

Looking back on it, I understood where her thoughts had been in the situation. If I had a future I felt was hopeless, would I willingly invite love into my life?

I knew I was a selfish motherfucker. I'd always been, but there was selfish and then there was cruel. If I were in her shoes, I probably would've lived my life much the same way I had —refusing attachment and fucking my way through life.

The problem had happened when we'd both realized how special the spark truly was. Neither of us had felt it before, and it kept bringing us back together, calling us to one another like the song of a siren and luring us to each other.

I wished things had been different. I wished we hadn't had the rocky start, but there was nothing I could do to change the past. Maybe it would help us become a stronger couple moving forward, but I knew I'd always have a sliver of fear inside me. Scared that she'd run away in a moment of panic if she were told that she was carrying the gene and would someday meet the same destiny her father had.

My heart ached at the thought. There was no way Max had the gene. I could feel it. She was too graceful, too beautiful, and too full of life to be robbed of her life by something so crippling as ataxia.

"Hey," she said as the door flew open. She had a sexy smile on her face.

I returned the smile and let my eyes wander down her body and take in her beauty. She had on a skintight pencil skirt and a crisp white dress shirt tucked into the waist. Black sling-back heels cradled her feet. I knew I shouldn't have known the term, but having Izzy as a sister made it impossible.

My eyes crept back up her body and settled

on her face. "You look stunning," I said as I reached out and held her face.

"Thanks. I want to make a good impression," she replied, as her smile grew larger.

"You could've done that in jeans and a T-shirt." I bowed, needing to kiss her lipstick-stained lips.

"Watch the makeup," she whispered, keeping her eyes locked on mine. "I don't want to have to go back upstairs and fix it."

"I'll be careful," I said above her lips before gently bringing mine down on her mouth. As I released her, I said, "Let's go. We're going to be late, and then you might as well have had a paper bag on. Maria Gallo doesn't do late."

She slammed the door and started to stomp away. "What are we waiting for, then? Oh my God, she's going to hate me already."

I laughed at her reaction. She already had the fear of Maria in her and she hadn't even met the woman yet.

"We have plenty of time," I replied as I followed her down the sidewalk.

"No, no," she called over her shoulder. "I want to be early. Brownie points always help."

"Suck-up. I'm never early," I said as I looked at my watch, and she laughed in response.

I'd picked her up a little early, hoping to make out a little before we headed to my parents' house. One look at her and I knew it wasn't going to happen. She looked too perfect to mess up. Once dinner was over, all bets were off.

I held open the car door for her, closing it behind her after she was situated. My parents had always taught me manners. I'd just chosen not to use any of them my entire life. It would have thrown off too many wrong vibes if I had.

We had a thirty-minute drive to my parents' house. I didn't know if I'd sat this close to Max alone and not had it lead to sex. I set my hand on her leg, needing to be connected to her as we drove. We talked about work and family. She and I were alike in that way.

Work and family were the two most important things in our lives. They took precedence over everything else. When my family asked me to do something, I dropped everything and helped. I was still the big brother, even though, at times, it didn't seem like it. They'd all grown, found their other halves, but only Joe had started a family. Sometimes, I acted like the youngest, unwilling to give up my freedom and totally join adulthood.

The drive flew by as we chatted about everything. She grew more talkative the closer we were to my parents'. I could tell she was nervous as she picked at her skirt, smoothing it over her legs, and fidgeted.

"Max," I said as I put the car in park and turned it off. "It's going to be okay." I'd never brought anyone to dinner, but I knew how everyone had embraced Suzy, Mia, James, and Angel. She wouldn't be any different.

She blew out a puff of air and closed her eyes before dragging in a breath through her nose. "Okay. I shouldn't be nervous. Got it."

I brushed the hair off her shoulder and ran my fingers up her neck. "It's okay to be nervous, but I promise they will love you."

"I'm sure your white family was over the

moon when they found out you're dating a black girl."

"Max, they were over the moon when they found out I'm in love with a woman. Color's inconsequential in the eyes of my family."

"Uh huh," she mumbled, and rolled her eyes.

"I'm creeping up on forty and have never brought a woman home to meet my family. I haven't had a girlfriend since high school by choice. You're different not because of your color, but because your heart. Shiiit," I drawled with a small laugh. "They're happy to know I'm not gay."

She giggled. "No!" she yelled, covering her mouth. "They didn't?"

"My siblings knew how I was. They'd seen the endless parade of women I'd been with, but not my parents. My mother secretly thought I was gay. It's not that they wouldn't have loved me, but I know she would've mourned for the children I'd probably never have with a partner."

I immediately regretted the words as soon as they left my mouth. I shifted in my seat, thinking of a way to stop the hurt I knew my sentence had caused. She didn't want to have children, and here I was, like a dumbass, saying that it was all my mother cared about. My stomach was in knots and no longer craved the pasta that was about to be dished out.

"Anthony," Max said as she placed her hand on top of mine.

I couldn't look her in the eyes. "What?" I whispered before trying to swallow past the lump in my throat.

"It's okay, baby. I know what you meant. We're going to have to talk about kids someday. We need to have that conversation before we get any deeper."

Before we get deeper? I was in as deep as I could be. There was no lifeline or turning back. I was sunk, with her as my anchor.

"Max, I want whatever you want. If you don't want to have kids, that's fine with me. I'm kind of old to even think about having a child. I'd be almost sixty by the time they'd graduate from high school. Now, if you said you wanted to have a baby, I'd make sure to give ya one to make you happy too."

"You'd have a baby to make me happy?" she asked as her eyebrows knitted together.

"I'd do anything to make you happy. Including a baby." I nodded, but I didn't know if I was trying to convince her or myself.

"You know it's not like a purse, right? I mean, you can't decide a baby doesn't suit you anymore or clashes with your lifestyle and get rid of it. There's no refund once the bundle of joy arrives," she replied, giving my hand a squeeze. I couldn't tell if she was trying to talk me out of it or trying to make sure it was something I wanted.

"Max," I said as the corners of my lips twitched. I wanted to kiss her and mess up that lipstick more than anything in that moment. "I know, Kitty Cat. It's not something I want, but I want whatever will make you happy."

"You make me happy, Anthony," she said before she bent down and planted a light kiss on my lips.

"I love you, Max," I whispered into her mouth as we sat in my car, parked in my parents' driveway.

"You're going to make me mess up my makeup," she whispered back. "I love you too, Anthony." She gave me a quick peck before blotting her eyes with her fingertips.

I smiled as I watched her dry her eyes without making a mess of her perfectly applied makeup. "Ready?" I asked as I glanced at the clock and realized we were five minutes early. "Or you wanna make out for a little bit?" I wiggled my eyebrows.

She slapped me on the shoulder. "We're going in before you ruin everything I've worked so hard to achieve."

"Max, you're even more stunning without makeup."

"You're a complete liar, Anthony Gallo, but thank you," she said as she grinned and swiped her thumb across my lips. "Let's go before I chicken out."

"Well, we're the first ones here, so it's probably good to go in now. They won't pile into the foyer to stare at you like you're a zoo animal."

"Oh, God," she muttered as she grabbed her face.

"You got this, beautiful. Let's go meet the Gallos," I said as I climbed out of the car.

Before I could get to her side, she opened the door and stood.

"Hey," I said. "I was going to get that for you."

"I got it, Anthony. I'm a big girl."

"I know," I said, nodding. "But my mother may be watching." I looked toward the house, trying to see if I could spot her face in the windows.

"You're really scared of her, aren't you?" she asked before laughing softly as she placed her hand in mine.

"No. I'm not scared of Ma. I just never want to disappoint her, Max."

She stopped walking, pulling me back by our connected hands. "Anthony, you're making it really hard today for me to see that asshole I met in the bar."

I grinned as I looked down at her. "I don't ever want to be that man again, Max."

"I like him. He's frisky. Bring him out every

once in a while for me. He's a freak in the sheets, and I adore the hell out of him."

"I can do that," I responded before brushing my thumb along her jaw line.

"Lipstick," she reminded me.

I blew out a breath and looked toward the sky. Today would be an exercise in self-control, and I could already feel it slipping.

I reached for the door handle as Max said, "You can't just go inside."

I looked at her, confused. "Yeah, I can. We do it all the time. I grew up in this house. Trust me. Everyone is beyond knocking at this point."

"Okay." She smiled at me and gave my hand a quick squeeze.

"Here we go," I said as I opened the door and took a step inside. "Ma! Pop!" I yelled in the foyer, and waited for them to come to us.

"Should I take my shoes off?" Max whispered as she glanced down at her feet.

"Nah. You're a guest."

"Anthony!" Pop called out before I heard the squeak of the recliner being righted.

Ma walked out of the kitchen, entering the foyer with her arms outstretched. "Baby," she said, motioning for us to come to her with her fingers.

As I reached for her, she grabbed Max and wrapped her into a giant hug. I stood there watching it as it happened. I no longer was the center of attention when I walked in the door. I now had another half, one who captured my parents' attention more than I did.

"Hi," Max said quietly. There was no doubt that the hug had cut off her ability to speak any louder.

"Son," Pop called out as he walked in and held his hand out to me.

"Pop." I shook his hand, stealing glances at the two most important women in my life.

"Let me get a good look at you," Ma said, holding Max by the shoulders and looking her over. "You're so beautiful."

Max beamed at the compliment. "Thank you, Mrs. Gallo."

"Maria, please. You're prettier than Anthony described you."

Max shot me a look over her shoulder. For

the love of God, why had Ma had to say that? I'd told everyone she was drop-dead gorgeous.

"Anthony said you looked like a grown-up Rudy from *The Cosby Show*, but I say you're a prettier version of Gabrielle Union."

Hold up a second. I couldn't believe that my mother had just told her about my Rudy comparison. I wanted to crawl into a hole. I'd never uttered those words to Max. I had been too worried about my balls to even drop it in passing. Beyond that, I was shocked my mother knew who Gabrielle Union was. The woman was full of surprises.

"He did, did he?" Max asked, glancing at me as I made my way next to them.

"Ma, we can drop the BET references. I think Pop needs to take away the controller."

Ma smiled and slapped me on the arm. "Baby, I don't know what BET is, but I know a beautiful woman when I see one."

"Who do I look like, Ma?" I asked, fishing for a compliment.

"What's that boy's name?" She tapped her lip as I pulled Max to my side.

"A boy? I'm kind of old for that." I squeezed her waist, feeling her body shake from laughter.

I glanced down at Max and smiled. I was glad she was enjoying herself. She looked more relaxed than she had when we'd walked in.

"Ahhh. Zac Efron. You look like him." She nodded excitedly.

"Ma, he's, like, twelve."

"Oh, no. He's all grown up now, Anthony. Your sister Googled him. He's almost thirty. He's very grown up," she said as she wiggled her eyebrows.

"Jesus," I mumbled. "Kind of pervy, Ma. Don't you think?" I felt a little uncomfortable.

"I may be old, son, but I'm not dead."

"Pop," I said, turning to face him. "What do you think of this?" I motioned toward Ma with my head.

"He sure is pretty," he replied, and snorted.

"Nice." I shook my head.

Pop cleared his throat, reminding me that I hadn't introduced him to Max. "Max, this is my pop, Mr. Gallo, and Pop, this is Max."

"Max," Pop said, holding out his arms for a hug.

"Mr. Gallo." Max smiled and returned the hug he'd wrapped her in.

"Sal." Pop smiled at me over her shoulder and gave a thumbs-up.

I chuckled to myself, trying not to ruin their moment.

"Sal," Max repeated.

"Shall we go into the living room?" Pop asked as he released Max.

"Sure." I nodded, holding Max. "Where is everyone?" I asked, surprised no one else had come barging through the door.

"I told them to come fifteen minutes later today," said Ma.

"You did?" I asked, in complete shock. Never, ever had that happened before.

"Yes. I wanted to meet Max before everyone arrived. I didn't want it to be crazy. I thought we could have a few minutes to ourselves before they showed up."

"But that's, like, sacrilegious or something, Ma."

"We don't want to overwhelm her, Anthony."

"I'm not breakable, Mrs. Gallo," Max said. "I have a very large, loud family. I'm used to a lot of people."

I knew about her mother and brother, but I didn't know how large the rest of her family was. Soon enough, I'd find out, and then neither of us would ever have a peaceful weekend alone.

"We're good, Max. It was for purely selfish reasons, I assure you," Ma said. "Why don't you and Sal go sit down and Anthony and I will grab some drinks before the others arrive."

I knew that confusion was written all over my face. My mother never needed help getting drinks. She must have wanted something or had something to say.

"Sure," Max said, giving me a small smile before following my pop into the living room.

"What are you up to?" I asked Ma.

"Nothing," she said flatly before turning her back and walking into the kitchen.

I followed her in and propped myself up on

the counter. "Don't lie, Ma. You have something to say."

"She's beautiful, Anthony. Stunning, actually. I'm so happy for you, son."

"That's it?" I asked with one eyebrow raised.

"Did you find out her test results yet?" Ma asked as she pulled down four drinking glasses from the cabinet.

"Not yet. It's been a couple of weeks, but we possibly still have weeks to go before we hear anything."

She sighed. "Tears me up, baby."

"What does, Ma?"

"Thinking of that beautiful girl and what she has to be going through inside."

"She's okay." I crossed my arms over my chest, knowing that I'd get swatted if I tried to help. My mother never liked any of her boys touching things in her kitchen when it could be avoided.

"Son. You've had good health your entire life. You've never had to wait for a test to hear your fate. I've been there. Your father has been there. I know how it's eating her up on the inside."

"What?" I asked. "When did you and Pop wait on test results?" I was confused. Clearly, there were things my parents had held out on in the sharing department.

"Sweetheart, you don't get to our age without a couple of scares. Don't worry. We're healthy. I've just been there. I know how it feels to wait to hear if you're going to be okay or if you should start planning a funeral. It's horrible." She shook her head as she poured the drinks.

"I know. It's eating me alive. Waiting to hear what her future holds is killing me slowly—I can't imagine what it's doing to her. I forced her into taking the test. I feel like shit because of it, too."

"Anthony," she said as she set the bottle of Pepsi on the counter and looked at me. "You're only doing what's best. Living with the assumption that you're going to be sick isn't a way to live. It's like a noose around your neck and waiting for the bottom to fall out. Once you two know the results, you can either rejoice in the good fortune or move forward with the knowledge and live every day like it's the most important day of your life. Things can change in an instant, but knowledge is power, baby."

"Yeah, you're right. I've always been a fly-by-the-seat-of-my-pants kind of guy." I pushed off the counter and grabbed two glasses. "Thanks, Ma."

"For what?" she asked as she picked up the last two drinks.

"For being you." I smiled down at her. "You always know the right thing to say to make me feel better."

"I love you, Anthony. I only want the best for you. I'll always support you in everything you do, even if that meant loving a man." She grinned and winked at me as she walked passed me into the living room.

"Jesus," I muttered to myself as I followed her.

When Izzy hadn't brought anybody home, no one had thought she was gay. Nope. She was a strong, independent woman. But me? My parents assumed I liked dick. Amazing how that worked.

Just as I was about to hand the pop to Max, the door opened and carried in loud voices. The rest of the Gallo crew had finally arrived. I wanted more time with my parents. The four of us was nice for a change, but it was too late at this point.

"Hey!" Izzy's voiced echoed through the house as the front door slammed. A couple of seconds later, she strolled into the living room, trying to act nonchalant.

I knew she was dying to meet Max. It had to take everything in her to keep calm. James walked in behind her wearing his typical workout shorts and tank top. Over time, his outfit had become more casual as he'd felt more comfortable. It'd been comical to watch the transition.

Izzy had dressed up for the occasion. Typically on Sunday, she wore jeans or sweats, but today, she had on dress pants and a pretty off-the-shoulder top. It wasn't her usual outfit. Max being a stylist was her wet dream. Not only was she ecstatic about me finally being "pussy-whipped," as she'd said, but another female in the family made her insides sing.

She kissed our parents and went right for Max. "Hi. I'm Izzy." She extended her hand. "Anthony's sister."

Max smiled and stood before placing her hand in Izzy's. "I'm Max, Anthony's friend." She looked out of the corner of her eye, glancing at me.

"Friend?" I asked as I crossed my arms over my chest.

"Fine," Max replied as she rolled her eyes. "He's my boyfriend." She gave me an "are you happy now" smile before turning her attention back to Izzy.

"I feel ya, Max. Men constantly need the affirmation." Izzy laughed and rolled her eyes like Max just had.

I sighed. The two of them together with their attitudes could only be trouble. Suzy and Mia were calmer women, more easygoing. Max and Izzy were spitfires and could cause trouble in any circumstance. I knew that the best course of action was to not let the two of them hang out too often together without male supervision.

"Max, this is my friend James." She grinned at Max before looking at James over her shoulder.

His eyes darted to mine. I knew by the single look that he was thinking exactly the same thing I had been thinking. They were trouble with a capital T.

"It's a pleasure to meet you, Max." James gently took her hand, bringing it to his lips. "I'm Izzy's man. Maybe I need to remind her of that later."

"Oh, you know I love your lessons, Jimmy." Izzy blew him a kiss and laughed.

Pop cleared his throat. Most likely, he wasn't entirely happy about the blatant sex talk in front of him. "Hey, baby girl. Come give your father a hug," he said, holding out his arms.

Izzy walked over to Pop and touched his shoulder. "Hey, Daddy."

I looked at James and mouthed, "Nice job."

He grinned at me and shrugged. James seemed to get away with more than anyone.

Maybe my family feared he was the only person who could put up with Izzy's shit. Either way, he got a pass more often than not.

"We're here," Joe called out as the front door opened.

Max walked over to me and nestled into my side.

"You okay?" I whispered as I looked at her.

She nodded, giving me a small smile. "I'm good."

Suzy waddled in first, looking like she was ready to burst. I hadn't known that the human body could expand that much and not explode. She still had some time left before the baby was due, but I didn't know how she could possibly grow more.

Joe rushed to her side, grabbing her by the arm as she stopped in the middle of the living room.

"I swear I've turned into a walking whale," Suzy whined as she rubbed her stomach. "I can't do this anymore."

"Sugar, you can do this. You look more beautiful than ever before." Joe kissed her on the forehead as he cradled her face.

I silently gagged. Suzy was stunning, but not more beautiful than she had been before the alien had started growing inside her. That statement could only come from a man who clearly loved his wife. Or maybe he liked his balls and had decided to give her a compliment to make his life simpler. Whatever his reason was, Suzy's face changed as he kissed her.

"Joe and Suzy, this is Max," I said, breaking up their moment.

They both turned as smiles crept across their faces. "Max," they both whispered, and glanced at each other.

"What?" I asked, confused by their response.

"Oh, nothing," Suzy sang, and shook her head.

"We thought Max was a dude. We made a bet," Joe added with a shit-eating grin on his face.

"Oh, go fuck yourself," I hissed. "You knew Max is a woman.

"I just like to see you get your panties in a

wad." Joe placed his hand on his chest and laughed.

"Nice to meet you, Max," Suzy said as she nodded toward Max. Then she smiled at me. "Still love me?"

"I don't have another choice, Suz. I'm stuck with your ass for the rest of my life," I replied as I kissed her cheek. It was almost acrobatic with her belly, but thankfully, Suzy was so short, it wasn't an issue.

"You are." She smiled at me and then looked Max over. "Wow. Your outfit is beautiful." Suzy touched her own dress, which wasn't as feminine as she typical wore, but it was of the "about to explode and can't fit into any other clothes" variety.

"Yo!" Mike said as he and Mia walked into the room.

For a moment, I thought the gang was complete, but then I remembered that Thomas and Angel weren't here yet. We'd been without him for so long that it was still weird and hard to get used to. It was a happy weird, though.

"Max, this is Mike, my brother, and his girlfriend, Mia," I said, motioning toward Mike and Mia. "She's a doctor," I added for no particular reason, but it had felt necessary.

She glanced up at me and then looked over at Mike and Mia. "Hi," she responded with a gracious smile.

"Max," Mike said, reaching out and pulling Max into a bear hug.

Her body looked tiny and fragile in his arms as her feet came off the ground. "Mike," Max squeaked out as her arms tried to grab on to his body.

As he set her on the ground, he peered over at me. "Good job, bro."

Mia smacked him on the shoulder. "Put the poor woman down, Mike. You're probably crushing her ribs."

"Sorry," Mike said.

Max shook her head and waved her arms. "I see that this family doesn't know how to grow a small man."

"Nope," Mia replied. "They're all big. Don't let their size scare you, though. They're all sweet as pie."

"So only I get the asshole Gallo?" Max asked as she giggled.

Her statement caused laughter to break out in the room.

"I'll embrace my assholiness, but I'm a changed man." I wasn't embarrassed by their statement or by my past. It was who I was, and I still loved myself.

As Joe sat down, he chimed in, "He acts like an asshole, but he's just as much of a pushover as the rest of us."

I even had them fooled. For my family, I'd give my life, and I treated each of them with respect at times. The other people roaming the earth had to earn my respect. Women, on the other hand, I often had treated like I was a complete asshole. Most of them loved it. When women say they want to settle down with a nice guy and live in a house with a picket fence, it's all a crock of bullshit.

I hadn't wanted to settle down—not until I'd met Max. That was why I'd perfected my asshole persona. I'd give the women what they wanted for a night but didn't want them coming back for more.

"I'm learning that fact, Joe," Max said as she squeezed my waist.

"Let me go get dinner finished. Who wants to help?" Ma asked as she stood from her chair. She'd been silently watching everyone and sipping her Pepsi.

"I can," Suzy said as she tried to get up from the couch, but she fell backward.

"You rest, Suzy dear. You're going to need all the strength you have soon enough. Izzy and Mia will help me."

"Great," Izzy mumbled. "What about Max?" she asked as she glanced over at her.

"She looks too pretty to ruin her outfit," Ma told Izzy.

"But—"

"I'd love to help if you have an apron," Max answered.

"I have an apron for you, love. We'd love for you to help." Ma walked next to me, sliding her arm through Max's and locking them together.

Just as my ass hit the couch, Thomas and

Angel walked in. "Sorry we're late. We got caught up doing something."

By the way their clothes were rumpled, I'd say they got busy in the car on the way over here. "I can see that," I said, pointing to his unzipped fly.

"Shit," he whispered as he zipped it up.

Angel blushed, smoothing out her hair. "Where's your girl?" she asked as she scanned the room.

"The women are in the kitchen, where they belong," I said with a grin.

"You're lucky Izzy didn't hear you say that," Angel said to me as a corner of her mouth twitched.

"I know." I stuck my tongue out at her before giving her a quick wink.

Thomas smacked Angel on the ass. "Go help out the ladies, babe."

"Sure," she said as she stood on her tiptoes and gave him a kiss.

"Lucky bastard," I muttered as she walked out of the room.

"What did you say?" Thomas asked as he sat

down in an empty chair.

"If I would've done that to Max or James to Izzy, we'd get a knee to the balls."

"Maybe you should've been more selective with your choice," Thomas replied as he rested his foot on the opposite knee.

"Shut it," I shot back at him, and stared at the television.

"How is she?" Mike asked.

I zoned out as I watched Jason Statham kicking some bad guy's ass.

"Yo! Earth to Anthony."

I glanced over at Mike and realized he was talking to me. "Sorry. I'm out of it."

"Clearly," he replied. "How's Max doing?"

"She seems okay. The waiting is making me crazy. I can't imagine how she feels."

"Yeah, Mia said it takes a while. That's tough, bro."

"Harder than anything I've ever done in my life." I tried to smile, but I didn't feel it. I took a deep breath and let out a silent exhale.

I felt a bit worn on the inside. Even though it wasn't my health at stake, I felt the heaviness of the situation. Max had been put on this earth to be with me, and to think that she could be ripped from my life at an early age just pissed me off. I wish I had met her earlier. We both had wasted so many years with bullshit.

"Dinner!" Izzy yelled from the dining room.

"Thank God. I'm starving," Suzy said as she tried to get off the couch again. Joe helped her up with a push on the back of her ass. "Thank you," she said as she tried to steady herself on her feet.

Weeble wobble.

She looked like a Weeble as she tried to stand and then stay upright. Her weight displacement was off, just like those damn toys I played with as a kid.

I walked into the dining room and saw Max holding the bowl of meatballs. She had a smile on her face. One that burned brighter than I'd seen in a long time. It had to be my mother, or maybe just being with the girls. They seemed to be a support system for each other.

I stared at her with a matching smile. Knowing that she was here with me and things were finally calm between us brought me a sense of peace. Maybe, just maybe, things would work out in our favor.

"You look sexy in that apron," I said as she placed the bowl down on the table next to me.

"Don't get used to it, buddy. I'm not a chef. I prefer to eat out."

"Lucky for you," I said with a sly smile, "so do I." I winked at her before pulling her to me and giving her a kiss.

For the first Sunday in a long time, I felt completely happy.

15

INTO THE FIRE

"Stop being such a baby," Max said as we approached her mother's house.

I'd never had to do this before. Meeting the family signified a relationship, and I hadn't been in one of those since high school.

"Last time I met your brother he was a total dick."

"You'd act the same if some asshole was bothering Izzy. Let's just try and move beyond that night. Denzel is a nice guy, and he knows that I like you."

She liked me? I had been hoping for a little

more than that as a description of how she felt about me.

"You just like me?

"You know how I feel about you, Anthony. Do we really need to get into this right now?" she asked as she knocked on the front door and glanced at me over her shoulder.

"Fine."

"Hey, sis," Denzel said as he opened the door. His smile faded when he saw me. "Hey," he said as he tipped his chin to me.

After Max walked past him, I held out my hand and hoped to make peace with Denzel.

"Hi, Denzel." My stomach dropped when he looked down at my hand before his eyes returned to mine.

"What's up?" he replied before taking my hand. "Scare ya for a minute?" He laughed, bending at the waist and slapping his leg.

"Hell yes, you did. Are we okay?" I asked. I wanted to be okay. I wanted everything to be smooth.

"Shit for real with my sister?" He gripped my hand tighter, trying to crush my fingers.

I knew the script. I'd done it more times than I could remember with men who'd wanted to be with my sister.

"I love your sister," I replied, still standing outside as he blocked the doorway.

"You love her?"

"I do."

"I've been trying to get her to take that damn test forever, man. She always refused, but for you, she did it. That's saying something."

I hadn't thought about how her family felt. Hell, I'd forgotten that Denzel could have it too.

"Did you get tested?"

He nodded and released my hand. "Yeah. About a year ago."

"And?"

He moved to the side. "Come on in."

As I walked into the house, he told me what he found out.

"I was negative. The test isn't one hundred percent accurate, though. There are forms of ataxia that don't show up through genetic testing. They said even though I was negative, there was a chance I could still develop it later in life.

It's going to depend on what my sister's results are."

"What do you mean?" There was a chance that Max's results could be negative too. Maybe she was just like her brother.

"It's like this, Anthony. If my sister tests positive, then my father had a type that's testable. If she's positive, then I'll always be negative. If she's negative, we can both still get it later because it's one of the types that they don't have a test for yet. Know what I mean?"

"Yeah, I think," I lied. I didn't want to seem like an idiot.

"I'll explain later after we have a beer." He smiled at me and slapped me on the back. "Let's get outside. They're all waiting to see you."

When we had been talking, I'd forgotten about everyone else, but as soon as he reminded me, I began to sweat.

"Right," I mumbled, and tucked my hands in my pockets.

"They aren't that bad."

"Who's this, baby?" a beautiful redhead asked as she slid her arm around Denzel.

"This here is Max's man, Anthony."

Her eyes raked over me, moving slowly from my feet to my face. "Hey," she said as a smile spread across her face. "It's nice to have a new face around here. You can be the new focus of the Washington family and take some of the heat off me."

"Heat?" I tilted my head, hoping I'd heard her wrong.

"Yeah." She giggled. "You'll see. They're good people. Don't ever think otherwise. I'm Brenda, by the way." She held out her hand and grinned.

"Nice to meet you, I think," I said as I placed a kiss on the top of her hand.

"That's enough touching my woman. You have one of your own. Let's go meet the family," Denzel said as he pushed down Brenda's arm as it hung in the air.

"Who's here?" I asked as I followed them through the house.

The smell was amazing and different than my parents' house. I could smell the South. Butter, bacon, cheese, and so many other great things that I craved when I went to dinner. Don't get me wrong. I loved Italian food, but sometimes, I needed something other than Ma's homemade sauce.

"Everyone is here. Aunts, uncles, cousins all came to meet the man who's dating Max. Nita and Malia are around here somewhere too."

"Is it that unusual?" I asked as we rounded the corner to the living room. Through the sliding glass doors, I could see more than a dozen people standing in the backyard.

"She hasn't dated anyone in a long time. So, yeah, it is." He didn't give me any more time to collect myself before he opened the sliding glass doors. "He's here!" he announced as all the eyes in the backyard focused on me.

I needed to play it cool. "Hey!" I said, pulling a hand from my pocket and waving.

"Anthony," Ruth said as she walked toward me. "It's good to see you fully clothed this time."

My face turned red. I really hated that she'd met me under those circumstances, but at least she could chuckle about it.

"It's good to see you too, Mrs. Washington."

"Ruth, please." She hugged me, running her hands down my back.

I felt a little molested.

Max was giggling behind her as she watched my face. "Mama, let him go," she said as she pulled her mother off me.

"It's just nice to feel a man in my arms again, Max."

Her statement made me sad. She'd lost her husband and had to be lonely.

"You can hug me any time, Ruth," I said before giving her a wink.

"Now, who do we have here?" an old man asked as he approached. He was hunched over and walking with a cane. Even though it was warm out, warm enough that I wished I'd worn shorts instead of jeans, he had on a flannel and pants that were pulled up way too high above his waist.

Ruth turned and smacked him on the arm. "It's Anthony, Earl. I told you about him."

"Who?" he asked as he came closer and squinted.

"Get those damn glasses fixed. It's Anthony!" she yelled in his ear.

"I'm not deaf, woman. I'm blind. Why are you yelling at me?"

"You ol' coot. I told you Max's boyfriend was coming over." She looked at me with a weak smile.

"But this here is a white man," Earl said as he looked me up and down.

"Not so blind now, are ya?" Ruth asked before she snorted.

"Does it matter, Uncle Earl?" Max asked as she walked next to me and hooked her arm with mine.

He shook his head as his brow furrowed. "Suppose it doesn't, Max."

"Good answer," Ruth said.

"Son, I'm not racist. No one told me you were white."

I felt a bit uneasy, but I chalked it up to his age. "It's okay, sir."

"Sir?" he asked, and smiled. "I like this boy already."

"I'm sorry," Max whispered, gripping my forearm tighter.

This was her family and I'd love them no matter what. I had some uncles that often spoke their mind too. I thought it was an age thing. People became freer with their words as they grew older. They didn't worry as much about offending anyone—or at least it seemed like it.

"Maybe if you'd get a damn hearing aid, you would've heard your sister say he was a white boy so you wouldn't act like an idiot like you are now, Earl," an older woman teased him as she walked up behind him. "I'm Clara, Earl's wife."

Earl rolled his eyes in much the same fashion Max always did. "Maybe I just don't want to hear what you have to say."

Clara smacked him on the back of the hand as Earl snickered. "Anthony, it's nice to meet you. Don't mind my husband. He's not entirely with it anymore." She smiled, and it was so warm and genuine that I couldn't help but smile back at her.

"Go make me a sandwich, woman!" Earl demanded as he pursed his lips. "Don't fawn over the boy."

"He's not a boy, Earl. That right there is a man." Clara's smiled changed, moving from sweet to flirty.

I cleared my throat, feeling the heat creep up my neck before filling my cheeks. I wanted to laugh, but I didn't want to seem like an idiot.

"You have yourself a man. I don't have me a sandwich."

"Earl," she said as she put her hands on her hips.

"Why don't you go introduce him to everyone else, baby, before you help me finish dinner," Ruth said.

"It's not ready?" Max asked before we walked away.

"Saved a few things for us to do together. When you're ready, Anthony can stay out here and get to know the family better."

"Do not leave me out here," I whispered to Max as I pulled her closer to me.

"You'll be okay," she said as she pulled me toward a large group sitting at a picnic table.

"Max, please. I'll come cook."

"You know you can't cook, and it's girls only in my mama's kitchen."

"Fuck," I muttered. It was like being at my mother's. Men weren't welcome to help prepare the food. I'd always been okay with that. It was less work for me, but at Ruth's, I wanted to run away and hide in the kitchen with Max instead of being left outside with strangers.

Max introduced me to her uncles and cousins, and I knew I'd never remember their names. Six men sat at the table, sipping their beers and looking at me with curiosity. Denzel stood at the opposite end of the table with a giant smile on his face. He seemed to sense my uneasiness and took pleasure in it.

"Guys, can you take care of Anthony while I go inside and help Mama finish up?" Max asked.

I stared at her, pleading for her to take me with her using only my eyes. My stomach knotted, and a nervous sweat broke out across my forehead.

"Sure, Max," Uncle Bob replied, shooing her with his hands. "We got him."

"I'm sure you do. Go easy on him, boys." Max took a step. "Malia and Nita, are you coming?" she asked, looking over at Nita and Malia, who were watching with big, sappy grins.

"Nah, we're good," Malia replied as she started to sit in an empty chair.

"Get your asses up. Let the guys have some time together," Max shot back at Malia, waving for her and Nita to follow.

I grabbed her hand, stopping her. "I can cook. Let me show you."

"No," she replied before standing on her tiptoes to give me a kiss. "You stay out here and get to know everyone."

My mouth felt dry and scratchy as I tried to swallow. I'd rather cook than deal with her family.

"You're such a bossy bitch," Nita said to Max as they walked away.

"Anthony, want a beer?" someone asked as I watched Max sashay toward the house.

"Sure," I said, closing my eyes for a moment before turning. "I'd love one."

Bob reached in the cooler, pulled out a

Coors Light, and held it out to me. I snatched the beer and refrained from holding it to my head to cool myself down.

"Want to sit down?" Denzel asked as he grabbed a lawn chair from under the tree.

"Sure," I said, because I thought maybe, if I were at eye level, I wouldn't feel like everyone was staring at me.

"Tell us about yourself," the man she'd called Junior asked.

I cracked the beer open and took a large gulp before I answered. "I'm a tattoo artist."

"That tells me what you do, son, but I want to know who you are."

The question threw me for a loop. I'd always described myself with my work. I didn't have anything else to really say about myself that most people were truly interested in hearing.

"Tell us about your family," Bob said.

Clearly, I hadn't hid the fact that his question had confused me. "I have a large Italian family with three brothers and a sister. We own a tattoo shop together."

"Parents still together?" Earl asked as he plopped down in a lawn chair next to me.

"Yes, sir. They are."

"How often do you see them?"

"Every week. My mother has dinner for the family on Sunday."

"So, family is important to you?" Bob asked as he rubbed his chin and studied me.

"Yes, very."

"Good answer. Max said she met you at a bar after you played a concert. Are you one of those crazy rock stars?"

"No. I just like to sing with my band on the weekends. It's more of a hobby." I toyed with the beer can. "My real passion is tattooing."

"Do you do drugs? I've heard those rock stars do a lot of drugs," Earl said.

"Yeah. And they have girls falling all over them," Bob added.

"That's not true," I lied. I wasn't into drugs, but the girls, they were real. "And no, I don't do drugs."

"I watched that *Behind the Music* on VH1

and I know how musicians are," Earl added as he ran his hands over his plaid pants.

Even though Earl was being difficult, I liked the man. He was funny and said the craziest shit.

"I can assure you that I haven't hit that status."

"If I were younger, I'd be a musician. They get all the women," Bob said as he tossed his beer can into a trashcan a few feet away. "Denzel, why don't you be a musician?"

Denzel blanched. "Uncle, you know I want nothing to do with music. I love my work, plus I have Brenda. I don't need other women." He grabbed two beers from the cooler and threw one toward Bob, who caught it.

"Son, it's always good to have options." Bob cracked open his beer, took a long sip, and sighed. "This is the life."

"I'm a one-woman man, uncle," Denzel said before he chugged the rest of his beer.

"I like the girl," Earl said. "But she has a flat ass. I don't trust any woman that doesn't have an ass to hold."

Denzel started to spit out his beer. "You must be shitting me."

Earl shook his head. "That's why I picked my Clara. Her ass was so round." He held out his hands, pretending to be grabbing an ass and squeezing. "I knew I was in love."

"What the hell does that have to do with trust?" Denzel snapped at his uncle as he gawked at him squeezing the air.

"It's like that song. I like big butts and I cannot lie."

"You make no fuckin' sense, old man." Denzel laughed, throwing an empty beer can toward his uncle, and it landed in his lap.

I couldn't help but laugh. This was one of the oddest conversations I'd heard in a while.

"I may make no sense, but I still like them round and juicy."

"There are other important things on a woman, Earl," Bob interrupted.

"Like what?" Earl said as he flicked the can to the ground.

"Tits," Bob answered with a smile.

"Jesus," Denzel muttered.

Just as I felt comfortable, I heard, "Dinner!"

As I climbed from my chair, I saw Max standing near the back door with her hand above her eyes to block the sun. She looked stunning as her skirt blew in the warm breeze.

With each step, butterflies filled my stomach. If they were anything like the Gallo family, the real questions wouldn't begin until we were at the dinner table.

"Everything go okay?" Max asked as I walked up to her.

"It went fine, love." I brushed my fingers along her cheek and gave her a small kiss.

"Earl behave?" she asked on my lips.

"He's a funny man."

"Earl may seem like he's crazy, but he's sharp as a tack."

"Noted." I held her hand as I gave her one more kiss.

"Enough of that now. Food's going to get cold," Bob said as he walked by us.

"Ever have chitlins?" Denzel asked as he bumped my shoulder.

I looked at Max with panic in my eyes. I

knew exactly what chitlins were and I couldn't stomach them. If I had to eat them, I'd vomit right at the dinner table.

"I can't eat those, Max." I could already feel my stomach turning over in my body.

"Don't listen to him, baby. Mama didn't make chitlins."

"Phew." I placed my forehead on hers. "I thought we were going to have a problem."

"Come on. You think your ma is bad when you take too long, you haven't seen that side of Ruth." She pulled on my hand to get my ass in gear.

We made our way through the family room to a dining room that had a card table set up at the end of the long wooden table. The table was covered with food. Unlike Ma, who would make a couple of dishes each week but in mass quantities, Ruth had prepared a feast. Ham, sweet potatoes, macaroni and cheese, fried okra, collard greens, cornbread, and more were waiting to be devoured.

When Ruth walked in, everyone grew silent.

I thought we were about to dig in, but then Max bowed her head.

"Heavenly Father, thank you for this amazing feast," she began.

My family never said a prayer. It was eat or be hungry. No one waited for a prayer to dig in.

"Thank you for bringing Anthony to be with us today. Lord, look over each of us and bless this family."

"Amen," Earl called out.

The rest of the family echoed his statement. I thought the prayer would have been longer, but I was happy it wasn't. My stomach was about to start speaking.

My plate was overflowing by the time I took a scoop of each food that had been prepared. I ate slowly, savoring the flavors. Just like the Gallos, the Washington family busted each other's balls, but they left me alone. No one asked me questions or put me on the spot. Maybe it was the way I was enjoying my food that told them to leave me alone.

"You enjoyin' what you're eating, Anthony?"

Ruth asked as I polished off the mac and cheese first.

The cheese was gooey and warm. It was the best mac and cheese I'd ever had in my life. I wanted more, but I didn't want to seem like a pig.

"It's amazing, Ruth. Best ever, in fact."

"You know what to say to tug at a girl's heartstrings," she said as she smiled. "Now I know why my Max loves you."

"Mama," Max said, and held up her hand.

"Actually, she thinks I'm a jerk most of the time." I wiped my mouth, hiding the amusement.

"I second that." Malia laughed as she slopped a heaping spoonful of macaroni and cheese on her plate.

"Max isn't happy unless she's complaining," Denzel teased before he was smacked in the head. "What the hell was that for?"

Ruth glared at him. "Be nice, Denzel."

"*Denzel Washington*. Seriously? Are you named after the actor?"

"That man is sin," Ruth said as she took a

deep breath. "I loved him on *St. Elsewhere*, and I knew when I had a boy I'd name him after him."

"Thanks, Ma. I get a lot of shit for it too."

"Watch your mouth, Denzel. You know you love it."

"I do get good reservations when I call a restaurant and give them my name. I'm better looking than he is too." He tipped his beer toward me and smiled.

Denzel reminded me of myself. The way he mouthed off during dinner and was met with a hand to the back of the head—I'd been there more times than I cared to remember.

By the time we finished eating, I thought I'd need to be rolled out of the Washington house. I wanted to sprawl out on the couch and fall into a food coma.

"Thank you for dinner, Ruth," I said as I rubbed my stomach. "It was the best meal I've had in a long time. Just don't tell my mother I said that."

"My mama always told me the way to a man's heart was through his stomach," Ruth replied.

"Your daughter hasn't learned that yet." I winked at Max.

"My girl is so beautiful she doesn't need to use food."

"I agree," I said as I pulled Max's hand to my mouth and kissed her soft skin. She smelled like cornbread and butter.

Denzel pushed back from the table and stretched. "I'm ready for a nap," he announced. "Anthony, want to come outside?"

I glimpsed at Max and received a brief nod of approval. "Just yell for me if you want help with the dishes, Max." I swept my hand behind her neck and kissed her.

"You go talk with Denzel." She smiled on my lips. "You two need to make friends."

"Okay." I placed my napkin on the table and followed Denzel outside.

He tossed me a beer as I approached the picnic table in the backyard. "I wanted to explain what I meant earlier."

"Good. I was a little confused," I admitted as I cracked the top open and sat down.

"Ataxia is complicated." He took a giant gulp

of beer before he set the can on the table. "There are only a couple of forms that are actually testable. If you have a possibility of having one of those forms, then your test results will be accurate. The problem lies in the types that do not fall in that spectrum. My results were negative, but maybe my dad had one of the untestable types. If that's the case, I can still develop it later in life even with the negative test."

"I get that." I moved the can between my palms, rubbing it back and forth. "What were you saying about Max?"

"If she tests positive, then that means my dad had a type that could be tested. It means she is positive and that I'll always be negative because it's a testable type and I didn't have it. Shit, does that make sense?"

"It does. I'm praying to God it's negative, Denzel." I took a sip, welcoming the ice-cold feeling of the beer sliding down my throat.

"Remember, even if she's negative, she could develop it later in life." He gave me a weak smile.

"But it's better than a positive result right away."

"True."

"Hey," I said. "I wanted to apologize for the night I met you."

He waved his hands. "It's forgotten."

"No," I said as I shook my head. "I want to apologize. I wasn't trying to be an asshole. I really liked your sister from the moment I saw her, man."

"I know that now. I thought she needed rescuing that night, but I think she had the situation under control. You have a sister, right?" He placed his elbows on the table and clasped his hands together.

"I do."

"So you understand. I'd protect my sister with my life."

"I do."

"We're cool, then."

I blew out a breath, feeling better about the whole situation. The last thing I needed was a pissed-off brother to deal with for years.

"As long as you keep my sister happy, we'll have no problems."

"I'm trying, Denzel. I'm trying."

We drank our beer as the sun began to set. For the first time that day, I felt calm. I liked her family, even Earl. When dinner was over and the kitchen was cleaned, we sat in the backyard and talked.

By the end of the night, I felt like I'd known them forever. It doesn't matter what color people are, family is family, and I could feel the love they had for each other. The Washingtons were good people. They'd welcomed me into their home and made me feel comfortable. Well, maybe not Earl right away.

As we walked down the driveway, I stopped and pulled Max to me. "I love your family," I whispered against her lips.

She smiled and smashed her lips to my mouth. She still tasted of sweet potato pie as her tongue mingled with mine.

"Take me home," she murmured into my mouth. "Make love to me."

My heart was full along with my stomach. Even if I hadn't liked her family, I'd still have loved her. Knowing that they were good people and much like my family made me happier than

I already was. No matter what the test said, I wanted Max to be mine. I wanted to spend my life loving her and making her happy. Soon, we'd have the results and better know what we faced. Either way, as long as we had each other, I'd do my best to make her life happy.

16

PATIENCE ISN'T MY MIDDLE NAME

SIX MOTHERFUCKIN' WEEKS.

Forty-two goddamn days.

One thousand eight freakin' hours.

Sixty thousand, four hundred and eighty excruciating minutes.

That's how long we waited until the doctor's office called to say that they'd received the results. Even though Max begged to be told the results, they wouldn't divulge the information over the phone. They stated that it was standard office procedure for her to come to the office to "discuss" the results with the doctor.

We'd already been stressed to the maximum

level possible. Every day, I'd felt like I could touch the tension and cut it with a knife. The time that felt the longest was when we sat in the waiting room at the doctor's office. I wanted to burst through the doors and demand to see the results.

To have come this far and know that the information was close enough to touch drove me crazier than I'd ever felt before. I couldn't stop shaking my legs and fidgeting in my seat. I didn't even have the patience to look at my phone. The only thing I could think about was the goddamn test.

I was the one who had made her do it. I'd been selfish in demanding her to get it done. The last six weeks had been absolute torture. We hadn't talked about it much, but it was always there.

I held her hand, which was stuck to mine from the nervous sweat that had formed. I could feel her trembling next to me as our arms and shoulders touched.

"It'll be okay, Max," I tried to reassure her with a small smile.

"Yep," she responded in a clipped tone as she stared straight ahead and didn't return my glance.

To the casual observer in the room, it would have seemed that we were here for me. I was the one more visibly nervous, but I knew she was a mess inside.

"We've been waiting here an hour. What's taking so damn long?" I complained as I looked at my watch.

"Look at all the people, Anthony. It's a busy office. It always takes this long here."

"Bullshit," I mumbled as I gnashed my teeth together.

"What's a couple more minutes when I've waited this long?"

"You can't mean that, Max. I know you're nervous."

"I am, Anthony. I know I have it. I can feel it. You wouldn't understand."

"I won't believe it until she says the words."

"Prepare yourself, then, Anthony. Are you ready for it?"

"We'll get a second opinion."

"No!" she yelled, causing people in the waiting room to look at us.

"Max," I said, leaning closer to her. "I'll go to the ends of the earth to give you a different fate."

"Can you give me a different body?" she asked as she looked at me.

"I'm in love with the one you have now, Max."

"Then it's what you need to accept."

"Ms. Washington," a nurse called out from across the room, standing near the doorway.

"Here," Max said as she stood.

I took a deep breath, holding it in as I climbed to my feet. I felt like I was doing the long march to the electric chair. I dreaded what I might hear in a few short minutes. Some invisible fist was inside my stomach and punching it. I could barely breathe as I moved on shaky legs.

I repeated to myself, "She will be okay," over and over again. Max squeezed my hand, never breaking contact as we were shown to the doctor's office.

"Please take a seat. The doctor will be in in a

moment," the nurse said before she gave Max a small smile and left us alone.

"I can't sit," I said as she started to move toward the seat.

"We can't just stand here," Max replied as she closed her eyes and exhaled.

"Let me hold you, Max. I need to hold you." I pulled her hand, bringing her to my chest.

I tried to memorize possibly the last normal moment we'd have. The moment where I felt we were just Max and Anthony. It would all change. We could be Max, Anthony, and ataxia. Not a relationship I wanted to enter into, but I might not have a choice.

"I'm scared," Max confessed into my shirt.

"I know, baby. Me too," I admitted. "Either way, I'm with you through it all, Max."

"Anthony," she whispered as she moved to look at me. As she toyed with my shirt, she said, "I don't blame you if you leave me. It's okay if you leave me. I'll totally understand."

"Are you giving me permission to leave you?" I tried to keep my voice steady, but inside, I was seething.

"Yes. No one wants to be with a sick person. Why should you be tied to me forever? I'm giving you an out," she said with tears in her eyes. "I love you, but I'll understand." As she gave me a weak smile, a single tear ran down her cheek.

"Max. I'm not going anywhere. No matter what the doctor says, I'm here to stay."

"Anthony—"

"Max." I grabbed her by the shoulders and stared at her. "You don't understand the depth of my feelings for you. There will never be another woman I'll ever love."

"Oh, that's horseshit."

I shook my head. "It's not. I've never found another person who makes me feel alive like you do. Touching you, kissing your lips is like that shock you get from touching something when the air's too dry."

"Never say never, Anthony."

"I would never let you go through this without me," I stated, holding her stare.

"Let's talk about this after the results." She

wiped the tears that had fallen down her face on my shirt.

Without even thinking, I dropped to one knee. It hadn't been planned. Fuck, I would've been more nervous than I already was if I had come up with the idea ahead of time. I knew what I wanted, and she was in front of me. There was no way I'd let her get away. I wouldn't let her excuse me or give me an out.

Her eyes widened as she noticed that I was balanced on one knee. Grabbing her hand, I stroked the top with my thumb. The only shitty part of not having planned this was that I didn't have a ring.

"Max," I said before clearing my throat. My voice was shaky, but I was more nervous about the results than asking her to marry me. "I love you more than anyone in the world. No matter the results, I want to go on the journey with you. It's taken me my entire life to meet someone who makes me a better person, and I want you to be mine forever. Will you marry me?"

She covered her mouth, the tears falling

faster than they had before. "No," she whispered.

"No?" I asked, the punch in my stomach feeling more like the slice of a knife as it cut up into my chest.

"Yes," she said. "Anthony. I just didn't dream of this being where I'd be proposed to someday."

"Thank Christ," I mumbled. "I don't care where we are, as long as you say yes."

"Anthony, I think I should wait to give you an answer until after we talk to the doctor. Let the information seep in before you ask me again. You may not feel the same once the enormity of the situation settles in your gut."

"It's settled. I've never told anyone before that I loved them. No one. Only you. It'll only ever be you."

"Hello," the doctor said as she walked in and then noticed that I was down on one knee. "Oh, I'm so sorry I interrupted."

"You didn't." She pulled her hand from my grip.

As the doctor rounded the desk to sit, Max sat

down. I pushed myself off the ground, feeling a bit wounded and even more nervous. I held on to the chair as I sat, making sure I didn't miss the seat.

Fuck. Everything about the day could fuck off.

"Sorry you had to wait so long," the doctor said as she opened a folder on her desk and began to study the contents.

I sucked in a breath, unable to release it. There wasn't a time in my life that I could recall where I'd felt more scared. Not when Angel had been kidnapped or when Thomas had been undercover. I felt completely helpless in this situation. When it came to brute force or kicking ass, I knew how to do it.

This was up to fate and genetics.

"It's okay," Max said with a fake smile as she looked at me.

I held her hand, gripping it tight. No matter what the doctor said, I wouldn't let her down. I needed to be her brace. I needed to be the man she could lean on. I needed to be her rock—the one thing to keep her steady and sane through this time in her life. Fuck, through this time in our lives.

"Well, let's get to it," the doctor said, flipping a page and skimming over it.

I swallowed hard, sucking in another breath and holding it in my lungs.

"Based on the results of your test," She flipped the page, moving over the words with her finger, "it states negative for ataxia, but as you know, there are some forms that can't be found through testing."

"So Max won't get it," I blurted out, giving her hand a squeeze.

"I can't say for certain, sir. Her brother tested negative, but her father was never tested before he died. We're unsure of what type of ataxia he had, therefore it makes the test results sketchy."

"Sketchy? That's not very helpful."

"Anthony," Max said, as she stroked my arm. "Doctor, so there's no real way to know if I'll get it or not."

The doctor shook her head as her brow furrowed. "I'm afraid not. It's a waiting game from here on out."

I thought I'd be happy to hear that she was negative, but all it did was make everything so uncertain.

I blew out the breath I'd been holding and gulped. I felt like my throat had closed, and even the simple act of breathing was difficult. I thought I had prepared myself for the worst, but knowing that it could still happen made my chest ache.

"How long?" I blurted out without thinking.

"Until the onset of symptoms if she'll develop it?" the doctor asked.

I blinked a couple of times, trying to focus. "Yes," I replied, and held Max's hand tighter.

"It's hard to say. Symptoms can begin at any time." She gave a half-smile that wasn't reassuring at all. "Max, how old was your father when he started to experience onset of symptoms?"

"His late fifties, and he died about ten years later."

"I'd say she'll probably follow the same timeline if you do develop the condition. You're only in your mid-thirties. You have probably twenty years before you'd start to notice major changes in your coordination. But remember, there's a chance you will never develop ataxia."

Twenty years. Only twenty fucking years. It seems like a long time when you're looking forward to something happy, but when it's bad news, twenty years isn't long enough. It feels like a heartbeat and passes in the blink of an eye.

"Twenty years," Max whispered, and closed her eyes.

"We're doing clinical trials at various clinics across the country. Hopefully in the next ten to twenty years, we'll have a cure or at least a treatment." The doctor folded her hands on top of the desk and leaned back.

"So, what do we do now, doc?" I asked.

"Just live life like normal, but there are things someone can do to possibly delay the onset of symptoms." She rubbed the arm of her chair with her hand as she looked across the desk.

"Such as?" My patience was hanging by a thread.

"It seems that alcohol and tobacco can have

an effect on the rapidity of symptoms. It's important to limit the consumption of both."

"Shiiit," Max drawled.

I looked at her with a steely stare. If it meant I'd have her healthier longer, then I didn't care to ever have another sip.

"Max," I said.

"I didn't say you couldn't have a drink. Just not every day and in large quantities."

"Fine," she snapped.

"What else?" I asked, ready to move on from the conversation about trivial shit like beer.

"It's important to keep the muscles strong. Regular workouts and weights will help when symptoms begin. Often, patients lose muscle tone as the symptoms progress. So having a good amount of muscle beforehand will help keep her stronger for a longer period of time."

I could do that. I worked out all the time and I could always get Mike to work with her. He'd love to help out in some way, and the man knew how to build muscle.

"So, I can't drink and I have to work out?"

"In the scheme of things, it's no big deal. We can work out together. We got this."

"I'm not a girl who spends time in a gym. I like my softness. I don't want to look like one of those hardcore bodybuilders. I embrace my curves."

"I embrace them too." I couldn't stop my smile. She'd left that open for me to comment. "We won't make you hard."

"Here's some literature about ataxia for you to read."

"Thank you, doctor," Max said before she let out a loud sigh.

"Make an appointment on the way out. We'll monitor you with yearly physicals to watch for coordination loss and other signs. That way, it doesn't sneak up on you if you start to develop any symptoms."

"I will." Max stood from her chair and gave me a weak smile. "Ready?"

"Yeah." I squeezed her hand as I climbed to my feet. I hadn't let go the entire time in the doctor's office, and I didn't want to let go now.

"Thank you," I said to the doctor as I followed Max out the door.

I wanted time with her. Twenty years, ten years—it didn't matter as long as we had some time together. She hadn't accepted my proposal —she'd brushed it off until later.

I still wanted to marry her.

I wouldn't leave her, and I wouldn't make it easy for her to leave me. She wasn't a selfish person. An individual who is truly selfish would've hid the condition and walked through life as if everything were fine. Max had done her best to push me away, but I didn't let her.

We walked to the car in silence, stealing small glances at each other as we wandered through the parking lot.

Was it better to know? I didn't know anymore. If I were ill, would I want a stopwatch placed on my life? I'd heard my entire life that knowledge was power, but I'd now say that it was crippling. I felt like the button had been pressed and each second that ticked by was one second less that I'd have a healthy Max.

When we approached the car, I smashed her into the door. "Are you okay, Max?"

She stared up at me with a half-smile. "Yeah."

I touched her cheek, resting my palm on her skin. "Max, it's okay if you're not okay."

She melted into my touch, closing her eyes. "I know I'll get it, Anthony. No matter what the test states. I dealt with it a long time ago."

"Hey," I said, needing to look into her eyes.

She opened them but looked at my shoulder.

"Look at me, Max," I commanded, not about to play a game as her eyes met mine. "You can play the hardass, Max, the one who doesn't give a fuck about anything, but I know the truth. We got great news today, baby. Stop being a pessimist." I placed my lips on her forehead, brushing my nose through her hair.

"I've just believed it for so long, it's hard to think anything different."

"It doesn't matter what she said, Max. I love you and want to spend the rest of my life loving you."

She grabbed my sides, digging her nails into my skin. "Take a day and think about it."

"I don't need a day." I backed away and stared down at her. "We've spent enough time dicking around."

"Can you take me home, Anthony? I'm tired and want to lie down." She peered down at the ground and squeezed me.

"Sure, but I'm staying with you. I need to hold you." I wanted to curl into a ball and bring her into my cocoon.

Before she could respond, I crushed my lips to hers. I inhaled her scent, the cherry lip gloss she'd used over her lipstick to give it the shine. I didn't care about that, but I enjoyed the smell and taste. The fullness of her lips on mine sent the expected sparks of electricity through my body.

By the time I broke the kiss, her breathing was ragged. I needed to bury myself inside her and get lost in the feel of our bodies together. It would help block everything else out and make it about us in that moment. There would be no illness, no future, just our bodies connected and working as one.

As I opened the door, I said, "I love you, Max, and I'm here to stay."

She just smiled, sliding into the seat before staring out the front window. I needed to remind her of the happy things in life.

No longer did I live life for me. Now, it was about us.

∗∗∗

Max

The man wouldn't take no for an answer.

I'd given him a final chance of bowing out of the entire clusterfuck that was my future. He refused, pressing forward and dropping to one knee. When he did, my knees became weak.

Never in my life did I think he'd propose. Especially since we hadn't known each other for that long. I couldn't even form a coherent thought when I realized what he was saying to me.

I know the doctor said I was negative, but I

couldn't shake the feeling that someday I'd face the same fate as my father. Maybe in time I'd feel at ease and be able to believe that I'd have my happy ending.

Anthony made me want to believe it was true. The impossible now felt probable, and for the first time in a long time, I felt hopeful.

No one knows their future, but it doesn't cripple them and stop them from finding their happiness. Why should I let it stop me? I needed to live my life one day at a time, loving Anthony, and being truly happy. I'd lived long enough with the cloud over my head.

17

MIRACLES

Max and I had been going back and forth about marriage since the day we'd received the results. Months ago, she hadn't wanted a boyfriend, but I hadn't given up and eventually got my way. Getting her to agree to be my wife was a much harder fight. Being who I was, I was willing to stick with it until the end. I wouldn't give up.

"Say yes," I commanded her through gritted teeth. "Say it." I slammed my dick into her. Fuck, she felt so damn good.

If I could have done it, I'd have stayed this way, with our bodies connected. There wasn't an hour of the day that I didn't think of her pussy, the feel, smell, and taste of it.

"No!" she said, shaking her head.

Max was in front of me, bent over on all fours. Her beautiful ass was on full display as I pulled out. I couldn't help but glance down and watch my cock as it moved in and out of her.

"Max, you know what I want to hear!" I rubbed both cheeks with my palms, caressing them as I waited for her response.

"No!" she yelled into the mattress.

My hand came down hard on her tender flesh. A loud crack echoed through the room as she howled.

"Say it, Kitty Cat. Whose pussy is this?" I kept rhythm, trying to keep her on the edge both mentally and physically until she relented.

Her side profile was visible over her shoulder as she sank down into the bed, but she kept her ass in the air. Then she sealed her eyes shut as she whispered, "Yours."

"Louder. I couldn't hear you. Whose?" I gripped her hips.

"Yours!" she screamed as I drove my rock-hard shaft into her wetness.

"Whose woman are you?" I trailed one hand down her spine, running my fingertips over each bone.

"Yours!" she called out before she sucked in a breath.

Seeing her this way, with my cock inside her and at my mercy, was such a heady feeling. I felt drunk on lust and power with her beneath me.

I pulled all the way out, hovering over her opening. "Whose wife are you going to be?" I figured that, maybe if I threw it in during the heat of passion, she'd finally say yes. I wouldn't let her forget it, either.

When she didn't respond, I released her hip and smacked her ass harder on the same exact spot I'd struck earlier.

"Ouch," she cried as she tried to crawl forward.

I didn't let her get away, dragging her back with a tight grip on her hips. I peppered her back with kisses until her body sagged into the mattress.

"Say you'll be my wife, Max." It was the only thing in the world I wanted to hear.

I slid my fingers between her legs, creating a V. I stroked her clit as I pounded into her. Her pussy contracted as the orgasm began to build inside her.

Just as her breathing changed, I cupped her sex and waited. I wouldn't let her come until she gave in and said yes. No fucking way would I give her that pleasure without hearing those words.

"I can't," she whined as she wiggled, trying to get friction from my fingers.

I still fucking hated that phrase. It was worse than no.

"You can," I whispered in her ear as I stuck my cock as far as it could go inside her.

"Anthony, please," she said, pushing her ass backward.

"Max," I said as I moved my fingers enough to make her body shudder, "if you want to come, you'll say yes."

"You're an asshole," she snarled as she glared at me over her shoulder.

I kept my voice low as I said into her ear, "I know. Now, say it, baby."

"Okay. Okay. I'll marry you," she said.

Not my shining moment, but I'd fucking take it.

Just as I started to move again, I tweaked her clit, feeling her body tremble, and my phone began to ring.

I ignored it, letting it ring until it went to voicemail. Nothing was going to stop me from fucking the shit out of her until we both collapsed into a sweaty pile. Seconds later, the phone began to ring again.

"Oh, God," she moaned as she fisted the sheets in her hands. Her ass began to sway as I continued to charge forward and chase the orgasm.

"Ignore it," I bit out, too deep to stop.

As my movement became sporadic, the phone began to ring again. I didn't stop. Hell, I couldn't stop. Pinching her clit between my fingers, I brought her over the edge with me as we both screamed through the pleasure.

By the time my body stopped shuddering

from the aftershocks, the phone had rung at least ten more times. She lay beneath me, breathing heavily.

"You better get that," she said as she collapsed.

I grabbed my phone off the nightstand and looked at the caller ID. "Damn it," I blurted out when I saw that it was my mother. Total cock-block move. She'd never called me over and over again. It wasn't her style.

I hit the call back button and waited. She picked up on the second ring.

"Anthony!" she shrieked.

"What the hell, Ma?" I asked as I moved the phone away from my ear.

"It's Suzy. She's in labor. Get to the hospital now."

I shook my head. "Ma, I understand you're excited, but it's going to be hours until she has the baby. I'll be there when I can."

"Come now, and bring Max," she said. Then she hung up.

I looked at the phone, wondering where my mother had gone and who the hell was occupying her body now. She'd become a ball of stress as Suzy's date had come closer.

"You don't even need to tell me." Max chuckled, trying to push her body up, but her arms were still too unsteady. "I guess we better go." She spread her arms out.

My legs were burning and my entire body felt like jelly. I didn't even know if I could move without falling down.

"We have time."

"Oh, no. We are not making your mother wait."

"Jesus, Max. Come on. Lie here with me for a minute."

"No," she said as she pushed me away.

I fell on to my back, sprawling out as she climbed to her feet. "You just had to lie there and enjoy the fucking. I was the one doing all the work." I smiled, knowing I'd get a shitstorm for that comment. Women had it easy. "Next time, you can hop on top and do the work."

"Puh-lease. It isn't that difficult, Anthony. Get your ass up," she demanded as she pulled at my foot.

"Maybe I need to fuck you again. You're way too mouthy."

She giggled, slapping the bottom of my foot. "Later. If you're good, I'll give you more pussy later."

"Shit, I'll just take it. You said it's mine, Max. I take possession very seriously." I placed my palms on the mattress and lifted myself up. "Give me five minutes."

"You have five minutes while I go get ready. Then we're leaving," she called out over her shoulder as she disappeared into the bathroom.

I stared at the ceiling and knew that the moment I brought up marriage again she'd deny ever saying it. Or she'd say that I'd blackmailed her to get the answer I wanted. We needed to announce it to the family. If Max cared that much about disappointing my mother, I'd find a way to make the wedding happen.

WE STROLLED INTO THE HOSPITAL FORTY-five minutes after my mother had demanded our presence. The maternity waiting room was filled with Gallos. We were the only ones missing.

"Anthony!" Ma called out as soon as she saw us. She hustled toward us with a giant smile on her face. "It's happening. I'm going to be a grandmother. Oh my God, I'm going to be Nona!"

"Ma," I whispered as I hugged her. "Breathe, woman." I chuckled. I didn't know the last time she had been so worked up.

"I am. I am." She rubbed my back, quiet giggles shaking her body. "She's been in labor for hours. She's already pushing. The baby will be here any time now."

"Hey, Pop," I said as I watched him over my mother's head.

He was pacing an invisible path across the waiting room. "Son." He nodded and continued on his endeavor to wear out the linoleum.

"Don't mind him. Births always make him nervous. This is such an exciting day. It couldn't get any better."

I smiled at her and felt that the moment was right. "It can, Ma. Everyone, Max and I have an announcement."

I didn't fucking dare to look at her. I could feel her stare boring a hole through my head.

She tugged on my arm and whispered, "What the fuck are you doing?"

I ignored her. "Today, Max agreed to be my wife," I announced.

Izzy clapped, Ma screamed, and my brothers and Pop smiled.

"Asshole," Max mumbled, loud enough for me to hear.

"Another daughter." Ma approached Max and pulled her into her arms.

Max spun with my ma in her arms and glared at me. I just smiled, knowing there was no way out for her now. She'd agreed earlier, and now the announcement had been made.

We were officially engaged.

Joe burst into the room before everyone had finished giving their congratulations to Max and me. "It's a girl!" he yelled, raking his hands through his hair. "A girl."

"Yes!" Izzy cheered, and raised her arms. "Thank you, God," she said as she fell to her knees and looked toward the ceiling.

"Congrats, brother." I held out my hand to him, grabbing his arm. I could see tears in his eyes.

"When can I see her?" Ma asked as she kissed Joe on the cheek.

"They just need a little time and then everyone can go in and see them."

"Do you have a name, son?" Pop asked as he stood beside Ma.

"Yes. It's Giovanna Bianca." He beamed as he said her name. He stood a bit straighter with his shoulders pushed back. The pride he felt at his new title of father was clearly evident.

"Gigi," Ma whispered. "You named her after my mother." She covered her mouth as she began to cry.

"We did." Joe grabbed my ma and stared down at her. "It's the perfect name for my little Italian princess."

Joe went into graphic detail describing the birth of his baby girl. At times, I felt faint. I'd seen plenty of crazy shit. Hell, I'd seen things come out of a pussy that weren't natural, but seeing a human being slide out, even a small one, was just wrong. He gushed over having been able to cut the umbilical cord and how a small piece of him would live on forever.

The entire time he spoke, I held Max's hand as she listened and seemed totally enthralled. For a woman who didn't want children, she was mesmerized and hung on every word.

Twenty minutes later, the family was given the go-ahead to see Suzy and Gigi. We let Ma and Pop go back first and spend time with the baby before we went in as a group.

"You doing okay, Max?" I asked as we waited.

"Yeah. I am," she answered quietly.

"You seem off." I stroked her hand as we sat side by side in the waiting room.

"I'm not. It's just..."

"What is it? You know you can tell me anything."

"Sometimes, I get sad when I think I'll never be a mother." She frowned as she stared down at our hands.

"You can be a mother. There's nothing stopping you, Max."

"I do not want to pass my bad genes on to a baby."

I sat there a moment, thinking about what she'd said. I could understand it. No one wants to give their child a life filled with illness. There isn't a person on the planet that has been guaranteed a lifetime of healthiness. We all experience some type of health issue in our life, whether it be cancer or some other ailment.

"Max, do you wish your parents never had you?" I asked her. It was the only thing I had thought to say.

"No."

"Have you had a happy life?"

"Yes. For the most part, I have."

"Even with knowing how your future could turn out, would you want it to end now?"

"No. Stop asking stupid questions."

"Listen to me. Just because the baby would have a small chance of getting the gene doesn't mean they shouldn't be born. If you had said you wished your parents had never had you, then I'd agree with you. But you said you've had a happy life and you want to live. Maybe being a mother will bring you more joy than anything else in your life. Maybe you can have a healthy baby."

She sighed and blew a puff of air through her lips. "I don't know, Anthony. It's a big decision. If the baby is born with the gene, I'd feel so guilty."

"Do you want your parents to feel guilty about your life? Are you mad at them for having had you?"

I didn't know where all of this was coming from. Six months ago, all I'd cared about was banging my way through life and living in blissful ignorance of love. Now, I was in deep. So far down that I couldn't imagine a life without Max anymore.

"Of course not."

"Then why would your baby feel that way about you? If you don't wish you weren't born, neither will they, no matter the outcome of their health. Nothing is guaranteed, Max. I could get hit by a bus tomorrow and die."

"What did you do with my boyfriend?" she asked as she peered up at me.

"Fiancé," I said. "I don't know what happened to me. You happened to me and mixed up my head."

"I kind of miss my asshole sometimes, but times like this, when you're so sweet and smart, I realize why I love you."

"Why is that?" I was fishing for a compliment. Max wasn't always so willing to hand them out. When she was in the mood, I made sure to get as much as I could.

"You have the perfect mix of asshole and lover. Just when I think you've hit your asshole streak, you come back saying such beautiful things that you make my heart melt."

"And what does the asshole do to you? I know it's that part of me that you were first attracted to."

"He makes my panties melt," she whispered, and bit her lip.

"Ahhh. I always knew that girls secretly wanted an asshole."

I had known it. Even though they all said that they wanted the nice guy, they really wanted a mix. They wanted the asshole in the bedroom, banging their brains out, and the sweet guy the other times. I could be both. Fuck, I had been my entire life.

"I only want one asshole, Anthony."

"I'm your man, then, Kitty Cat." I grinned, bringing her hand to my mouth and kissing the top.

"Anthony and Max," Joe said from the doorway as he watched us. "You want to see Gigi?"

"Hell yes," I said.

We followed Joe down the hallway past a set of windows behind which little babies slept peacefully in their small plastic beds. They looked so sweet and quiet, but I remembered how loud a baby actually was, since I'd lived through the infancy of my siblings. Izzy had screamed the loudest and most. We should've known then that she'd be nothing but trouble.

I held Max's hand as we entered the room. Suzy had Gigi in her arms as she looked up at us and smiled.

"Ah, look who came to see you, Gigi. It's your asshole uncle, Anthony." Suzy giggled.

"Don't mind her," Joe said as he patted my

shoulder. "She's on some pain meds from the birth."

I chuckled, liking the calmer side of Suzy.

"It's cool, man." I patted him on the stomach and walked toward Suzy. "Can I hold her?" I asked, holding out my arms as I stood at her bedside.

"Sure." Suzy gently placed her in my arms.

I sat down on the edge and cradled her. She was so tiny—much smaller than I remembered my siblings being. Maybe it was because I was bigger that she seemed that much smaller.

Gigi was wrapped in a pink blanket with one hand sticking out. Her long fingers moved as if searching for something. Holding her tight to my chest, I stared at her and instantly fell in love. Her straight, dark hair was like Izzy had when she was born—full and wild.

I bounced her lightly and touched her hand with my finger. Her tiny digits clamped down on my finger with force.

"Isn't she beautiful?" Joe asked as he stood next to Suzy on the other side of the bed.

"She is," I agreed, and looked at Ma. "Look

how perfect she is." I stared down at Gigi and rubbed the back of her hand in the same motion I used when I wanted to reassure Max. "It's amazing."

"Look at you getting all mushy, Anthony," Suzy said, but I didn't bother to look at her.

"She's a Gallo. I have a right to be mushy."

"God, she's gorgeous," Max cooed as she touched her cheek.

Gigi turned and tried to latch on to Max's finger as she stroked her cheek.

"You can hold her if you want, Max," Joe said.

For a moment, I felt a pang of jealously. I didn't want to let her go. I wasn't ready to share her with anyone else, even Max.

When Max said, "I'd love to," and held out her arms, I gently handed her over.

I'd have a lifetime to spoil the little girl. I could be the cool uncle who bought her the best toys and let her run wild. I wanted to be that guy. I didn't want to be the self-consumed douchebag I had probably been months ago.

As I scanned the room, I realized how much

love I'd always had in my life. Suzy and Joe gazed at each other. Their love shined brightly and seemed to grow over time. I'd always secretly envied them for the way they loved each other. I hadn't thought I'd find someone who would make my heart skip a beat until I'd met Max.

"It's a miracle," Max whispered, brushing her lips to Gigi's head and inhaling. "There's nothing like the smell of a new baby."

I smiled at her, feeling everything inside of me warm. I loved this woman. I wanted to make babies with her. I wanted to watch her blow up like a balloon like Suzy had and carry a piece of me inside her.

More importantly, I wanted a piece of us to live on long after we were gone. It was the only way to have us be remembered.

"You want one?" I asked Max with one eyebrow raised.

"It's not that simple."

"It is," I said. "I think we should go home and get to work on that ASAP." I clutched Max's hips, trying to convey the sense of urgency.

"Anthony," she said as she glanced down at me and pulled Gigi closer to her chest.

"Did you two hear the news?" I asked Suzy and Joe.

"No," they replied at the same time.

"Max and I are getting married."

"Oh. My. God!" Suzy yelled.

"Way to go, man." Joe said as he hung over the bed and shook my hand. "You better marry her fast before she realizes what an asshole you really are."

"Nah," I said. "She loves when I'm an asshole. It's how I plan to get her knocked up."

Suzy and Joe cracked up.

"Let's let them have some time with Gigi before the rest of the family comes in, Max."

She nodded and gave Gigi a kiss on the cheek. I dipped down, kissing her too as I took one last chance to hold her hand.

"Night, little Gigi," I whispered against her face.

She let out a small cry and turned her mouth toward me. Cool baby spit landed on my nose. I was done for, and there was no turning back.

She'd given me her first kiss, and it would be forever seared in my brain.

"Are you tearing up?" Max asked as she started to hand Gigi back to Suzy.

"No!" I shot back as I tried to blink away the mist that had formed in my eyes. "It's the air in here. It's killing my contacts."

"Um, I didn't know you wore contacts," Max said with her face all scrunched up like she knew I was full of shit.

"He doesn't," Joe piped in.

"Shut up." I stood from the bed and hooked my arm over Max's shoulder. "Let's get out of here. We have a wedding to plan and a baby to make."

"Fuck me," Max blurted.

"I plan to, Kitty Cat. I plan to," I said as I waved goodbye over my shoulder.

When we walked out of the room, we could hear Suzy and Joe laughing their asses off. Nothing in the world could get me down. I had my woman by my side, my family tighter than ever, and a little niece who had captured my heart forever.

Karma had finally switched teams.

***

Max

What the hell happened to my life? Oh yeah, Hurricane Anthony made landfall and wreaked havoc on my life. Months ago I was alone, and for the most part I was okay with that. Now he had me dreaming of babies and planning a trip down the aisle.

I would've never imagined him to look so damn good with a baby in his arms. When I saw him hold Gigi, the way he looked at her as he talked to her made my heart melt. I couldn't deny him the chance of having one of his own. It would be a way to leave a piece of us on this earth forever.

Even facing an uncertain future, I couldn't say no to a baby any longer. I wouldn't give up any bit of my life even with the knowledge of a crappy future. There's no guarantee when having a baby that they'll be healthy and have the most amazing life. Our only job is to love them and give them every opportunity at happiness. Anthony had made me believe this. Seeing the way he held Gigi made me believe it. To deny him of the ability to love a baby with his whole being would be wrong.

The one thing I knew for sure: I no longer wanted to wait to start living my life. I was on the high board and ready to do the biggest belly flop of my life and welcome the impact it would have on my future.

18

GIVING IN

I THOUGHT I ALWAYS LOOKED GOOD, BUT I was wrong.

At least, that was what Max told me after she agreed to be my wife.

"You need some new clothes," she declared one night as we walked along the beach, letting the waves lap at our feet.

"Why? What's wrong with what I have?"

"You wear decent clothes, but you need to look more..." She looked out over the ocean.

"More what, Max?" I asked as I stopped walking and pulled her back with her hand.

Her chest collided with mine as she began to

laugh. "I just want to dress you. It's what I do for a living, Anthony. Jeans and a T-shirt are good sometimes, but at other times, I want a man of style by my side."

"I always look good."

"I never said you didn't." She brushed her lips against my chin as her fingers crept up the back of my shirt.

A shiver cascaded over my body as her nails grazed my lower back. "So then why?" I kissed the top of her nose, looking down in her chocolate eyes.

"It will be fun. Please, baby. Let me take you shopping and dress you up."

"Like I'm a real-life Ken doll?" I cradled her face in my hands and smiled.

"Exactly. Think of how much fun it'll be." She smiled.

I'd found it hard to say no to anything she asked me ever since she agreed to be my wife. I was sure there's a line somewhere I wouldn't cross, but I hadn't found it yet.

"Okay, but it doesn't sound like fun at all," I whined before I crushed my lips to hers.

The waves crashed against our legs as I held her in my arms. The beach was empty and the sun was setting with a brilliant orange and red glow behind us. When I released her lips, her eyes remained closed and her lips stayed puckered.

Before she opened them, I pulled away and removed the ring from my pocket. I'd let her pick it out and had finally picked it up from the jewelers. It was a brilliant three-carat princess-cut diamond set in a platinum band. I'd felt shitty about how I'd asked her. It was so unromantic to drop down on one knee in the doctor's office, but I wanted her to know how serious I was about our relationship.

"Max," I said as I kneeled in the sand and held her left hand.

Her eyes fluttered open as her face drifted down.

I held the ring up and kissed her fingertips one by one. "I'm so in love with you, Max. I've never had a woman who has driven me as crazy as you have."

"Is this supposed to be good?" she interrupted.

"Shush, woman. I'm not done." I cleared my throat and she laughed. "I knew from the first time I touched you that there was something different about you. I couldn't get you out of my mind, no matter how hard I tried. Your sassy mouth and bitchy attitude hooked me."

"I should've been like Candy," she teased.

"Never mention her name again." I tugged her arm, pulling her down in the sand with me as she threw her arms around my neck. "You're the only woman for me. Even to this day, months later, I still feel the spark when I kiss your lips. There isn't an hour of the day that goes by when I don't think of you. No matter what happens in the future, I want to be there with you. Max, I'm asking today if you'll marry me and be mine forever?"

Her grin turned into a giant smile as she sniffled. "I love you, Anthony Gallo. There isn't anything I want more in the world than to become Mrs. Anthony Gallo."

"Yeah?" I asked as I slipped the ring on her finger.

"Yeah, baby. You're the only man in the world who would put up with my bullshit. Now if I can only get you to dress a little better, we'll have a bright future." She laughed as she waved her fingers and stared down at the rock that glistened in the vanishing sunlight.

"Such a shit," I said as I grabbed her sides and started to tickler her.

"Anthony!" She giggled and lost her balance, falling backward.

I landed on top of her and pushed myself up so I wouldn't crush her. "I love you," I whispered against her soft lips.

She ran her hand through my hair. "I love you too. Thank you."

"For what?"

"Being a cocky asshole," she murmured against my mouth.

"Speaking of assholes." I wiggled my eyebrows.

"After I say I do."

"Let's elope," I declared, feeling like it couldn't get here soon enough.

"No way! I'm going to wear the prettiest dress I can find. I'm not missing my walk down the aisle in a designer gown just so you can fuck me in the ass."

"You make it sounds so tawdry. I do remember you violating me the first night we spent together."

"And you fucking loved it. You were all twitchy and gasping for air."

"Enough," I said, feeling slightly embarrassed.

"When you were all, 'Oh God. Yes, Max. Deeper, Max.'" She laughed.

"I never said deeper," I said as my cheeks heated.

"We'll see if you do tonight," she added as she pulled my face against hers and kissed me.

"Mm," I mumbled into her kiss as my stiff prick pressed into her thigh.

"Take me home," she said as she released my lips.

"Gladly, but only if you're going to do that special thing with your finger."

She snickered, pressing her head into the sand. "I knew you liked it."

"Only when you do it, baby," I said as I pushed myself up to my knees.

"Tonight you get what you want and tomorrow I get what I want."

"Anal?" I asked, feeling hopeful.

"Clothes." She smiled as she used my arm to pull herself up.

"Fuck me," I muttered, and rolled my eyes.

WELL, SHE HAD THAT SHIT RIGHT. SHE'D GET exactly what she wanted, but only after I had a few mind-blowing orgasms. Even though I hated shopping, I felt completely okay with it as I stood in Nordstrom.

"Would you like me to start a dressing room?" the salesman asked Max.

I stood there with my arm outstretched as I

held at least ten hangers of clothes that didn't look comfortable.

"Yes please." She took the hangers from my arms and handed them to the man before he disappeared.

"Got enough?" I asked, hoping that her answer would be yes.

"Nope. Only a few more things."

I sighed and followed her to the next rack that held Armani suits. "What do I need a suit for?"

She paid no attention to me as she looked through the jackets.

"Do you just want to torture me?" I whined.

"It's for the rehearsal dinner."

She pulled the wedding card and she knew damn well I wouldn't argue. "Okay," I answered and felt completely pussy-whipped. "Can I wear a fedora?"

She stopped dead and gawked at me. "You can't be serious."

I nodded with my mouth set in a firm line. "Dead serious, woman."

"No hats."

"I heard they're in style."

"Where? In the Rolling Stone?"

"I think I look good in hats."

"This is my show, buddy. I say no hats. Especially for the rehearsal dinner."

"Wedding?"

"No," she snapped.

"Bossy."

"Cocky."

"Hey, Max, if you're really good, we can christen that dressing room with all my cockiness."

She laid her hand on my chest and brought her lips within an inch of mine. "You are not going to derail today with sex."

"Think of it as an accessory."

"It's not happening."

"Killjoy."

"I am, and that's why you love me." She gave me a quick peck before turning her attention back to the rack of suits that cost more than I'd spent on my entire wardrobe to date.

"Yeah, that must be it. It wouldn't have anything to do with your amazing body and tight pussy. It was entirely your sparkling personality that made me fall in love."

"Anthony."

I could see her smile from the side profile as I watched her in her glory. "You owe me big for today."

"You owe me big for being your wife."

"Anal, baby." I laughed as she hit me on the chest.

I couldn't be a happier man.

This magnificent creature before me was going to be mine. Even with my bad sense of style—her words, not mine—and my checkered past, she still loved me. On paper we didn't work. White boy with tattoos and a total asshole and a black girl with a chip on her shoulder.

Hell, sometimes I wondered how we got to the point where she was my fiancée. But when my assholishness met her feisty attitude, everything clicked together.

Honestly, I was drawn to her since she was the only female who hadn't thrown themselves at me. I had to work for her love. Shit, I had to work just to get her name.

I felt completely at peace and excited to see what the future held for us. I felt like I was starting life over again. Now I looked forward to each day with an open heart and a good woman by my side.

Maxine Washington was mine, along with an Armani suit and about twenty other pieces of clothing by people I'd never heard of. My life overfloweth.

19

CELEBRATE GOOD TIMES

"We're so sad you couldn't make it to girls' night out last week," Izzy told Max as we slid into the booth along the back wall.

Max smiled at Izzy. "Yeah?"

"It wasn't the same without you," Suzy added, sitting in a chair across from Izzy.

After Max couldn't make it to girls' night out because of some work event, which I found a way to skip, we decided to get together as a group. Everyone came. Max's brother brought Brenda and all the Gallos, including James. My parents agreed to watch Gigi for the night so we could have a celebration.

On one side of the table sat Izzy, James, Denzel, Brenda, Max, and myself. In the chairs across from us were Mike, Mia, Thomas, Angel, Suzy, and Joe. Malia and Nita took opposite ends of the table for "maximum view," as they liked to call it.

"I'm just glad Suzy could make it out again," Max said as she brushed Suzy's long blond hair away from her shoulder.

Max had grown close to the girls over the last months or so. They rallied around her through text messages, phone calls, and lunch while we were waiting for her results and even afterward. I could never thank them enough for everything they did to make her feel welcome and like a member of the family, especially after the results were given to us.

"I wouldn't miss this for the world. I swear that baby is going to be the death of me."

"Sugar, you're the best mother in the world," Joe said before giving her a kiss on the cheek.

"Enough of me whining, we're here to celebrate. Champagne?" Suzy asked with raised eyebrows.

"Yes!" I said as I slammed my open palm down on the table. "Wait. Can you drink while breastfeeding?"

She laughed and shook her head. "Technically no, but I have a stock pile of breast milk saved for occasions just like this."

"Really?" Mike asked as he blanched. "That's just so..."

"Responsible," Mia added before he could finish his statement.

"How does that work exactly?" I asked, trying to visualize how the milk goes from breast to bottle. "I mean, do you milk yourself by hand?"

"Oh, Jesus," Mia said, slapping her forehead as everyone groaned.

"You are not that dense." Thomas shook his head.

"Yo!" I yelled, pointing at myself. "I know nothing about babies. Women, yes. Breasts, yes. Milking, um, no."

"It's okay, Anthony." Suzy laughed, reaching across Max to touch my hand. "There's a machine that pumps the milk out."

I scratched my chin, trying to picture it. "Does it look like the breast pumps I can get at Todd Couples Superstore? You know those ones you can use," I said as I pretended to attach them to my chest, "to get your kink on while you're eating—" A hard slap to the back of my head stopped me. I glared at Joe, knowing exactly where that hand came from.

"Just stop."

"You've turned into a prude fucker, Joe," I spat.

"Yep, they're almost exactly like that," Suzy replied as she swatted Joe's arm. "Be nice to him."

"Why?" he growled, peering down at her. "He says dumb shit."

"He's curious, baby." Suzy patted his arm before looking over at me. "They aren't as fun as the ones you're talking about, though, Anthony. Your brother can attest to that." Suzy broke into laughter.

"I don't want to know, Suzy," I said as I blanched. "I like to think of you as an angel." I smiled as she blushed.

"What a crock of horseshit," Izzy declared. "Suzy is one of the dirtiest bitches out there."

"Am not," Suzy said.

"Are too," Mia agreed, and threw a sugar packet at Suzy.

"Izzy, shall we discuss your necklace?" Suzy asked as she raised one eyebrow and gave Izzy a cocky grin.

"No!" Izzy snapped with wide eyes.

"What's she talking about?" Thomas asked, looking between James and Izzy.

"Nothing," Izzy said without giving James a chance to respond.

"I'm not stupid. I know James too well," Thomas said as he mouthed "we're going to talk later" to James, who gave him a nod.

"Why do I always think I'm missing something?" I asked Max.

"It's okay, babe. I'll tell you about it later," she whispered, and kissed my lips.

"So," Izzy drawled, "where's the waitress so we can get some champagne?"

Just then a woman popped up out of

nowhere as if she was summoned. "What can I get y'all?" she asked as she stared at me.

I closed my eyes. It was Candy—the Candy whom I slept with more than once and regretted with every fiber of my being. She was a train wreck and I couldn't shake her. I had to remember to scratch this place off my list.

"Anthony," she said. "Long time no see."

"Candy," I replied, avoiding eye contact.

"Candy," Max snarled, and squeezed my leg, digging her nails into my skin.

"Are we celebrating?" Candy asked.

"Yeah," I said, and raised my eyes to meet hers. "We're celebrating my engagement." I smiled at her, not feeling an ounce of guilt.

Her face fell as she narrowed her eyes at me. "Well hell, just a few months ago we were—"

My stomach dropped. "Stop right there," I said, holding up my hand. "You will not disrespect Max. Candy, I don't know who you think you are, but this is a family affair and I'd prefer another waitress." I put my arm around Max, drawing her head to mine and placing a kiss on her cheek.

"So would I," Max inserted as she glared at Candy.

"I was going to say that we were at the Ritz and you two were talking. Jesus, I'm not total trash. Congrats, asshole," she retorted before stomping off.

"What the fuck was that about?" Denzel asked, turning to watch Candy storm away.

"Anthony always had problems with the ladies," Mike answered for me.

"There weren't any problems, that's the issue," Max said.

"Enough about Candy, for shit's sake. I have the woman I want sitting next to me and nothing and no one will ruin it," I declared.

"I'll go get another waitress," Denzel said as he left the table.

As the girls began to chat, I kept my eyes trained on Denzel. He spoke with the bartender, motioning to our table with his head as their eyes found their way to our spot. Before he walked back to the table, he found Candy and grabbed her by the arm. They were having a heated conversation from the looks of it. She kept glancing toward our table as she spoke to him.

"All set," Denzel said as he sat back in his chair.

"What was that about?" Max asked, tilting her head toward where Candy and Denzel had just spoken.

"Nothing. Just making sure we're left alone."

"Denzel, you don't always have to come to my rescue," she said as she rolled her eyes.

"You'll always be my baby sister, and I'm sure as these fine gentleman sitting here can attest to, I'll protect you forever, Max."

"Men are impossible."

"We've known that for years." Mia snickered. "Welcome to the Gallos."

"Don't worry," Izzy told Max. "They think they run the show, but we know who really holds the power."

"Lies," I muttered as a new waitress set down three bottles of Dom Pérignon chilling in ice buckets at the center of the table and another girl placed champagne flutes in front of each person.

Joe, James and I grabbed a bottle and started to fill the glasses. When everyone had a full glass, Joe stood from his chair and held the champagne in the air, clearing his throat.

"We have a lot to celebrate tonight. First to Max and Anthony and their upcoming wedding: may you find the happiness that only lives in the movies. I never thought I'd live to see the day, but I'm damn proud of you. Max, welcome to the family and I hope you always find it in your heart to forgive my brother for being such an asshole."

"It's what I love about him most," Max added as she raised her glass higher.

"I thought it was my giant cock?" I teased, which earned me an elbow to the ribs.

Joe continued, ignoring my comment, "We'd also like to celebrate Thomas returning safely to the family. Angel, thank you for making my brother happier than I've seen him in a long time." Thomas and Angel both nodded at Joe with smiles. "Denzel and Brenda, welcome to the family. What used to be five is now twelve.

We've been blessed and the best is yet to come." He raised his glass and everyone followed suit.

"Big pansy," Mike muttered as he lifted the glass to his lips.

"Don't fuckin' start with me," Joe growled, setting his glass on the table.

"So, Max," Mia said between sips. "What kind of dress are you going to wear?"

"I don't want to know," I said quickly. "It's bad luck."

"Dumbass, its bad luck to *see* the bride in the dress before the wedding." James sighed and rubbed his forehead.

"I don't give a shit. I'm taking no chances."

"Why don't we switch places so the girls can all gab while you boys talk about whatever it is you talk about?" Brenda said.

"Fantastic plan," Mia said, shooing Mike away. "Everyone switch."

"But I want to sit next to my fiancée," I whined, and didn't move.

"Fine," Izzy said with a groan. "You two stay where you are and the rest of us will move. Because, ya know, the universe revolves around your ass."

"I know it does. At least for tonight, since it's *our* celebration, little sister."

"Whatever," she whispered, and rolled her eyes again.

James leaned over, speaking in Izzy's ear. "If you roll your eyes one more time, I swear I'm going to spank your ass."

I sat up straight. James had threatened Izzy. I'd never heard him say he'd spank her. I thought about standing and intervening, but I changed my mind when she looked him right in the eyes and rolled her beautiful blues backward.

He bit his lip, hiding his amusement as he gripped her arm. "Excuse us. I need to talk to Izzy really quick," he said as he tipped his head to everyone. Izzy smiled and almost skipped away as James kept hold of her.

"What the fuck was that about?" Mike asked as he sat down next to me.

"You don't want to fuckin' know," I replied as I shook my head. "Some shit you just can't unhear."

"Shit is the truth, brother."

It was the first night in a long time that everything seemed to fall into place. As a group, we just fit together. The additions of our significant others didn't make our love diminish or alter the way we felt for each other. No. It had made us a stronger unit and a force to be reckoned with. We were the Gallos—even Denzel would get his honorary membership for the way he handled Candy.

After their conversation, I didn't see her face again the rest of the night. I didn't know until afterward that he offered her three hundred bucks to get lost for the night or else he'd unleash his sister on her ass. Candy was at least smart enough to take the offer and tell her boss she was too sick to finish her shift.

As I looked around the table, I realized that much of our wedding party sat around us. The only two people who were missing were a couple of the guys from the band who were going to partner with Nita and Malia. I'd paired them with men who would be able to handle their type of aggression. When they saw pictures of the guys, Nita and Malia both thanked Max. I guess they figured they'd be able to paw a tattooed man and maybe get lucky in the process.

I sat back, listening to everyone chat as their voices faded. I was the luckiest son of a bitch on the planet. There was so much love at this table that I felt like my heart would burst.

No longer was I an asshole, but I had drowned in love so deep that I couldn't remember what life was like without Max by my side.

In a few short weeks she'd be mine for eternity.

20

WHEN OPPOSITES ATTRACT

"Ma, this is Mrs. Washington," I said as I held out my hand to Ruth.

"Ruth," she said with a small grin.

"Ruth, this is my ma, Maria."

The two women smiled at each other.

"Ruth?" Ma asked, her eyebrows knitting together.

"Maria," Ruth replied as she held out her arms to my ma.

I looked at Max and she shrugged. Good thing I wasn't the only one lost.

"You look so good, Ruthie. I haven't seen you in what?"

"Five years," Ruth replied as she squeezed Ma.

"Anyone want to share?" Max said.

"Oh, child," Ruth said as she let my mother go.

"Well, Ruth and I used to be part of a ladies' group. I joined when we moved here years ago. Sal thought it would be a great way for me to make new friends. We'd meet for lunch once a week and sometimes have drinks when we needed to lean on one another."

"So you two, like, know each other?" I asked as I tried to hide my shock.

"We do," they answered together.

"Maria and I would talk often, but when your father started to get sick I didn't have as much free time. We'd lost contact."

"I'm so sorry to hear about your husband, Ruth. I can't imagine."

"Thank you, Maria," Ruth replied with a small smile. "It was the most difficult thing I've ever been through in my life."

"Ruth?" Pop asked as he approached. "What are you doing here?" He kissed her on the cheek.

"Max is my daughter, Sal."

Pops eyes grew wide as a giant smile crept across his face. "What a small world. I never put two and two together."

"We're going to be related," Ma added as she clapped her hands.

"Who would've known, Maria? Those times when we shared pictures of our kids and bitched about them that they'd end up together."

"You bitched about us?" Max asked as her body stiffened.

"You two were a handful, if I remember correctly. Don't even get me started on the other kids." Ma laughed and was quickly joined by Ruth.

"I'm sorry I never called, Maria. Time got away from me after he passed and I barely made it through most days."

"All is forgiven, Ruth. I'm sorry I wasn't there for you through that time in your life."

"Let's make sure to get back to lunch and drinks. We're going to have so much fun planning this wedding."

"Right?" Ma agreed. "I'm not letting you out

of my life again. We're going to be family. I can't wait to have more grandbabies."

"Can we get married first?" I asked as I watched the two grow excited at the thought of more little ones.

"Phew," Earl called out as he walked into the private room at Morton's Steakhouse and stared at my mother. "That right there is a fine specimen."

Clara gave him a crack in the back of the head. "Behave, Earl."

"Clara, I was talking about the steak," he said as he pointed at the display sitting behind where my mother stood.

"You're a horrible liar."

"I'm Earl," he said as he held out his hand to Ma.

"Maria," she replied as she slid her hand into his.

"I'm Sal, Maria's husband," Pop interjected before Earl had a chance to kiss Ma's hand.

"Lucky bastard," he whispered against Ma's hand. "That's mine," he said as he tipped his head backward. "Clara."

"It's a pleasure to meet you, Clara." Pop wrapped her into a hug and kissed her cheek.

Clara slid her hands up and down my father's back as he embraced her. The entire time, a giant smile clung to her face. "There's entirely too many good-looking men in this room," Clara added as she glanced around and zoomed in on my brothers.

"We're Gallos," I added, being my cocky asshole self.

"You sure do grow them right," she said as she cleared her throat.

"What did you say?" Earl asked as he stared at her and then followed her line of sight.

"I said I don't wanna fight."

"What would we fight about?" he asked as he glared at her.

"Everything."

Watching the two of them made my head hurt. I wondered if they ever had a serious conversation.

He slapped her on the ass as her body jolted forward. "Get me a drink, woman."

"That right there," she said as she looked

down at his arm, "will make you never wake up from your sleep again."

"You keep promising, but I always wake up to your sparkling personality."

"Why don't we find our seats," I said as I held out my arm, hoping to get everyone moving. They followed my cue and headed toward the tables.

"Thank you," Max whispered as she slid her arm around mine.

"Can you believe our mothers know each other?"

"It's so weird. How did we not know about each other and how did they not notice us when we met them?" I asked, thinking about how funny life could be.

"I've seen the pictures of you when you were younger, Anthony. You weren't quite as handsome as you are now."

"Puhlease. I've always been a lady-killer." I pinched her ass as she yelped.

"Keep telling yourself that. It's a good thing teenage girls don't have such high standards."

"Yeah, 'cause you were hot with your mouth

filled with metal and your dorky oversized glasses."

"I was in style even then."

"Max, baby. You're a beautiful woman today, but then, I would've run away from you," I teased as I pulled out her chair.

"Keep believing that, Anthony."

I was lying through my teeth. Even in the pictures where she looked like a gawky teenager, she was still stunning. Her features were so pronounced and exotic that not even giant glasses could hide her beauty.

I moved my chair closer to hers as we faced the room full of our closest friends and family.

Pop stood, tapping a knife against his wineglass. "I'd like to propose a toast." The room grew silent as all eyes focused on him. "I want to thank each and every one of you for coming tonight to celebrate the joining of our two families. Until tonight Maria and I hadn't realized that we'd known Max for many years. Ruth and Maria had been close friends who had lost touch. This is not only a joining of Max and Anthony, but a reunion of families. We couldn't be happier to be gaining a daughter as beautiful and loving as Max to our oldest son, Anthony." He raised his glass and finished with a *"salute."*

Max grabbed my thigh under the table and gave it a hard squeeze as we sipped our champagne.

"Kiss," Nita said, clanking her silverware against the glass.

Without hesitation, I grabbed Max by the back of the neck before she had a chance to set the glass down on the table and crushed my lips to hers.

"Babies," Ma called out from down the table.

I laughed, pulling away from Max. "And so it begins," I whispered, and looked into the eyes of my future.

LIFE CHANGES WHEN WE LEAST EXPECT IT

THE RECEPTION

"Jesus. I was so nervous," I said as Max and I took a moment to ourselves in my parents' bedroom. I had been more than nervous. I had sweated through my dress shirt as my heart hammered in my chest. I had been worried it would burst before I heard her say "I do."

Throwing Max under the proverbial bus with my mother had worked. After the day at the hospital, we started to plan the wedding. Actually, I left the planning up to the women in my life, including Max's mother.

They decided we'd marry on my parents'

property in their backyard. Max wanted a nighttime wedding and dancing under the stars.

Who was I to say no?

The fact that she had agreed to be my wife was enough for me to cave into anything she ever wanted.

I was wearing a suit instead of a tuxedo. Her choice, not mine, but I couldn't have been happier. I loosened my tie and stared at my wife. My wife. She was now my wife. There was a Mrs. Anthony Gallo in the world.

She had on a strapless Stella York gown with jewels decorating the waist. It showed off her curves and accentuated her breasts. The bottom of the dress puffed out with layers of material. The ivory color made her skin look more radiant. She was simply stunning. She had said that the dress was timeless and wanted it to be something she could hand down to our future daughter someday.

No, we weren't pregnant yet, but I took every opportunity to make it happen.

"We did it," I said as I pulled her to me. "You're mine forever."

"No, baby. You're mine." She kissed my cheek without having to stand on her tiptoes for once. The heels she had on made her only a couple of inches shorter than I was, but they had to be painful.

I smiled down at her, feeling content. The only other time in my life that I'd felt that way was when I was on stage. I felt everything else melt away and it was just my music and me. No one had ever given me that feeling before I'd met her.

She had torn me down, making me a better man than I used to be. I hadn't known I had been missing something in my life until I'd found her and then she'd gotten rid of me.

The pain she'd caused me had been necessary. It had made me love her more, cherish our time together, and altered how I looked at life and love.

"Thank you," she whispered into my neck as she squeezed me.

"For what?" I asked as I squeezed her tight and toyed with the ends of her hair that had cascaded down her back.

"For saving me, Anthony."

All the warm, gushy feelings I already had amplified. "Max, you're the one who saved me."

"I was such a pissed-off person. You don't even understand how angry I was about everything in my life. When I found you, I felt even more upset. I cursed God for letting me find you when I knew it wasn't right for me to have you. I could have dealt with being alone when there wasn't someone out there for me."

"I didn't know what love was until I met you. You drove me crazy, but I knew there was something I couldn't let go. The moment I kissed your lips, I knew life would never be the same."

"We did it, huh?" she said, resting her hand on my ass.

"I plan to do it a lot tonight. I mean a lot. If you're not knocked up by the end of the honeymoon, I'm tying your ass to the bed until you have my seed growing inside you."

"I was talking about being husband and wife." She shrieked as she pinched my ass.

"I know." I kissed the top of her hair.

"Do not mess up my hair, Anthony Gallo."

"Shhh," I whispered. "You look beautiful, Maxine Gallo. I meant what I said, too, about the tying you to the bed."

"It sounds like the perfect way to spend a honeymoon," she replied, groping my ass cheeks in her hands.

"You guys ready?" my ma asked as she knocked on the door and stood in the doorway.

"Yeah, Ma. I think we are."

"Yes, Mrs. Gallo. We're ready."

"Ma."

"Ma." Max smiled brightly as she released my ass from her grip.

"I'll tell the band to make the announcement for your first dance."

"Okay," I said as she grinned at us and walked away.

"What song did you pick?" Max asked me as she smoothed out her dress.

"I'm not telling. It's a surprise."

It was the only thing I'd asked to plan for the entire wedding. I had wanted to be in charge of the music. I'd needed the song to be special, and I'd found the perfect one for us.

"Am I going to cry?" she asked, checking her makeup in the mirror over my parents' dresser.

"Maybe." I smiled and shrugged.

"Damn it, Anthony. I don't want to mess up my face."

I gripped her from behind, staring at her reflection in the mirror. "You look amazing, Max. You couldn't mess up that beautiful face with a few tears."

"Thank God I wore waterproof mascara. It would be running down my face by now." She glided a fresh coat of lipstick on and then smacked her lips together.

"Come on, Mrs. Gallo. I want to hold you in my arms and dance with you tonight."

She smiled, setting the lipstick on the dresser, and turned in my arms. "I love you, Anthony."

"I love you too, Max," I whispered as I gently kissed her on the lips, trying to avoid leaving the room with a fresh coat on my lips too.

When we made our way to the dance floor, I took in the beauty of the backyard. Small lanterns were strung through the trees along with white, twinkling lights. Round white tables filled with the guests framed the makeshift wooden dance floor in the center. We hadn't done assigned seating, hoping that the families would mingle.

Our families seemed to be getting along as they had drinks and chatted. Our mothers had formed a solid bond while planning the wedding. They had chatted daily on the phone and met for lunch once a week. It was something my mother hadn't had the chance to do with the other women's parents.

Even Denzel, Max's brother and the man who had threatened to knock my teeth out, was part of the wedding party. He'd given me his blessing to marry his sister, and it had meant more to me than anything else in the world.

As the lead singer of the band announced us, we walked to the center of the dance floor. All eyes moved in our direction, and the chatter of the guests stopped.

The song I'd picked for our dance was to be played via recording. I wanted the original, not a version recreated by the band that had been hired to play for our reception.

As the music began, I moved my mouth next to her ear. I wanted to sing the words to her.

I could feel her breathing change as her chest moved with mine. Her heartbeat sped up and thundered so hard that I could feel the vibration in my torso.

I brushed my lips to her ear and began to sing along with the music—"Thinking Out Loud" by Ed Sheeran. It fit our relationship and the love we had for each other perfectly.

I sang softly as I moved with her in my arms.

"Oh, Anthony," she whispered as she peered up at me with tears in her eyes.

I kissed her forehead, swaying with her in my grip. I kept singing and blocked everyone else out.

God, I loved this woman. I didn't care what happened in our future. I was too lost in the here and now to worry about anything else. I wanted to enjoy every day we had together. I wanted to dance with her as long as I could and hold her in my arms.

Even if she was confined to a wheelchair, I'd carry her in my arms and dance with her. I'd never let her be alone.

"Anthony," she cried as I sang the last lines of the song.

When the song ended, I kissed her on the lips, holding her face in my hands. Max had become my everything. I'd remember this night for the rest of my life.

I'd remember it as the day I married my soul mate.

The day I'd become a different man.

She'd forever changed me.

I'd had to fall hard and deep to come out on the other side a changed man.

I'd never go back to where I had been before Max.

I didn't want to be that man.

I had a purpose in life, and she was in my arms.

Nothing else mattered but living every day to the fullest and never regretting a moment of our lives together.

She was my salvation.

FIVE YEARS LATER

"Daddy." A tiny hand tugged on my pants leg. "Daddy," she repeated.

I looked down at her, and instantly, my heart melted. The little girl had me wrapped around her finger. Her wild, curly black hair framed her face and made her look bigger than she was. Her hazel eyes sparkled with mischief, and she puffed her lips into a frown. At almost four years old, she could already play me like a fiddle.

"What, baby doll?" I asked her as I picked her up and set her on my lap.

"Gigi is being mean, Daddy." She hugged

me, resting her forehead on my cheek. Her tiny fingers found my ear and tugged on my earlobe.

"What's that bad Gigi doing, Tamara?" I kissed her soft tanned cheeks, inhaling the sweet candy smell of her skin.

We'd made a monster out of Gigi. For a long while she was the only baby in the family. We doted on her and gave her everything she wanted. Even after Tamara was born, Gigi was still spoiled. Everything she did was a big deal. The first time she walked, I swear my mother called everyone in the family and had a celebration.

Even today, I still look at Gigi with a special love. She wasn't mine, but she was the first baby that tugged at my heartstrings. She was the reason that Max said she wanted a baby. Without Gigi we wouldn't have Tamara. The first time I held Gigi I knew I'd never be the same. The first time she smiled at me when I made a funny face, I was a total goner.

When Tamara came into my life I thanked my lucky stars. I'd felt a little jealous of Joe when he became a father. I wasn't through the entire

Suzy "eat everything in my wake" pregnancy, but when I saw that little girl, I understood it. He'd have someone who would love him unconditionally and for life. I wanted that. That pure love and someone to call me "Daddy" until the day I died.

"She won't let me play with her dolly." She pouted and glanced toward the floor as she toyed with my ear.

"Sweetheart, you have a doll too," I replied, brushing the stray hairs away from her face.

"I like hers more." She batted her eyelashes, something she had learned at a young age from her mother.

"It's Gigi's doll, Tamara. If she doesn't want to share it, she doesn't have to, and it looks just like yours."

"But hers has a pink dress, Daddy." She laid her head on my shoulder, resting her forehead on my neck.

"Want to stay with me and watch television?"

"*Frozen?*" she asked.

"Baseball," I replied.

"Ew." She picked her head up and pulled at her lips.

"Why don't you go see if Aunt Izzy is okay or go see Nona outside with the girls?" I rubbed Tamara's back as I looked out the sliding glass doors and watched my wife.

Max sat outside, talking as she unconsciously stroked her belly. After Tamara had been born, we'd decided we wanted one more child, but we wanted to wait until we were past the diaper point to have another.

When I'd held Tamara in my arms the first time, I had known I wanted more. As she had grown, she'd become more and more like her mother. Both girls had me. They could get away with murder, and I'd help them cover it up too. I loved them so much, more than I had ever thought possible.

Max's greatest fear was passing on the disease to her baby, but we decided it was a risk worth taking. No one had a certain future, and we all walked through life with an unexpected fate.

My biggest regret in life was not having children sooner. I wished I'd met Max sooner and started a family. I was an old father. Now that I was in my forties, everything was a little harder. By the time Tamara graduated from high school, I'd be pushing sixty. It'd be tough to chase the boys away, but with the help of a gun, I'd be able to protect her.

"Lemme down," Tamara said as she kicked her feet and pushed my chest. She slid down my leg, placing her feet on the floor. "Ice cream?" she asked with her eyes big and a smile on her face.

"Not yet. Nona will give you some later, baby."

"I'm not a baby, Daddy."

"You'll always be my baby."

She shook her head slowly as she frowned. "I won't be. Mommy's having a baby."

I bent down and cradled her face. "Tamara, sweetheart, you'll always be Daddy's baby girl."

"Always?"

"Always."

"Ice cream?"

"No." I shook my head and sighed. It was

already hard to say no to her. I was totally fucked when she got older.

"Nona will give me ice cream." She smiled and stuck out her tongue. Tamara marched off and headed right toward Ma to get exactly what she wanted.

She hadn't picked up the eye rolling yet. I figured I had another eight years or so until that became a habit. She had nailed sticking her tongue out, though. When words failed her, she went with that damn tongue. I couldn't be mad. It always made me laugh.

"Amazing, isn't it?" Joe asked as he sat down.

"What?" I asked as I sank back into the couch and watched Tamara while she tried to push the giant sliding glass door open.

"How much our lives have changed in five years."

"Yeah," I said as I kicked my feet up on the coffee table after Izzy slid the door open for Tamara. "Everything has changed, but in the best way possible."

"I can't believe Izzy is having twins. God has

a sense of humor." Joe slapped me on the leg. "She'll get hers."

"The fact that she's having boys is the best thing ever."

"It's her curse for always bitching about us."

I nodded with a laugh. "It is. It's going to be interesting to see how she deals with them."

"James is going to have his hands full."

"He already does."

"I what?" James asked as he walked into the room with a cup of coffee.

"Have your hands full with our sister."

"Ugh," he whined as he sat down. "She's a beast."

"They all are," Joe said.

"I don't know how much longer I can take the pregnancy deal. She's so damn demanding."

"That's Izzy."

"Dude, it's so much fucking worse. Oh, and while you're all laughing at me, ever think God is cursing you two because he gave ya girls?"

Joe and I looked at each other and grimaced. We'd pay penance for all the havoc we wreaked on womankind. Hopefully the baby inside Max was a boy. I didn't know how I could deal with two girls. I needed a boy to even things out.

Just then, Lily ran into the room screaming and headed straight for Mike.

"Lily," he called out as he held out his arms. "What's wrong?" He searched her face and wiped away a tear.

"Daddy, Tommy." She pointed toward the kitchen.

"What did Uncle Tommy do now?" Mike asked as Thomas walked into the living room.

"I was just having fun with the kids. Chasing them, but I snuck up on her and scared her." He grimaced.

"Lily, it's just Uncle Tommy. He won't ever hurt you." Mike stroked her blond hair, holding her head to his chest. "You'll be okay, sweetheart."

"Sorry, Lily," Thomas said as he kneeled down in front of her and Mike. "I won't do it again."

"Okay." She sniffled, wiping her nose with the back of her hand.

"Soon, you can scare your own kid," Mike said as he kissed the top of Lily's head.

"He's barely walking. I don't think I'll be able to scare Nick for a while."

"He'll be running before you know it," I replied as I thought about how rapidly time had passed.

Five years ago, I was alone and not looking for love. Today, I had a beautiful wife, an amazing daughter, and a baby on the way. Everything about the family had changed. We were all parents, or about to be. It was no longer about us, but about our kids.

Ma was beyond ecstatic. She had become the official babysitter, begging for us to drop off the kids and go out for a night. She spoiled the kids, but then again, we all did. The Gallo kids would grow up not wanting for anything. They'd probably be monsters by the time they were teenagers.

Life couldn't get any better than it was right now. I was thankful to have a beautiful daughter, a loving wife, and an amazing family. The house had been bursting at the seams every Sunday since the kids started to arrive. They'd be close cousins and probably give us heart attacks as they grew. I hoped to God that Tamara would be a calm child and a recluse as a teenager. The thought of her having a boyfriend someday made me break out into a cold sweat.

I tried to enjoy the little moments in life, savoring the small things, such as tiny kisses from my daughter, the way she laughed with Max when they played on the floor during the day, and holding my wife in my arms. I'd worry about the future when it arrived, but for now, I'd bask in the happiness that surrounded me.

THANK YOU FOR READING WITHOUT ME! *I hope you loved Anthony, Max, and the Gallo Family. The family' s story continues in* **HONOR ME!**

City & Suzy are back! I had everything I ever wanted—a wife, a kid, with two more on the way. I was living the American dream. **One-click Honor Me...**

And sign up for my newsletter to find out about new books... *menofinked.com/news*

You can also join my Facebook group, *Chelle Bliss Books*, for exclusive giveaways and sneak peeks of future books.

I appreciate you help in spreading the word, including telling a friend. Word of mouth is everything.

Reviews help readers find books too! Please leave a review on your favorite book site.

Turn the page for an excerpt from **Honor Me...**

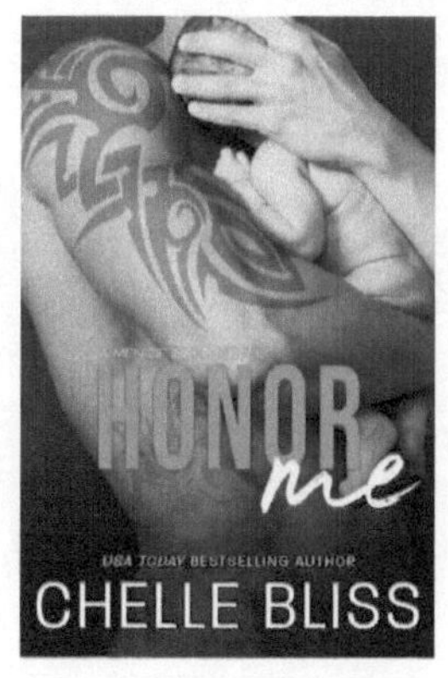

God clearly had a sense of humor.

First, he dropped an innocent blond bombshell into my lap, which changed my life forever. Never in a million years would I have guessed I'd fall head over heels in love with someone so innocent, but it happened.

I corrupted her thoroughly.

Quickly, too.

I made her mine and never looked back. There wasn't a day that passed that I didn't take stock of my life. I was the luckiest son of a bitch in the world.

Next thing I knew, we had a baby, Gigi. She

wasn't just a kid, but one who had me wrapped around her little finger.

She said, "Jump."

My response, "How high, baby girl?"

Gigi rocked my world.

Seriously turned everything upside down.

The moment she was born, nothing else mattered. I never knew that type of love existed until she came screaming into my life. It altered the way I looked at everything, making me more protective of my family than ever before.

When she was just a tiny bundle, I'd sit up with her at night and rock her, telling her my hopes and dreams for her entire life. I had big plans too—the kid was going to be president someday. Actually, she could be anything she wanted. I'd make sure of it.

I spoiled her, too much probably, and it turned her into a tiny monster. She was now my cross to bear, my demon child. The first time she said "Daddy," I knew I was a goner—completely and utterly in love.

Don't get me wrong, Suzy was the love of my life...my soul mate.

She was the one person who truly got me and understood who I was on the inside without judging me for my past indiscretions. She was the mother of my children and would always be the one who did it for me.

When Suzy told me she was pregnant again, I was over the fuckin' moon happy. I mean, more kids meant more love, right?

But if I was being honest, it terrified me too. Especially when the doctor dropped the news that we were having twins.

Twins.

Double the feedings and even less sleep; nothing would ever be the same again. But like with any kid, whether having one or six, they had a way of creating chaos and havoc out of any situation.

Family had always been my number one priority. It was the thing that kept me moving and helped me stay out of trouble most of my life.

I'd been known to have a temper. I couldn't help that shit. If someone was dumb enough to talk shit, they'd better be willing to put up their fists and back their words up with some strength.

Understand this—I was a good guy.

I'd bend over backward to help a friend.

But cross me, and I'd fuck you up. Hurt someone I love, and I'd put you in the ground.

It was that simple. I was like most red-blooded American men.

Years ago, if you'd told me I'd live in a house filled with women and pink shit everywhere, I would've laughed in your face. But it was my lot in life. Pink had replaced the white space, filling up every corner of my world.

But the journey to get to the place of peace hadn't been an easy one. My road to happiness wasn't paved in gold. It was more like a cobblestone walkway, filled with dips and ridges.

One-click Honor Me and read now...

My entire audiobook collection is available on your audio retailer. Tap here to see where you can download your next favorite listen.

MEN OF INKED: SOUTHSIDE SERIES

Join the Chicago Gallo Family with their strong alphas, sassy women, and tons of fun.

- Book 1 - Maneuver (Lucio)
- Book 2 - Flow (Daphne)
- Book 3 - Hook (Angelo)
- Book 4 - Hustle (Vinnie)
- Book 5 - Love (Angelo)

MEN OF INKED SERIES

"One of the sexiest series of all-time"

-Bookbub Reviewers

Download book 1 for FREE!

- Book 1 - Throttle Me (Joe aka City)
- Book 2 - Hook Me (Mike)
- Book 3 - Resist Me (Izzy)
- Book 4 - Uncover Me (Thomas)

- Book 5 - Without Me (Anthony)
- Book 6 - Honor Me (City)
- Book 7 - Worship Me (Izzy)

ALFA INVESTIGATIONS SERIES

Wickedly hot alphas with tons of heart pounding suspense!

- Book 1 - Sinful Intent (Morgan)
- Book 2 - Unlawful Desire (Frisco)
- Book 3 - Wicked Impulse (Bear)
- Book 4 - Guilty Sin (Ret)

SINGLE READS

- Mend
- Enshrine
- Misadventures of a City Girl
- Misadventures with a Speed Demon
- Rebound (Flash aka Sam)
- Top Bottom Switch (Ret)

NAILED DOWN SERIES

- Book 1 - Nailed Down
- Book 2 - Tied Down
- Book 3 - Kneel Down

TAKEOVER DUET

What happens when you sleep with your biggest enemy?

- Book 1 - Acquisition
- Book 2 - Merger

FILTHY SERIES

- Dirty Work
- Dirty Secret
- Dirty Defiance

LOVE AT LAST SERIES

- Book 1 - Untangle Me
- Book 2 - Kayden

BOX SETS & COLLECTIONS

- Men of Inked Volume 1
- Men of Inked Volume 2
- Love at Last Series
- ALFA Investigations Series
- Filthy Series
- Takeover Duet

View Chelle's entire collection of books at menofinked.com/books

To learn more about Chelle's books visit *menofinked.com* or *chellebliss.com*

ABOUT THE AUTHOR

Chelle Bliss is the *Wall Street Journal* and *USA Today* bestselling author of Men of Inked: Southside Series, Misadventures of a City Girl, the Men of Inked, and ALFA Investigations series.

She hails from the Midwest, but currently lives near the beach even though she hates sand. She's a full-time writer, time-waster extraordinaire, social media addict, coffee fiend, and ex history teacher.

She loves spending time with her two cats, alpha boyfriend, and chatting with readers. To learn more about Chelle, please visit menofinked.com or chellebliss.com.

JOIN MY NEWSLETTER

Text Notifications (US only)
→ Text **BLISS** to **24587**

WHERE TO FOLLOW CHELLE:

WEBSITE | TWITTER | FACEBOOK |
INSTAGRAM
JOIN MY PRIVATE FACEBOOK GROUP

Want to drop me a line?
authorchellebliss@gmail.com
www.chellebliss.com

facebook.com/authorchellebliss1

bookbub.com/authors/chelle-bliss

instagram.com/authorchellebliss

twitter.com/ChelleBliss1

AFTERWORD

Dear Reader,

I thought long and hard about the storyline in *Without Me*. I didn't want his story to be the classic "boy meets girl" and they eventually live happily ever after. One day, I was driving to my parent's and Ed Sheeran—Thinking Out Loud started to play on the radio. For the first time, I really listened to the words. Inspiration hit me.

Ataxia is personal to me. My father has ataxia and was diagnosed about five years ago after having symptoms for over ten years. He'd always assumed he had a stroke and other people always thought he was drunk.

When we heard the news, it was devastating. He went through extensive testing, but we've never been able to find out what type of ataxia he has even to this day. He still walks, but with the assistance of a walker. He refuses to give up on life. He still washes the floors on his hands and knees to help my mother and does other household chores to stay active.

I struggle with the decision each day about being tested. His insurance turned his claim down years ago to have genetic testing completed. I can have the test done today on myself, but do I want to? I don't know if I want to know. I know sometimes it's best to hear the worst and plan, but I just can't. At this point in my life, I just can't. I'm a little like Max in that way.

It's not that I feel I'll develop it, but I don't know if I want to know with certainty. It's too scary for me. Someday I may be strong enough to face my fear and be tested. Today isn't that day.

My father is my hero. He's faced this illness with grace and courage. He never complains or shows sadness, but I know it's changed him. A man who could once do anything, at least in my eyes, now has trouble carrying a cup of coffee. I want to do everything in my power to help him. If I could make him better, no matter the cost, I'd do it. He was my first love and will always be my daddy.

Hold the ones closest to you a little tighter, love them a little more, and protect them with all the strength you have. No one knows how long we have on this planet and we need to enjoy each moment. There's nothing sweeter than life.

Thank you for taking the time to read my letter and to fall in love with Anthony and Max. I hope you'll take a moment and leave a review. Don't worry. I have more stories up my sleeve.

Sincerely,
Chelle Bliss

ACKNOWLEDGMENTS

I don't even know where to start. There are so many people who have helped me along the way that it surprises me to this day. Here it goes in no particular order:

Thanks to Eric Battershell and his amazing cover photo of Thomas Yarborough. I wanted something different, a model whose skin had never been seen. Eric delivered in spades with the fantastic photo of TJ. I had the photo before I wrote a single word and it had the right feel for my Anthony. I appreciate Thomas for agreeing to be on a Men of Inked cover.

Melissa Gill has been a great friend and cover designer. She's been with me since the start of the Men of Inked series. She's a very patient person mostly when we're trying to get a cover just perfect. I'm not easy to deal with. When I have a cover vision, I can't stop until it's perfect. Thanks Mel for putting up with my shit.

Mickey Reed and Arran of Editing 720, thank you for making my words flow better and correcting my crazy-ass writing. Both of you have been the best editors a girl could ask for. I wish you both success and prosperity in 2015.

Fiona and Candy, thank you for reading through the book prior to release to make it as clean as possinle. I'm demanding and cranky when I'm waiting. Thank you for putting up with my ass.

Becca Dawn you're amazing. Thank you for reading through the medical jargon and ensuring that I have the details correct about Ataxia. You're going to be a rockstar doctor.

My awesome beta girls always made me smile while I wrote. I know I kept sending you bits and pieces and leaving it at the most agonizing part, but you took it like champs. Thanks for loving Anthony and helping make it the best novel possible. In no particular order: Patti, Mandee, Malia, Renita, Maggie, Ashley, Kathy, Stefanie, and Deb.

Thank you to my fellow indie authors and friends Cat Mason and Tracy McKay. Your love of the Gallos has always brought a smile to my face. Your willingness to drop everything and read Anthony was more than I'd expected. It's authors like you who make the indie community something special.

Thank you for amazing Aurora Rose Reynolds for reading Anthony and Max's story. You've always been an amazing friend and supporter. I love your BOOM!

I can't forget the bloggers. Your support and ability to help spread the word about the Gallos has been humbling. I appreciate your hard work and kindness for the last year. And thank you for never spoiling a book before release. Each and every one of you mean the world to me.

I don't know who else to thank, but I'm sure I've missed dozens of people. The last year of my life has been a crazy fun. I can't wait to bring you more alphas.